# When Memories Fade:

## Victory Gospel Series

# When Memories Fade:

## Victory Gospel Series

Tyora Moody

**www.urbanchristianonline.com**

Urban Books, LLC
78 East Industry Court
Deer Park, NY 11729

ISBN 13: 978-1-60162-753-7
ISBN 10: 1-60162-753-X

First Printing April 2013
Printed in the United States of America

10 9 8 7 6 5 4 3 2 1

*This is a work of fiction. Any references or similarities
to actual events, real people, living or dead, or to real
locales are intended to give the novel a sense of reality. Any similarity in other names, characters, places,
and incidents is entirely coincidental.*

Distributed by Kensington Corp.
Submit Wholesale Orders to:
Kensington Publishing Corp.
C/O Penguin Group (USA) Inc.
Attention: Order Processing
405 Murray Hill Parkway
East Rutherford, NJ 07073-2316
Phone: 1-800-526-0275
Fax: 1-800-227-9604

# When Memories Fade:

## Victory Gospel Series

**Tyora Moody**

# Dedication

This book is dedicated to caregivers. Please know your sacrifice and love are highly appreciated by your loved one.

# Acknowledgments

God is amazing! I sensed as I was writing the first book in the Victory Gospel Series that there were minor characters that had stories to tell. As I entered this fictional world, I was led to research and then develop characters with very relatable issues that any of us could face at some point in our lives.

Did you know African Americans are twice as likely to die from a stroke as Caucasians?According to a 2010 special report by the Alzheimer's Association, older African Americans are probably about two times more likely than older Caucasians to have Alzheimer's and other dementias.

I knew when I started this novel, the story line would be centered around a missing person's case. Over the years, when an African American woman goes missing, her plight does not always receive the same attention as that of a Caucasian woman. Did you know that according to FBI figures, nearly 40 percent of all missing persons are people of color? That's an incredible percentage. The cable network TV One broadcasts a much-needed program about African Americans who have vanished under suspicious circumstances, *Finding Our Missing*. This is a start.

If you find at any time while you are reading this book that you have more questions about the subject matter, I have included online resources at the end of the book to provide some answers.

# Acknowledgments

Now, there are a few people I want to acknowledge. Thank you to Robin Caldwell for reading through the manuscript. Your friendship, advice, and encouragement are priceless. To Dr. Jeffrey Brown, M.D., thank you so much for taking the time out of your busy schedule to answer my questions about stroke and Alzheimer's. I can Google all I want, but there's nothing like talking to a medical professional. Joylynn Ross, thank you for always being available to address my many questions as a newly published author. I've learned so much from you and look forward to continuing to work with you.

I want to take a moment to acknowledge the people who helped me push the first book in this series, *When Rain Falls*. I can't name everyone, but to all my family and friends, book reviewers, bloggers, online radio hosts, book clubs, and readers, thank you for your support of *When Rain Falls*. It's truly appreciated.

Thanks, Dad, for helping me spread the word about *When Rain Falls* locally. Your enthusiasm and support mean the world to me.

Last, but not least, I want to acknowledge my two best friends, my mom and my sister. You two have been the best with helping me get galleys out, finding readers and venues to promote the book, and being traveling companions. You two are my bookends.

Thank you, readers, for taking the time to read the second book in the Victory Gospel Series.

# Prologue

She gripped the steering wheel in fear as she calculated every move he made. For the last hour, he had held the gun in her direction. What if she jerked the car off the road? No. She *wanted* to live. Still, a car accident had to be better than what he would do to her. She had no idea where they were going.

"Pull over right up here." He turned his hot breath on her. "Do it now."

With as much ease as her trembling body allowed, she slowed the car and pulled to the side of the road. There hadn't been another car for miles on this back road. The sun had disappeared as cloudy dark gray skies loomed ahead.

He cocked the gun toward her chest. "Get out."

Her hands felt ice cold as she struggled to grasp the door handle.

"Come on," he growled.

She yanked the door handle and scrambled out of the car to face her abductor.

The man waved the gun and yelled, "Start walking."

Sticks and leaves crunched as they walked into the mass of trees. From a distance, she saw lightning streak across the sky. A cool breeze whipped through the trees, but it brought no comfort. Her heart raced as if she had just run a marathon. She choked back a sob. He was going to kill her.

To think how much she had trusted him. It never would have crossed her mind that he would hurt her. More lightning split the sky, followed by an intense rumble of thunder. The trees shook their limbs, as if taunting her for being so naive.

"Stop."

She turned and noticed he'd cocked his head like he'd heard something. Was someone else out here?

He swung the gun an inch from her temple. "Get down."

"What?"

"Get on your knees," he snarled.

She fell on her knees, feeling the earth beneath her. Her heart lurched as the thunder roared like an angry lion above their heads. Big drops of rain began to crash down around them. She shut her eyes tight, not believing this was her fate. "Please, God, help me," she prayed fervently.

When she opened her eyes, an answer lay near her, barely covered by leaves. She glanced up at him. His eyes had grown wilder as he paced around her. He seemed to be having a conversation, but she couldn't understand a word he was saying. The rain was falling harder now, soaking her clothes. She peered down at the ground again. Why not? What did she have to lose? She had to do something.

She scooped the smooth rock up from the muddy ground. Her dormant softball skills kicked in as she homed in on his hand. Not waiting another second, she swung the rock with all her might.

The rock smacked him square on the hand, and he dropped the gun. "No, you . . ."

She leapt forward like a track runner and headed into the trees. As she ran, the oddest memory of a Sunday school lesson entered her mind. The one about

Lot's wife. God told her not to look back, but she did and lost her life.

His voice bellowed behind her.

"Don't look back," she told herself as she ran. "Don't. Look. Back."

# Chapter One

*Charlotte, North Carolina, 2011*

"We both know she's dead." Angel Roberts tightened her grip around the steering wheel, realizing too late she'd destroyed a beautiful evening. A harsh silence sucked the air from inside the car. After a minute, her grandmother responded softly, but firmly. "Angel, I can never give up hope."

Angel took her eyes off the road to peer at her grandmother's face. A warmth of shame washed over Angel as she witnessed the pain in Fredricka Roberts's eyes. *Why now? It's my birthday.*

Less than fifteen minutes ago, Angel had driven away from Victory Gospel Church, still grateful for the love shown to her. A year ago, Angel would have never imagined herself regularly attending church, and definitely not Bible study. Tonight the members of the Overcomers Women's Ministry had presented Angel with a surprise twenty-fifth birthday celebration. Angel had loaded the remains of the almost eaten butter cream cake and birthday gifts into the backseat, not realizing her joy would be short-lived.

Angel slowed the car down as she approached the red light. All had been well until her grandmother had said, "You look so much like your mother when she was twenty-five."

Despite confessing her faith in Christ nine months ago at Victory Gospel Church, Angel had continued to struggle with resentment. It seemed like every year, Angel's birthday turned into more of a memorial for her mother. There was this gap between Angel and her grandmother where her mother should have been. Angel barely remembered the woman who had disappeared twenty years ago.

The question that haunted Angel the most was the same one that brought her grandmother hope. What if her mother were alive? To Angel that meant Elisa Roberts had abandoned her daughter. That night after Angel's fifth birthday party, her mother had walked out and had never returned. Elisa had provided no clue about where she was going or whether she was going to meet someone. Just vanished. Due to foul play or on purpose. Surely, her grandmother didn't want to hope to find a woman who had done the latter.

As she drove through the green light, Angel chided herself for getting angry with her grandmother. It was just her and Grams now. She cleared her throat. "Grams, I'm sorry. I didn't mean to blurt out that we know my mother's dead. We don't really know."

No response.

She glanced at her grandmother. Fredricka's face was turned toward the passenger window. Not wanting to upset her grandmother any more tonight, Angel became engrossed in her own thoughts. What Angel didn't want was for Grams to find out what she was doing. She was on a mission to find out what or who had led to her mother's disappearance. Five years ago, she'd started working on a documentary of her mother's life, but various circumstances led her off track and she abandoned the project. Now she was determined to complete it. Anything to bring attention to her mother's short-lived legacy.

Her grandparents had raised her, doing their best to keep memories of her mother alive. Even though she was young, Angel remembered her mother being sad all the time. Angel was born a few months after a devastating breakup between Angel's mother and father. It didn't help that her mother, a protégée, had struggled to regain her footing in a once promising singing career while trying to raise Angel.

In many ways, Elisa had shown signs of either desperately wanting a new life or ending the dismal life she perceived she had. Reaching her own breaking point four years ago, Angel longed for a connection with her mother.

Angel maneuvered her grandfather's old Buick into the driveway of the only place she called home. Her grandmother shuffled behind her as they made their way down the cobblestone walkway toward the front door. Once inside, Angel headed toward the kitchen to find a spot for the leftover cake inside the refrigerator. She had an urge to leave the cake out and eat the rest of it, but weariness invaded her body. She slammed the fridge door shut and turned around.

"Whoa, Grams." Her grandmother had managed to sneak up behind her. Angel didn't remember hearing her walk in the kitchen.

Her grandmother sputtered, "Angel, we should have stopped by the store on the way home."

Angel frowned. Maybe she had agitated her grandmother too much with her outburst in the car. "I can go back out, Grams. It's not a problem. What do you need?"

"Aspirin." Fredricka held her hand to head. "I'm not feeling well."

Angel placed her hand on her grandmother's shoulder. "Why don't you lie down? I will bring you some aspirin. I'm sure we already have a bottle."

Angel walked across the kitchen to the cabinet where they kept a medicine supply. She searched among the orange and white labeled bottles. There were so many bottles. A lot of the labels bore her deceased grandfather's name. She really needed to work with Grams to throw away his old medicine. Finally, Angel saw a bottle of aspirin.

"Here is the bottle." Angel flipped the bottle in her hand to check the expiration date. A forceful thump startled her. Angel turned around. "Grams!" she cried out. She ran over and knelt beside her grandmother on the linoleum floor.

The right side of her grandmother's face twitched. "Ang . . ."

Before Angel could stop them, tears sprang to life, blurring her vision. "Grams, hang in there. You are going to be okay."

Angel sprinted to the phone on the wall, and with trembling fingers, she dialed 9-1-1.

*Oh, God, please don't take Grams yet.*

# Chapter Two

Grateful for the interruption, Wes Cade removed Serena's arms from around his neck and pulled himself up from the couch. What was he thinking? He crossed the room to where his suit jacket was lying across a chair. He wrestled the ringing BlackBerry out of his jacket pocket.

From behind him on the couch, Serena Manchester hissed at him. "Did you really need to answer *that* call?"

Wes ignored Serena, like he should have done earlier, when she requested he come inside her apartment. He glanced at his phone. Voice mail had already kicked in. The missed call was from his mother's cell. He clicked the voice mail button and then held the phone to his ear to listen to his mother's message.

Wanda Cade's panic-stricken voice alarmed him. "Wes, I need you. Your grandfather . . . I can't find him."

He groaned. *Not again.* Wes Cade clicked the button on his phone to end the voice mail. His mother's voice sounded tired and panicked at the same time. What would it take to convince his mother that Pops had grown to be too much for her? The old man's memory had been affected for years. Some days he no longer recognized his daughter or his grandson. He turned around to his female companion for the evening. She glared at him.

"Is everything okay?" Serena sounded more like she wanted to slap him.

Wes was drawn to her steely but seductive brown eyes. "I'm sorry. You know my grandfather has Alzheimer's. He's missing again, so I need to go."

Serena's eyes softened as she rose from the couch. She slinked toward him, placing her hand on his arm. "Again? Shouldn't you put him in a place where he's safe?"

Wes stepped away from her and started putting his jacket on. "Believe me, I know." He'd been fighting an uphill battle with his mother, a nurse for eighteen years, who was convinced she could handle everything. As a single mother, Wanda Cade was a strong woman, but at this rate he needed her to be around for a few more years. The woman was killing herself trying to keep up with Pops.

"I have to go." He moved toward the door, but not before Serena placed her hand on his shoulder. Before he could protest, she squeezed in front of him, blocking his hand from reaching the doorknob on the front door.

"We need to finish this. Soon." She reached for his neck and drew his head down toward her lips.

Knowing in his mind that he shouldn't, he kissed her back. When she moved away, he refused to look at her. "I'll see you in the newsroom tomorrow."

Not until he was safe inside his Honda did he exhale. Wasn't there a rule that said a person shouldn't get involved with a coworker? Especially one as hot as Serena. More importantly, what had happened to him practicing celibacy? If the phone hadn't rung, he doubted he would have stopped. This was what he got for being super busy and not honoring his commitments.

It had been a year and a half since his last relationship, and he really wanted to settle down and find the right woman. He was approaching thirty, and something in him longed for family life. At a men's conference last year, he'd made a commitment to stop dating and remain celibate. He'd been doing great until Serena started messing with his head. There was no doubt in his mind, Serena was not a woman he wanted to get involved with, but he kept being drawn toward her.

He blew out his breath and dialed his mom's cell number.

"Hello."

"Mom, did you find Pops yet?"

His mother let out a deep, long sigh. "We found him. Praise the Lord! My next-door neighbor and I went looking for him. He was sitting at the park with some of his old buddies. Bless their hearts, they looked out for him. I just can't figure out if he walked there or hitched a ride. It's almost a mile from the house."

"Mom, don't you think it's time?" Wes couldn't picture Pops sitting in a nursing home. They both knew Pops preferred being around family. He used to be such a vibrant and fun-loving man. At least when he was sober. Despite Pops's love for alcohol, the man was the father Wes never had.

He nudged her. "Mom, did you even look at the brochures I dropped off last week? Those nursing homes are well rated. One of the reporters at the station did a broadcast series on them not too long ago."

"I'm still not ready."

"What is it? Money? You know I would help you."

"No. I'm just not—"

"Ready. I know," Wes responded sharply. He couldn't stand this arguing every week. "I know he's your dad, but he's my grandfather. You're my mother. You got to think about you now. Don't think I haven't noticed how worn-out you've been. I can't lose both of you."

"Wesley Cade. I will be just fine. I just need to pray about it some more. Don't worry about me. Okay. Look, if you get a chance, come by and see him on Sunday."

Knowing he'd hit a nerve, Wes adjusted his tone before responding. "Sure, Mom." He added, "I love you."

"I love you too, son. Have a good night."

Wes disconnected the call. He didn't enjoy visiting with Pops these days. The man rarely remembered him. That hurt more than Wes wanted to admit.

He glanced over at the home he'd just left. What did Serena want from him, really?

Wes had heard that Serena's vice was to get what she wanted using any tactic necessary. What bothered him more was Serena's curiosity about Pops. If there was one thing he had in common with Serena, it was that they both loved investigating a good story. What reporter didn't?

But there were some parts of his grandfather's life that were a mystery even to Wes, and he wanted to protect Pops from Serena's digging. For many years, Pops was a detective in the Charlotte-Mecklenburg Missing Persons Unit. Even as his memories were fading, Pops could remember some of the cases with a vividness at the oddest moments.

From what Wes remembered, when he was about nine years old, there was one particular case that seemed to change Pops. He drank more and grew further and further apart from both Wes and his mom. About six months ago, Wes found out from his mother that the case that had haunted Pops involved the missing daughter of an old friend, guitar legend Nick Roberts, with whom Pops had played for about ten years in a band. When Roberts died, Pops had been lucid enough to attend the funeral. Since the funeral Pops seemed more depressed, tumbling farther down the slippery slope of Alzheimer's disease.

Why that particular case? Was it because the missing young woman hit so close to home? Wes, the grandson and investigative reporter, felt a strong need to help put his grandfather's ailing mind at rest.

# Chapter Three

Melanie Stowe woke to darkness. As she shook the sleep away, a stale, musty odor grabbed her nostrils. The room's temperature was uncomfortably warm, and her clothes were soaked with her sweat. What alarmed her more was the mattress against her back. This wasn't her bed. Where was she? In a panic she sat up. Her eyes adjusted to the darkness, processing strange shapes around her. This couldn't be happening. How did she get here?

She swung her legs off the bed to the floor, where she felt wood flooring beneath her bare feet. Melanie stood and then quickly sat back down as nausea swept over her. As her dizziness subsided, she thought back to last night.

She had not wanted to leave the house. But her best friend, Lisa Sloan, had wanted to go to the Paradise Club. She could see Lisa's pouty face. "Mel, come on. We haven't been out in ages." As she always did with her longtime friend, she caved.

For most of the time at the club Melanie had stood staring at her so-called friends on the dance floor. Lisa, who danced like there was no tomorrow, did come to check on her a few times. As Melanie stood there, people kept coming up to her, wanting her autograph. She had smiled and signed, but inside she'd wanted to climb back in her bed. Ever since she was a contestant on *American Voices,* her life had never been the same. She had auditioned for the national talent show with the hopes of becoming the singer she had always dreamed of being since she was a little girl. With each failed record company offer, her quest for stardom had faded.

Clutching her stomach, Melanie bent her body forward and whimpered. She stopped when she thought she heard a sound. Melanie shouted, "Is anyone there? Hello. Please why are you doing this?" Her voice sounded muffled in her ears. She waited, her body tense from fear, to hear the sound again. Nothing. A swift burst of pain around her right temple caused her to cry out. The tears rolled down her face and into her shirt collar as she willed the pain to stop. She had to get out of here. As she concentrated as much as she could, bits and pieces of last night flooded her mind.

She had been so tired. The only thing good about going out was the virgin strawberry daiquiri she drank. Melanie had finally gone to Lisa and told her she was ready to go. Lisa had offered to go with her, but knowing how hard it was for her friend to get a babysitter, Melanie had told her to stay and have fun. Plus, Melanie knew Lisa wouldn't have a problem getting a ride home.

Maybe she should have stayed longer, instead of leaving the club by herself. She'd walked past the bouncer. He had smiled and nodded at her. His smile had felt like the only genuine smile all evening. At least he hadn't stopped her to get her autograph.

Outside it was cool, a nice spring night, with a slight breeze. Normally, she would love the smell of the blossoming cherry trees that lined the sidewalk outside the club, but she was in no mood to enjoy. It was dark in the parking lot. She liked to park near the lampposts, but they had arrived later than usual, missing all the good parking spaces. Her heels clicked on the asphalt.

Funny, before *American Voices,* she would never wear heels. She couldn't walk in them. Being up on that stage, she'd sung her heart out every week in three-inch stilettos. Apparently, the experience hadn't helped her learn how to walk very well, as she stumbled over a rock. She caught herself and looked around, waiting for the laughter. These days everyone was laughing at her or looking at her with pity.

There were conversations going on in the parking lot. She noticed a couple cuddled up near a car. Their faces were so close, she was pretty sure they were in their own world. Melanie also remembered a group of guys hanging out. Smoke wafted around them as they laughed and talked smack. At the time she had been grateful for being invisible to them.

The last thought she could remember from last night was having her car keys in her hand. There was the familiar chirp after she pressed the button on her keys to unlock the car door. But before her hand touched the door handle, she sensed a presence behind her. There was no time to turn around before her mouth was covered. She struggled and then fell into unconsciousness.

So here she sat on a strange bed, in a strange place. Melanie squinted and focused on the room. In the semidarkness now, she could make out a door, because there was a thin stream of light coming from underneath. On the other side of the room, there was a small window, but it was covered with plywood from the outside. She couldn't tell if it was daytime or nighttime from where she sat. Her life hadn't turned out the way she'd wanted, but she wasn't going to die here, not like this.

She opened her mouth to yell again. "Hello. Is anyone here? Why are you doing this?" *Who are you?*

# Chapter Four

Angel shook herself awake, struggling to remember the day. *Friday*. She'd spent all Wednesday night and Thursday at the hospital, going home briefly yesterday afternoon to take a shower. As she sat up, the blanket she had had wrapped around her all night slid to the floor. She noticed the sunlight peeking from around the window blinds, casting a comforting glow across the stark hospital room. Angel turned her head and focused her drowsy eyes on Fredricka's chest, to ensure it rose and fell. Grams was all she had.

Now, Angel was a granddaddy's girl for sure. Despite losing his legs to diabetes, Nick Roberts never lost his spirit for life and God. He had been so proud of her the day she walked down the aisle at church to confess her faith in Christ. Grams had pushed his wheelchair toward the front of the church so he could be beside *his* Angel. He wouldn't have been happy at the way she had lashed out at Grams Wednesday night.

She took a deep breath, exhaled, and lifted her head. She had gone to sleep in the chair with the television playing. She turned her attention to the television in the corner. Wes Cade was the anchorman for the morning news today. Now, there was a day brightener. Angel couldn't remember the last time she had a crush, but Wes's boyish good looks made her smile.

As she watched the news, footage of a young, pretty black woman appeared on the television screen. The woman appeared to be holding a microphone in her hand. She looked familiar. Curious, Angel leaned forward to hear the woman singing a rendition of "I Will Always Love You" by Whitney Houston. The young woman's voice was hauntingly close to the popular singer's.

Wes continued the story. "This morning's lead story focuses on the disappearance of Melanie Stowe. Melanie, known simply as Mel to family and friends, went out with friends on Wednesday evening. Melanie left the Paradise Club before her friends but never arrived home. Some may recognize Melanie as a local celebrity here in Charlotte. She was recently a contestant on the national talent show *American Voices*. Even though Melanie didn't make it as a finalist, her fan base increased each week she remained on the show. If you have any tips that could lead to Melanie's whereabouts, please call the phone number on your screen."

Angel sat back in her seat, thinking Melanie's small celebrity status could help or hurt her. Oftentimes adult missing person cases weren't given as much seriousness as child cases. Adults could come and go as they pleased. So many adult missing person cases were reported for a few days on the news and then disappeared from the media headlines. Angel prayed for Melanie's safety. The young woman had been in the spotlight so much this year that maybe she wanted to disappear for a while.

For a brief moment, the news story strangely reminded Angel of her mother's disappearance. Elisa could have been a superstar. Her mother's voice would have easily blown away the competition on a show like *American Voices*.

Angel jumped in the chair when a chubby-cheeked nurse entered the room.

"Honey, you been here all night again? That chair can't be comfortable. You should go home." The nurse nodded toward Angel's grandmother. "We can call you if anything changes."

Angel shook her head. "No, that's okay. I want to be here."

"Is this your grandmother?"

She looked at the nurse and then back at Grams. "Yes, but she has been more like a mother. She raised me."

"Oh my. Bless her heart. I'm a grandmother myself. I became one way before I was planning to be one, if you catch my drift. I do love my grandbabies, though."

Angel had often wondered if she was more of a burden than a joy to her grandparents. She knew they loved her, but she imagined their life had turned out differently than they had planned. When she was younger, Fredricka had traveled with dance troupes across the country. Angel's grandmother had enjoyed her dance career until she met up with Nick, a popular guitar player in the North Carolina–based band Southern Soul. The couple had left their respective roles in the entertainment business to raise Angel's mother and uncle.

Angel reached over and smoothed her grandmother's silvery hair, now a bit tangled from the ordeal. The doctor had said she might have been experiencing a headache and even dizziness prior to her fall. All signs of a stroke. This one was a minor one, but nonetheless still dangerous. Angel couldn't help but think this was her fault. Grams had meant no harm with her comment.

The nurse invaded Angel's thoughts. "Honey, do you have some family and friends who can come be with you? This can be really stressful."

"Thanks for asking. Yes, I have been trying to contact my uncle." Angel reached into her bag and pulled out her iPhone. Her uncle hadn't responded to a single voice mail. Usually, if something was happening with Fredricka, Jacob would be on a plane or in a car immediately.

She walked out into the hallway and dialed Jacob's cell number again. This time there was no voice mail greeting. It was weird for his voice mail box to be full. Her uncle was all about the business, with his Bluetooth wrapped around his ear like some body part. Angel leaned against the wall, pondering what to do. *Aunt Liz.* She searched through her phone, hoping she still had her aunt's cell phone number.

Angel listened to the rings, trying to recall if her uncle and his family had any out-of-town plans.

"Hello." Her aunt answered like she was out of breath.

"Aunt Liz, it's Angel." For a moment, Angel thought the call had dropped. "Hello?"

"Angel. I'm sorry. I was on the treadmill. I had to catch my breath. This is a surprise. Is everything okay?"

She answered, "No! Grams had a stroke Wednesday night. I've been calling Jacob for, like, two days now. Is there something wrong?"

Her aunt's voice faltered again before she answered. "Angel, I'm sorry to hear about Fredricka. Is she okay?"

"She's stable." Angel huffed, "Liz, where is my uncle?" *This is not like him.*

"I don't know."

Liz spoke so low, Angel almost didn't hear her. "What do you mean?"

"I guess Jacob hasn't told anyone yet. Angel, I asked your uncle to move out a few weeks ago."

"Are you serious?" Angel knew her uncle Jacob was not an easy man to be around, but she knew he loved Liz. The man worshipped the ground his wife walked on.

"I can't go into it right now, Angel. It's best your uncle talks to you. I'm sorry about Miss Fredricka. I will see if I can help you track down Jacob, okay?"

"Okay." Angel ended the call and stared at the phone, still trying to comprehend what Liz had told her. Jacob and Liz had been married all of Angel's life. No one was perfect, but her uncle and aunt had always embodied the perfect life. What had caused them to unravel?

Whatever was going on, she needed Jacob to show up soon. Grams would need some serious care and attention now. She couldn't make these decisions on her own. Since her birthday, Angel had felt like she had crossed over into a new level of adulthood. Loneliness and fear crept into her mind as she leaned against the wall outside her grandmother's hospital room.

Just as Angel was trying to get her life together, it seemed like her world was falling apart. Again.

# Chapter Five

"Candace, I just don't know if I can handle this. I just lost Granddad," Angel confided on the phone.

"Honey, I know. It's only been about six months, right? Look, Fredricka is strong, and she's going to come through. God won't give you more than you can bear."

Angel felt grateful that Candace Johnson had taken the time from her busy Saturday morning schedule at the Crown of Beauty Salon to encourage her. If anyone knew about going through difficulties, it would be the woman who had become her surrogate big sister in the past year. Angel had observed Candace's strength through the trial of the woman who had murdered both Candace's husband and best friend. It was because of Candace that Angel began participating in the Overcomers Women's Ministry, a ministry that Candace had started at Victory Gospel Church.

Angel confessed, "When we left the church the other night, we argued about my mother."

"Did you tell her about the project you are working on?" Candace asked.

"No. When I started working on the documentary years ago, everyone seemed to be uptight about me digging up the past. I think Grams thinks my mother is going to walk back into our lives after all this time."

"Angel, you know your grandmother is a woman of faith, but she would want you to do what you needed to do. Lord knows this has to be hard. I've lost loved ones, but I can't imagine one of them simply disappearing and not knowing what happened to them." Candace grew quiet and then inquired, "Angel, do you need me to come sit with you? I have a new stylist in the salon now, and she's working out pretty good."

"No, no. I appreciate you taking the time to talk to me. I know Saturday mornings are busy."

"You know how much I love you and Fredricka. You both are family and were there for me and the kids this past year. Be sure to let Fredricka know I will stop by and take care of her hair. I know how she likes to be looking foxy."

Angel laughed. "She would love that. Thanks, Candace." After saying good-bye, Angel thought about Wednesday night's birthday surprise, which she now knew Candace had secretly planned. Angel smiled. She'd missed what it felt like to have a genuine friend who cared.

She checked the clock on the wall. Right now Grams needed her. Angel rose from the chair to head back toward the hospital room. The CT scan and MRI had determined that the type of stroke Grams had Wednesday night was the result of a blood clot. Blessedly, they were able to arrive at the hospital in the crucial three-hour time frame for stroke victims, allowing the emergency room doctors to restore Grams's blood flow. Now it was all about preventing a second stroke from occurring.

A bit of aphasia had set in, causing Grams to slur her words, and her right arm was not cooperating. The doctor seemed optimistic that with rehabilitation, Grams's brain would rewire itself, giving her her mobility back. They needed to prepare for rehabilitation for a few weeks in the hospital before Grams could return home.

Angel walked into the hospital room and was startled by a figure in the room. At first she thought her uncle Jacob had snuck past her, but her uncle would never be caught in a cowboy hat. She grinned as the man rose from the seat in the corner, where she'd slept the night before.

"Uncle Eddie." She crossed the room and hugged the tall, dark man. Eddie Gowins, better known as Eddie G., wasn't really her uncle, but a longtime family friend. He had played the drums in the band with her granddad.

Angel stepped back to look up at him. "I haven't seen you in ages." Eddie was well over six feet tall, muscular, and almost imposing, especially today with his cowboy hat and boots.

Eddie had stopped smoking a few years ago, but the raspiness remained in his voice. "I heard through the grapevine, Fredricka wasn't doing too good. You know I had to come see about Nick's girl."

Angel chuckled at Eddie's reference to her almost eighty-year-old grandmother as her granddad's girl. "She will be happy to see you." Angel sat down at the bottom of the bed.

Eddie G. shook his head. "Man, I miss Nick. He knew how to live life to the fullest. Always admired your grandparents."

"I miss him too, Eddie."

For an awkward moment, they sat quietly. Angel folded and then unfolded her arms.

She peered at Eddie and asked, "So how's Denise doing?" She cleared her throat so she wouldn't choke on her next comment about Eddie's daughter. "I hear she is getting married soon."

Eddie stared at her for a moment before he answered. He shook his head. "Yes. The wedding is later this summer. I was just talking about you the other day. Would be nice if you could film the wedding. I've heard great things about your video business."

Her business, Angel Media, was booming due to the fact that the wedding season had just begun. She'd worked hard last year starting up the company and putting together a portfolio. Angel felt she brought a unique style to the footage she shot and edited. Despite reservations from her family, she was doing the entre-preneurial thing, something that awed her sometimes.

Angel crossed her arms. Despite her success, she couldn't see offering her services to Denise. How could she when three years ago, Kenneth Morgan, now De-nise's fiancé, was the love of Angel's life? That day when Angel walked in on Denise and Kenneth together at his apartment, she'd lost her best friend and boyfriend. Later, when she found out Denise had had a baby boy with Kenneth, Angel lost herself. It had only been by building her business and becoming a Christian in the past year that she'd found her footing.

She shook her head. "Sorry, Eddie. I'm not sure if I could. Don't get me wrong. Things worked out the way they needed to. I just don't know if I should be anywhere near the wedding." For years, both she and Denise had talked about how they would be the maid of honor at each other's wedding. All that was history now.

"I'm so sorry to see you two girls are not friends any-more. You were like sisters."

Before she could respond, Angel heard movement behind her. The nurse was rolling Grams back in from rehab. Her grandmother looked at her, but Angel couldn't read Grams's expression, because her eyes lacked the usual spark.

Eddie bowed his head toward Grams, not speaking a word until the nurse helped her back into the bed.

Grams quietly nodded in Eddie's direction.

Eddie bowed his head again. "Fredricka, I just wanted to check on you. You know I promised Nick I would look after you and Angel. I'll come back when you are up to it." He winked at her and then placed his cowboy hat on his head. "Angel, let's talk soon. I'd like to help you get some business."

"Thanks, Uncle Eddie."

As Eddie approached the door, a man swooped in. Both men almost collided with each other.

Her uncle Jacob looked like he hadn't slept in days. His chocolate brown face was covered with a several days old beard peppered with gray. Jacob glared at Eddie. "Eddie. What are you doing here?"

Eddie retorted, "I'm leaving, Jake. No need to upset your mother."

Angel could hear the tap of Eddie's cowboy boots as he made his way down the hallway. She had never understood why Jacob disliked Eddie. The feelings were mutual. Eddie wasn't too fond of Jacob, either. She had often wondered if the rivalry stemmed from Granddaddy always including Eddie in family events, almost like he was a son.

Grams sputtered, "Jake . . ."

Jacob moved to the side of the bed and leaned his head against Fredricka's forehead. "Mom, it's okay. I'm here. You are going to be all right."

Angel was glad he was there, but wanted an explanation. "Jacob, I've been trying to reach you."

Her uncle kept his attention on his mother. "I'm here now, Angel. I will take over from here. Go home and get some rest."

*What?* He was just going to sail in here and dismiss her? Where had he been? He could at least reveal what was up with him and Aunt Liz. Angel's rising emotions were interrupted by her vibrating phone. She reached in her pocket and pulled out the phone. When she looked down at the caller ID, her anger toward her uncle switched to anxiety.

Angel glanced at her family and then slipped out into the hallway to answer the call. "Hello."

"Angel? Angel Roberts?"

Angel answered, "Yes."

"Hello. This is Jennifer from the Bring Them Home Foundation. We used to keep in touch with Nick Roberts about cases that came in."

A few weeks before he passed away, Angel's granddad had given Angel a shoe box full of correspondence, most of it from this organization. "Yes. He passed away late last year. I touched base with someone in your office a few months ago to let you know that I wanted to receive those updates."

"I will be happy to work with you. I worked with Mr. Roberts for many years. Now Elisa, she's your mother.

"Yes."

The woman on the other end of the line was quiet for a few seconds. "I do want to warn you this process can be difficult, and it's been a number of years now."

"I understand. I need to do this."

"Okay. We have had a few Jane Doe cases come in."

Angel leaned against the wall and gripped the phone.

"But I'm sorry none of them were a match for your mother."

Angel let out the breath she didn't realize she had been holding. "Okay."

"You know, I preferred not to dash Mr. Roberts's hopes, but he wanted any information we had. I think it was important to him to know we were still actively working to find your mother."

"We appreciate your organization doing this. Please keep me updated too."

After saying good-bye, Angel clicked the phone off. It was definitely time for her to move forward. She needed to start by putting together the events that led up to the night her mother disappeared. There had to be some clues people have been overlooking all these years.

There was one man who could help her. Her grand-dad had lost faith in him, but when Angel started on the documentary a few years back, she realized Detective Lenny Cade's obsession would become her main connection to the past.

# Chapter Six

Wes turned into the drive of the home where he grew up. It resembled most of the other brick homes with one-car garages in the cul-de-sac. His mother used to spend a lot of time in the garden. As he exited his Honda, Wes noticed a few of the annuals, but the yard definitely had a neglected feel to it.

He unlocked the front door, expecting the smells of a home-cooked meal. Instead he was met by a gloomy quietness. The blinds were closed shut in the living room. Everything about his childhood home seemed so different. Maybe because he was different.

He called out, "Mom!" His mother knew he was coming by. Wes strained his ears and heard voices coming from the bedroom down the hallway. He walked hesitantly toward the open bedroom door with his ear cocked to catch the conversation.

"Dad, Baxter isn't here. Look, please let's get you dressed."

"Well, where is he? Wanda, we have to find him."

Wes entered the room. "Mom. Pops."

Wanda turned toward him, her face weary. "Hey, Wes."

"Let me help you." He moved to the other side of his grandfather and grabbed the sleeve that his mother had been trying to help guide Pops's arm through.

Pops looked at him with a faint smile. "Boy, where you been? Did you bring the girl home with you?"

Wes grinned. "Nope. No girl this time, Pops."

"Wes, you got to help me find Baxter." Pops's eyes were drooping, and his speech was slurred.

Wes patted his grandfather's shoulder. "Don't worry, Pops. Baxter is fine. Why don't you lay back and enjoy a nap?" Pops seemed to be drifting in and out of a memory from a decade ago. The last time Wes had brought a girl home was when he was in college, right around the time Pops's chocolate Lab, Baxter, had died.

Wanda switched the channels on the television until she found what appeared to be an old black-and-white Western. She turned and smiled. "His favorite." She nodded for Wes to move toward the door.

Once they both were outside in the hallway, his mom touched his arm. She eyed him. "Seems like every time he sees you, he is asking about some girl. Is there something I should know?"

Wes laughed. "Believe me, I'd like to know too."

His mother smiled. "Oh, hon, the right girl will come along when you are not looking. I can tell you this here girl is sorry I haven't had a chance to start dinner yet."

"Mom, don't even sweat it." Besides, what he really needed was some spiritual food today. After joining Serena at her apartment on Friday night, Wes realized he had grown lethargic about his commitments.

His mother walked ahead down the hall. "Tell me about church. I've missed too many Sundays with Dad needing care. The younger Freeman is pretty much pastoring now, right?"

Reverend Jonathan Freeman had been filling in for his ailing father, senior pastor of Victory Gospel Church, for a year now. Wes followed behind her into the kitchen. "Yes. The older reverend still attends when he is able, but his son delivers the sermons most Sundays now."

As they entered the small kitchen, Wes stopped and looked around. He had spent many afternoons working on homework at the round country table. He watched his mother open and close cabinets and then open the fridge to stare at the shelves. Wanda put her hands on her hips. "My goodness, Wes, I should have gone grocery shopping. It just slipped my mind."

Wes responded, "Why don't we eat out?"

Wanda turned and shook her head. "Wes, I can't leave him."

"Yes, of course. I will pick up some food." Wes scolded himself for not thinking to grab some food after he left church. He should have known not to expect his mother to fix a Sunday meal. Life was no longer the same.

His mother touched his cheek. "My sweet boy. I sure could put my feet up right about now." Wanda entered the living room and turned the lamps on. A warmth radiated from the golden lamp shades, pushing the gloominess away. As Wanda sank into the recliner, she said with a sigh, "Honey, whatever you find to eat works for me."

Wes left the house. As he drove away from the house, he fought back emotions. Pops lost in the past. His mother's weary spirit. He had always had a small family, just Mom and Pops. Both of them seemed so fragile now. He felt like he should be doing more.

Wes pulled into a nearby Chinese restaurant. The restaurant was packed with people dressed in their church clothes. He walked up to the counter and ordered broccoli and chicken, pork fried rice, egg rolls, and wings from the menu. Not the most healthy selections, but this was the kind of meal his mom would bring home after working a long shift at the hospital. He liked seeing her come through the door with the brown paper bag, oftentimes with one side soaked from the food cartons inside.

As he sat waiting for his order, some people recognized him. That was one of the benefits of being a local reporter. He usually liked to talk, but he was in a subdued mood at the moment and just wanted to get back to his family. Like the curious reporter he was, he checked his phone. He wanted to keep up with any leads in the disappearance of that local celebrity, Melanie. Back in the day, his pops would have been on a missing case like this.

"Sir, your order is ready." The cashier interrupted his scrolling through e-mail.

Wes inhaled the smells coming from the brown bag as he drove back to his mother's house. He was hungrier than he thought. As Wes approached the house, he saw a small white car, what looked like a Toyota Corolla, parked in front of the house. He didn't remember his mother mentioning anything about company. He turned into the drive, cut off the car, and then grabbed the bag. As he headed toward the front door, he noticed a young woman had stepped out of the driver's side of the car. There was something about her face that seemed so familiar. Where had he seen her before?

His reporter's senses kicked in as she approached.

It was hard to tell her age. She was about four inches shorter than him, and her curly black hair was pulled back into a ponytail. Her face appeared apprehensive as she approached him.

"Can I help you?" he asked.

She stared at his face and then finally stuttered, "Yes, I'm l-looking for Detective Lenny Cade."

Wes frowned. No one had referred to his grandfather as a detective in years. Pops had been retired about seven years now. "That's my grandfather. May I ask why you are looking for him?"

She looked down at the restaurant bag in his hand. "I'm sorry. I don't mean to intrude. I wondered if this was a good idea." The woman clasped her small hands and then pulled them apart as she talked. "I just left church, and I've been driving around and around. I thought I would try to see him. Is he here?"

Now more curious, Wes studied the young woman. She looked so familiar to him, but he could not figure out why. "He's not up for company today."

"Okay. Well, when is a good time to see him?"

Feeling a bit protective of Pops, Wes narrowed his eyes. "Who did you say you were again?"

"I didn't. I'm sorry. I'm being so rude," she blurted. "My name is Angel. Angel Roberts. Detective Cade was a friend of my grandfather, Nick Roberts. I wanted to ask him some questions about my mother's case. Elisa Roberts."

Speechless, Wes stared at the woman. That was where the familiarity was coming from. He'd recently seen pictures of Elisa Roberts. He remembered a photo of a little girl. Well, here she was, all grown up. She had definitely inherited her mother's beautiful bone structure.

Wes responded, "Why don't you come in? Maybe I can help you." Maybe they could help each other.

# Chapter Seven

*Now what?* Angel had had no clue the reporter Wes Cade was related to Detective Lenny Cade. She followed Wes into the house, wondering if this was a good idea. Her goal was to do her investigation without letting anyone in her family know. This guy's whole career was based on reporting stories. Not that it would be a bad idea. Maybe she needed some media attention on her mother's disappearance. It had been so long.

Her beautiful African American mother had been in the news for a few weeks only because her granddad was a famous local musician. It angered her that the media gave attention to certain high-profile missing person cases, while others were barely mentioned. Thankfully, today there was the Internet and social media, which helped with spreading the news.

Angel focused on the cozy living room she had stepped into. A woman who resembled Wes was sitting in a recliner and appeared to have been disturbed from a nap. Her curly sister locks were peppered with gray and positioned high on the top of her head.

The woman blinked several times and said, "Wes, honey, you were supposed to come back with food. I didn't know you planned to come back with a guest." Despite her comment, a smile spread across the older woman's face, putting Angel at ease.

"I will explain. Let me put this food in the kitchen," Wes replied.

Wes disappeared through a doorway off the living room. Angel wondered if he had had second thoughts about inviting her inside. She didn't have long to ponder this before he returned. He stared intently at her.

"This is my mother, Wanda. Mom, this is—"

"I know who she is, Wes. It's Angel, right?"

Startled, both Angel and Wes eyed Wanda.

Wes blurted, "Mom, how did you know who she was?"

Wanda lifted herself from the recliner and walked around the coffee table, which was covered with family photos and African American figurines, and extended her hand toward Angel. "I knew your mother. You look so much like her. She was a beautiful woman. Your grandmother too. Beauty runs in the family."

Angel's face grew warm. She knew her fair skin had probably turned visibly red around her ears and cheeks. She shook Wanda's hand. "Thank you. I really hate to intrude on your Sunday afternoon. I've been working up the nerve to do this for some time."

"No problem. We haven't had guests in some time on Sunday. Why don't you sit down?" Wanda took her arm and guided her to the couch.

Angel glanced at Wes, who stood watching the exchange between his mother and her. She didn't want to look at his face too long. This was the same man she stared at, instead of listening to, when he reported the news. His clean-shaven face was stunningly handsome up close, kind of reminiscent of one of her favorite actors, Columbus Short. Wes must have been to church today, because he still was dressed in a suit, minus the jacket.

She'd gone to the eight o'clock service, despite not having Grams beside her. The absence of Grams had weighed heavily on her as she listened to the morning message. A few years ago, she wouldn't have cared about having her grandparents around, but she missed both of them today. They had been a major force in her life, always there when she needed them, even when she'd been rebellious.

After the call from the Bring Them Home Foundation, she didn't sleep, not that she'd been sleeping much, anyway. She decided today was the day she would try to see Detective Cade. Angel had met him twice in her life. Once with her granddad. She remembered the depth of sadness and the tears that did not fall as Granddad asked Detective Cade if he would continue to look for her mother. Angel was almost seven years old then, and she remembered that the conversation took place a few weeks before she started second grade.

The second time she met Detective Cade was at the opening of Southern Soul Café. Her granddad and the detective had gathered there with other members of the popular North Carolina–based band. What she remembered most was the coldness her granddad displayed toward Detective Cade. She'd always thought of her granddad as warm and funny. It never occurred to her that he would not speak to someone. At some point, Detective Cade came over to her to introduce himself. He was the first person who commented about how much she resembled her mother. She didn't think so.

Wanda returned to the recliner, while Wes sat down in a chair. Angel sat on the couch and turned her body slightly toward Wanda. "I really appreciate this. My granddad passed away about six months ago. Unfortunately, my grandmother suffered a minor stroke this past week."

"Oh, you poor thing. Is your grandmother going to be okay?" Wanda leaned forward, her eyes filled with concern.

"Yes, she is expected to recover after some rehab."

"Pops and I were able to attend your granddad's funeral. Nick and my dad were good friends back in the day. It was hard for him to be there," Wanda said.

"I was hoping to talk to Detective Cade." Angel lowered her voice. "I had some questions about the day my mother disappeared."

Wes, who had been very quiet, spoke up. "You don't remember anything about that day?"

Angel turned to face him. "My memory is pretty fuzzy."

Wanda added, "Well, you were young. I remember it was your fifth birthday." Wanda pointed at Wes. "Wes had received an invitation to your birthday party, but he opted to go fishing with Pops."

Wes cocked his head to the side. "Really? I didn't know that."

Wanda smiled. "You and Angel hung out a few times. You were older. Wes was almost nine when you turned five."

Angel smiled. "Small world." Maybe that was why she had always felt like Wes was a familiar face to her.

Wes shook his head. "I guess. I just don't remember."

"Angel, I attended your birthday party. From what I remember, there were more adults there than children," Wanda noted.

Angel frowned. "I remember that too." As a matter of fact, she couldn't remember there being many children at the party at all. Or if there was a special theme. Growing up, she had had friends who had birthday parties with cool themes that included a princess or a superhero. What really bothered Angel was the lack of photos. *Who doesn't have photos from a kid's birthday party?*

Wanda twisted her hands like she was nervous. "It's not a great time in my father's life right now. He's suffering from Alzheimer's. I don't know if there is much he can help you with, although some days he thinks he is still working a case."

Angel's hopes were crushed. Detective Cade was the one person she had been counting on. "I'm so sorry to hear that. I touched bases with him about four years ago, when I started working on a documentary about my mother. I just lost focus. Now I wish I had stayed on course."

Wanda clasped her hands together. "I'm so sorry. I can't imagine what you and your family have gone through. My dad worked a lot of missing cases over the years, but I know because he watched your mother growing up, he really was determined to help find her."

Not wanting to waste her visit, Angel inquired, "What do you remember about my mother? Was she happy or sad the day of my birthday?"

Wanda sighed deeply. "I couldn't tell. She seemed happy to be giving you a party. You were all dressed up in a pink sundress. I think she was wearing pink too. I know she was telling everyone she had finally received an offer for a record deal."

"Mom, I didn't realize you knew the Robertses so well. Were you close to Angel's mom?" Wes asked.

"Oh no." Wanda shook her head. "I actually graduated with Jake. Angel, it was your uncle who invited me. I mean us. Wes and me." Wanda smiled nervously as she spoke about Jacob.

"Oh." Angel wondered how close Wanda was to her uncle. She had never seen Jacob with any woman other than Liz and really didn't know much about his early years.

"Elisa?"

Angel's heart skipped a beat. A voice from behind her had called out her mother's name. She turned to find an older man standing in his bare feet and pajamas. His shock of gray hair resembled a halo on his head.

Wes jumped up from the chair and moved toward the older man. "Pops, you're awake. Let's get you back in your room."

Pops moved his head back and forth and pointed at Angel. "Elisa?"

Angel rose from the couch. "I'm sorry. Maybe I should come back another time." *Or not at all.*

The detective continued to try to communicate with her. "Elisa, where have you been? We've been looking for you."

Wanda moved beside her father and gripped his arm. "Pops, that's not her. That's Elisa's daughter. Now, let's get you back to your room."

"I told Nick, he did it," Pops shouted. "Nick wouldn't believe me." Suddenly looking confused, he whispered as he stared at her with wild eyes. "Maybe I was wrong."

Angel's eyes connected with Pops's. She knew she should leave, but she had to ask him a question. "Who? Detective Cade, who did what?"

She tried to move closer, but Wes stepped in front of her. "I think it's best you go now."

Angel looked over Wes's shoulder and watched as Wanda guided the ailing man back down the hallway. She looked at Wes. "I'm sorry."

Wes walked over to open the front door. He stared at her intently, his face displaying a mixture of emotions. "Don't be sorry. I'm sorry Pops can't help you. Maybe I can. Let's stay in touch."

She nodded and then walked briskly out the door, with Pops's voice filling her head. "I told Nick, he did it." Angel doubted Wes meant what he'd said. The reporter probably just wanted to get rid of her. Could she blame him?

Pops's statement pounded her until she was inside her car. She struggled through tears as she fiddled with the keys. Finally, she found the right key, pushed it in, and turned the ignition. She pulled off, tears streaking down her face.

At least the detective had confirmed what she had always known in her heart. Her mother was dead. In the back of her mind, she was scared the person responsible was someone close to her mother. The same person who had abandoned Angel the night her mother vanished into thin air. What really was his excuse for never contacting his own daughter?

# Chapter Eight

Wes unloosened his tie as he sank down into his desk chair. This morning the top news story continued to be about the missing *American Voices* contestant, Melanie Stowe. He couldn't help but think back to yesterday afternoon with Angel Roberts. He meant what he'd told her. Wes wanted to help her and felt horrible about asking her to leave. Pops's confusion was not only upsetting, but disturbing. Despite his affected mind, Pops was still determined to bring the person responsible for Elisa Roberts's disappearance to justice. But who?

He sensed a real story right under his nose. The last story Wes followed was the trial of Hillary Green. The woman was sentenced to life for the murder of defense lawyers Pamela Coleman and Mitch Harris and Detective Frank Johnson. Twenty years had passed, so it was doubtful Elisa hadn't fallen victim to foul play. Where were her remains?

Growing up without her mother and not knowing what happened had to have been tough for Angel. His dad had died in a car accident when he was still a toddler. While Wes didn't remember his father, he visited the grave site with his mom each year.

Wes tapped his keyboard to wake up the sleeping monitor. He clicked on a folder he'd created a few months ago. Inside the folder were photos and a few video clips from the station's archives. He studied the last photo taken of Elisa Roberts. Angel had inherited her mother's sculptured cheekbones and big brown eyes—the kind of eyes that made his heart flip-flop. Angel had a fairer skin tone, but she could have been her mother's identical twin.

He decided to see what else he could find on Angel. Wes did a quick search on Facebook. Everybody, including his own mother, had a Facebook page. Sure enough, several Angel Robertses appeared in the search results. After a quick scroll, he found her avatar. She didn't post on her wall much. Every few days she shared an inspirational post and videos. Most of the recent videos posted on her wall were from weddings. He noticed her Facebook profile gave him a link to her Web site.

He clicked the link and watched the Web site load. Angel Media. He remembered her mentioning she was working on a documentary. It appeared there were even more wedding videos in her portfolio. He put on his headphones and clicked on a video. He loved the camera angles Angel used as she focused on the bride and then the groom. She was good, capturing the romance and joy of the couple's special day. He wondered if he would have that moment. As he approached thirty, the bachelor status had grown pretty lame.

A tap on his shoulder interrupted his musings about possible nuptials. He pulled off the headphones and spun around. He groaned inside as Serena stood with her hand on her hip, looking way too seductive for the work environment.

"Are we looking to march down the aisle soon? I certainly hope not. I would be really disappointed."

"Hey, Serena. I was just checking out something for a friend." He closed the Web site. The last thing he needed was Serena snooping in his business. He was entirely clear what her motivation was for being so friendly lately. "What can I do for you?"

"That's a dangerous question, Wes. There are a lot of things you can do for me."

Wes sputtered, "Work related, Serena."

Serena laughed. "Wes Cade, you are so fun to mess with." She flipped her hair over her back and smiled down at him. "I was going to head down to Melanie Stowe's high school to talk to some of her former teachers, but I have had a change of plans."

"Yeah? How's the story coming?" As the senior reporter, Serena took on the big stories and was known to dig deep and sometimes too far. He could never figure out why someone with her incredible looks didn't go for the anchor role. She'd been at the station for at least five years, two years more than him. The two anchors at the station had both been here for ten years. Maybe Serena was just waiting. Whenever he had a chance to fill in in the anchor role, he could see himself being there one day. If it wasn't for his mom and Pops, he'd consider moving to another market.

Wes tuned back into Serena's update. "Melanie's ex-boyfriend is of interest. He sounds like he is the jealous type and was not too crazy about her being on a national talent show. You know the deal. An abusive boyfriend. Girlfriend goes missing. In this case, the girlfriend was a Charlotte native who had her fifteen minutes of fame on a national talent contest. Sounds like a real winner to me, but I will leave it to you to find out the dirt."

"Me?" Wes responded. "What's going on?"

Serena licked her lips. "I have another story to pursue."

Wes raised his eyebrow. "Really? A bigger story than Melanie Stowe?"

Serena leaned forward. She was close enough for Wes to smell her expensive perfume. He slid his chair back. Serena looked him in the eyes. "This missing person case is right up your alley. If you can get the real truth, this will boost your career beyond what you can imagine." She stood upright and then asked, "By the way, how's your grandfather doing?"

Wes swallowed before answering. He was still grasping the fact that Serena had just dropped her assignment in his lap. "Uh, not too good."

"That's a shame. It sure would be nice to know his take on the case."

He frowned. "There are others folks in the missing persons unit we can talk to, Serena."

"Yeah, I know."

"Is there a reason in particular why you are interested in my grandfather?"

"I'm just curious about an old case. That's all. Look, I will catch you later, kiddo." Before walking away, she pointed a manicured red-tipped finger at him. "Get the truth."

Wes watched as Serena sauntered out of the newsroom. *What is she up to?*

He walked across the newsroom and knocked on the news producer's door. Alan James called out, "Come in."

"Hey, Alan. What's going on?"

Alan put down his cup of coffee and looked up from his laptop. "I should ask that of you. I take it Serena has shared her news."

"I'm shocked. She must have a pretty big assignment to let this opportunity go."

"Something she's been working on for a while."

Wes threw up his hands. "Any clues?"

"The only thing I can tell you is she will be leaving for New York tonight."

"New York?"

"Yep. You, in the meantime, need to pursue any leads about Melanie. She's a Charlotte native. We need to be at the head of this story."

Wes shook his head. "I'm well aware. Serena dropped a hint about the boyfriend."

"I think we should pursue him hard. Right now, he's been dodging interviews. We need an exclusive with him. Can you pull it off?"

"Hey, I'm on it."

"All right. I'm counting on you, Wes."

"Yes, sir." Wes walked out of his producer's office. He wasn't sure how he would pull it off. While the way Serena went after a story was a bit manipulative, Wes chose to use his good guy charms. When he sat back down at his desk, he opened the Internet browser to surf to the Facebook Web site. Social media had become an excellent source of information for him. Being the web-savvy guy he was, he had been the first one in the newsroom to open accounts at all the popular social networks. He liked talking to fans and getting information. Sometimes the information didn't pan out, but he had verified several leads in the past and had brought the story back to Alan later.

Right now he wasn't so much looking for any leads. He would after he connected with someone who was on his mind all night. He wasn't sure if Angel was interested in hearing from him again, but he pulled up her Facebook profile and made a friend request. Wes wanted another face-to-face with her. Their first meeting was pretty awkward.

He still couldn't believe he'd hung out with her when they were children. At nine years of age, he was pretty sure he still didn't like girls. Yet he had to admit there was a familiarity with her yesterday. It had more to do with the fact that she looked like her missing mother.

He clicked open a folder to access a video clip. There was one person that was questioned extensively about Elisa's disappearance. Wes pressed PLAY and then paused the video to study the face of Angelino Mancini as he was escorted into the police department for questioning. This was twenty years before, but Angelino could have been cast as a *Jersey Shore* cast member. He had a bronze tan, and his muscles rippled through the polo shirt he was wearing. Angelino and Elisa, with her deep chocolate complexion, were definitely the most striking couple Wes had ever seen. Wes jotted down some questions. *How did this interracial couple meet? Did their cultural differences drive them apart?*

Wes could see which parent gave Angel her strong jaw structure. When she left yesterday, he noticed how her face was set as she tried to contain her emotions. Had she ever talked to the former street-tough boxer, who some thought was responsible for Elisa's disappearance? What kind of relationship did Angel have with her Italian American father?

# Chapter Nine

Angel hummed and then sang the chorus of one of her favorite songs. "I need more, more, more, Jesus more of you. I need so much more, Jesus more, more, more." She didn't dare sing in front of others, but in the car she felt free to sing and worship.

After leaving the Cades' home yesterday, she had stopped to visit with Grams. The entire time she had wanted to lean across Grams's shoulder, like she did when she was a little girl, but she couldn't. Even after losing her granddad, Angel wasn't prepared to see Grams struggling. She'd gone home feeling the weight of change.

Then there was Wes Cade. She would have never made that connection. He was kind to her in spite of her awkward interruption of his family's Sunday afternoon. She could relate to the tension on his face as he observed his grandfather's confusion. Angel wasn't so sure she wanted Wes's offer to help, though. She had decided she wanted to continue to find out what she could about her mother, but without telling her family. This was something she needed to do, even if it meant she had to face the man who could have been responsible.

Angel put on her turn signal as she approached her exit. It was Monday, and bills still needed to be paid. When she first joined the Bible study, Candace taught about the importance of keeping on your garment of praise. Angel felt the heaviness lift as she continued to sing along with JoAnn Rosario. "Fill me like an empty cup, and when it seems I have had enough, I still need more, more, more."

By the time she arrived in the parking lot of Lenora's Bridal Boutique, her anxiety had lost the battle and she felt energized despite her lack of sleep. She parked her car and headed toward the boutique's door. Lenora had recently changed the window to display formal wear. *It's that time of the year again.* Just as she anticipated, when Angel walked through the entrance, several young women were waiting for a consultation with a member of Lenora Freeman's staff. Some were there to be fitted for a wedding gown, but the high-pitched chatter indicated that most were looking for a prom gown.

Angel squeezed her way through the teenagers to find the queen of the shop. Lenora Freeman was well known as the first lady of Victory Gospel Church, but she was also a popular wedding planner and bridal shop owner. Lenora needed a videographer on her staff. Thanks to Candace's swift introduction, Angel no longer worried about her next video production. This time of year, wedding season was in full swing.

Angel walked toward the dressing area in the back and found Lenora talking to a teary-eyed young woman. Angel was surprised at how down to earth Lenora could be, despite the fact that she was the most elegant woman she had ever met. Always dressed in an impeccable skirt suit or pantsuit, her makeup flawless, the woman handled her business, her brides, and her role as a first lady with perfection.

Lenora rubbed the shoulders of the young woman, who was now visibly crying. "Honey, you want this to be your day. Make sure this is the dress for you, and not what your family wants you to wear. Now, do you think you found the dress you wanted today?"

The young woman nodded. "Yes, I really liked the first one."

"Then that's your dress, honey. Let me talk to your mother."

Angel smiled at the sternness of Lenora's words but the soft passion in her eyes. She knew Lenora was for the bride, and she would make sure her bride felt secure about *her* day.

Lenora looked over and spotted her. "Oh, Angel. I'm glad you were able to come. Florence, take care of my little bride here. Make sure she gets the dress *she* wants. If the mother has questions, she can see me. Angel, let's go to my office."

Angel took long strides to keep up with Lenora, who, with the stilettos she was wearing, had to be nearly six feet in height. All business, Lenora closed the door and reached out her arms. "How are you doing?"

Angel accepted the hug. "I'm doing okay. Thank you for asking."

"Bless your heart. You know, I would have understood if you couldn't make it. How's your grandmother doing? Pastor and I are both praying for her."

"She's stable. I appreciate the prayers, Mrs. Freeman—"

"Uh-uh." The woman cut Angel off with her finger. "When are you going to learn? Call me Lenora."

Angel grinned. "Lenora. My grandmother has some rehabilitation to go through. The stroke has affected her right side a bit, and she is understandably frustrated."

"I can imagine. Ms. Fredricka is a ball of fire, even at her age. We are praying for a full recovery. Your grandmother has been such a blessing to so many people."

Lenora walked over behind her desk. "Look, I don't want to hold you. I know you need to get back to the hospital. I just want to go over the wedding details for this weekend."

Angel took the seat across from Lenora's desk, which was filled with neatly stacked and organized catalogs. Lenora quickly flipped through her appointment book, which occupied the middle of the desk. From where she sat, Angel could see the perfect handwriting. Angel wished she could say her desk looked like this, but instead it was full of sticky notes, scribbled-in notebooks, and DVD cases.

"Now, I have scheduled a couple more weddings for the summer, and they all indicated they would love a videographer. I will check with you about those before you leave."

Angel responded, "Sounds good. So the couple this week is Tommy and Sharise?"

"Yes, they both like the package where you interview them individually before and after the wedding. If you can arrive a bit early, they also want you to interview some of the guests as they arrive and then again at the reception. By the way, Brad took some great shots. Aren't they a beautiful couple?" Lenora passed an envelope to her.

Angel took the envelope and slid out a few photos. Tom, the groom, was slender, tall, and reminded her of the actor Morris Chestnut. The bride was simply stunning. Sharise was equally as tall and had long, flowing hair. "These are beautiful. You indicated last week that they want to do some footage in another location."

"Yes. They are college sweethearts, so they are interested in doing a shoot at UNC Charlotte. They want footage of the places where they first met. Will you be okay with meeting them on the campus Thursday?"

"Yes, that's fine." It would be a busy week, but Angel looked forward to filming the couple. Her mind whirled like a movie projector as she began thinking of how the final production would come together. It felt good to focus on work.

"Okay, now, here are the names of weddings I have coming up. Let me know if you are able to add these to your calendar. They all loved your portfolio."

Angel reached over and took the list from Lenora. There were about five couples listed, but one couple leapt off the page.

"Angel, is something wrong?"

She had sucked in a breath sharply, but she didn't realize how her reaction appeared to Lenora. "I'm fine."

"Are you sure?" Lenora eyed her. A knock on the door saved Angel from having to explain. Not that she even knew what to say. She folded the list and stuffed the paper into the side pocket of her bag.

A woman burst into the office. "Mrs. Freeman, I need to have a word with you."

Lenora lifted a well-groomed arched eyebrow at the woman. "Excuse me. I have someone in my office right now. Can you please wait outside? I will be with you shortly."

"Yes, but—" The woman stopped and stared at Angel. She was petite, probably just a few inches shorter than Angel. Her blond hair was pulled back, showing off intense blue eyes. The woman stepped back and placed her hand on her chest. "Oh, I'm sorry."

Angel stood from her chair. "It's okay. Lenora, I will meet with Tommy and Sharise on Thursday and will see you on Saturday, before the ceremony begins."

Lenora had a smile on her face, but her eyes displayed displeasure as she focused first on the woman who had burst in and then on Angel. "Okay. Thank you for stopping by, and tell your grandmother we are praying for her."

Angel turned to walk out of the office, but the woman remained standing at the door, still staring at her. *This woman clearly has some issues.* "Excuse me. I need to get by."

"Yes, of course." The strange woman stepped to the side.

Angel slid by her and out the door. As she turned the corner, she looked back to find that the woman continued to stare at her. Angel felt sorry that Lenora had to deal with the creepy woman. Angel couldn't leave fast enough. All she wanted was to breathe fresh air.

# Chapter Ten

Angel closed the front door behind her a bit hard, rattling the picture frames in the hallway. *Really?* All the wedding planners in Charlotte, and *they* had to pick Lenora? Okay, okay, granted, Lenora was the best. If Angel ever had the opportunity to walk down the aisle, she would choose Lenora to plan the wedding. The woman was good at what she did. Angel enjoyed having the opportunity to work with her, but she was not going to be working with Denise and Kenneth.

She threw her bag on the couch and sat down in a huff. Angel wanted to kick herself for not speaking up during her meeting with Lenora. She wanted to make the money, but Angel knew she couldn't seriously document the marriage of two people who had betrayed her trust. What really upset Angel was the fact that Denise and Kenneth knew she did the video productions. Lenora had Angel's bio with a link to Angel Media on the bridal Web site. Maybe she should just get over it. This happened four years ago. *Life goes on, right?*

"Angel, what are you doing home?"

Angel jumped at her uncle's voice. "I think I should get to ask the questions. Where have you been? Why are you so hard to find?"

This morning she had tried to catch up with her uncle Jacob, but it was almost like he was avoiding her on purpose. Even though she didn't hear his arrival last night or his departure this morning, the guest bedroom was occupied with his suitcases and the bed was unmade.

She got up from the couch and peeked out the window. "I didn't see your car out there. Why aren't you with Grams?"

"I don't need the twenty questions. I came to get a shower. She's in rehab now, anyway. Shouldn't you be working?"

Angel stared at her uncle like he had grown horns. "I *am* working. I just came back from consulting with one of my biggest clients." Why did they go through this every time? For some reason, her uncle couldn't get it in his head that she ran a business. He should be proud of what she'd accomplished at a young age.

As a media arts major, Angel had been determined to be a film producer. She was a big movie fan, and her most treasured gift was the Sony video camera her granddad had given her at the age of thirteen. Grams didn't get the reason for such an expensive gift, but during family reunions, birthdays, and parties, Angel loved capturing people in action. Movie production was a big dream, but she still loved producing videos and was getting paid to do it.

"I just want to be sure you can carry your own weight," Jacob said and smirked. "My mother doesn't need to be carrying you. You're an adult now."

Angel rolled her eyes and grabbed her bag off the couch. "I know that! I work just like anybody else and pay my own bills. By the way, I'm here taking care of things for Grams. I did the same with Granddaddy. Why do you insist on insulting me?" By this time Angel was yelling. She knew she needed to calm down, but Angel hated when he treated her like a child. Of course, she had clearly lost it.

Jacob continued without even looking at her. "My parents spoiled you, just like they spoiled your mother. I need to make sure you are doing the right thing."

Angel's mouth dropped open. "Why are you so mean? Why would you throw something like that in my face?"

Jacob looked at her. "I'm not throwing anything in your face. I just want you to . . . Never mind." He walked out of the room, leaving the smell of his cologne in the air.

She shouted at his back as he went out the front door. "No wonder Liz asked you to leave." She didn't know if Jacob heard what she said. All she heard was the door close.

What was wrong with her? That was a low blow, even if Jacob deserved it. A swift cloud of shame fell over Angel. She had entered the house feeling rattled about seeing Kenneth's and Denise's names. Jacob had just added to the mix. She dragged her feet to her room and sat on the edge of her bed.

When did life become so complicated? If she was over Kenneth and Denise, why was the pain of the betrayal just as fierce today as it was four years ago? When did Jacob stop being a fun uncle and begin treating her like she was her mother all over again? Was her mother that bad?

She took a deep breath and prayed. *Lord, please help me. I thought I was over being angry at Denise and Kenneth. I'm not. I think I just shoved down my emotions and tried to put it behind me. But I haven't.* Then Angel thought of herself. Jacob wasn't the only one who had uptight issues. Why was she so angry? *Last week I blew up at Grams, before she had the stroke. Was that caused by me? I need you, God, to help me stop being so angry. What's really eating me? I thought when I accepted you, I would be different. Help me. I don't want to feel and act like this. In Jesus's name, amen.*

Angel climbed back on the bed and reached for her Bible and notebook on her nightstand. They were starting a new topic of study this week, forgiveness. She turned to the verse for this week in the book of Philippians. *Forgetting what is behind and straining toward what is ahead, I press on toward the goal to win the prize for which God has called me heavenward in Christ Jesus* (Philippians 3:13–14 New International Version). Angel broke out in a laugh mixed with tears. That was all she could do, move forward. Tomorrow would be a better day.

Angel went over to her computer and decided to e-mail Lenora. She carefully worded her e-mail. Lenora didn't need to know the whole story, and there would be plenty of other weddings this summer. Denise and Kenneth could find another videographer. Before Angel hit SEND, she read the e-mail again. And again. Instead of sending the e-mail, she saved it as a draft. She wasn't sure why, but sitting on it another day wouldn't hurt.

Angel clicked over to Facebook so she could read and respond to any new messages. When she logged in, she had a few new friend requests. To her surprise, one of her friend requests was from Wes Cade. He was actually serious about wanting to help. She tapped her fingers on the desk.

Wes might be her only avenue to getting some of the information she needed. Hopefully, this wouldn't be a decision she would regret. She confirmed his friend request and then surfed to his profile page. He looked really handsome in his profile photo. She noticed on his wall that most of the messages were from women and that he personally responded to everyone.

Not that she cared.

She clicked on the message button and typed. Hello, Wes. You mentioned on Sunday about staying in touch. Can we meet to talk? Without a bit of hesitancy, she sent the message. It occurred to her as she logged off the computer that she had delayed sending a message to get out of a potentially painful situation. Instead, she had chosen to contact a man who could lead her to some truths that would bring more pain.

*Forgetting what is behind and straining toward what is ahead.*

# Chapter Eleven

Melanie had since lost track of the days, but she knew it was daytime. While the window in the room had been boarded up from the outside, inside the bathroom that was off from the bedroom, there was a window made of glass blocks. She had figured out she was in a cabin. Years ago, she remembered visiting a cabin with Lisa and her family. The cabin was up in the mountains, with nothing but trees around it. Melanie placed her face against the glass, feeling the warmth of the sun. She couldn't see clearly but could hear birds fluttering and singing nearby.

Whoever took her wanted to keep her around for a while. She just couldn't figure out why. She tried to think about the people who had come up to her in the club. No one had followed her out of the club that she could remember. There were a lot of creeps who had asked her to dance, but no one stood out to her as a horror movie–type creep. That was exactly the way she felt, like she had been snatched up and dropped in a scene. She laughed out loud. "Could this be another reality show? Let's take a peek inside the life of a woman as she slowly loses her mind."

She kept leaning her head against the thick glass. Melanie never heard vehicles or voices. Her throat was still raw from yelling over and over again that first day. Melanie returned to the bedroom. The bedroom was at one time probably used a lot. It was decorated like any other cabin bedroom. The quilt on the bed was quaint. She could tell from the dust that adhered to her hands when she touched the furniture that the room had not been used in a while. This didn't help her. There was no telling how far this place was off the map if no one used the place.

She didn't know what was beyond the door. Was anyone else here? She wished there was a television on the stand across from the bed.

Melanie didn't have the best relationship with her stepmother, but she'd let her move back in until she could get a new apartment. Hopefully, she had noticed that Melanie was gone. Even if she hadn't, Lisa would have noticed. She called without fail every day. Melanie sat on the bed. He'd taken her bag and her phone. He'd even taken her shoes. *Smart man*. Those three-inch heels would have come in handy.

She reached for the bottled water on the table beside the bed. When she'd explored the room, she'd found water and other snack items, like you would in a hotel room. She twisted the cap and gulped down the liquid. The smell of roasted peanuts filled her nostrils as she pulled the packet open. She'd never eaten this many peanuts in her life. It wasn't a four-course meal, but she was so hungry. She'd waited as long as she could to open it. It was the last bag of peanuts.

As she drank and ate, she prayed.

This wasn't her first prayer, but one of several. The first time she'd prayed, her words had sounded so foreign in her ears. Praying was something she did when she was a little girl. *Now I lay me down to sleep, I pray the Lord my soul to keep. If I should die before I wake, I pray the Lord my soul to take.*

Now she just prayed, *God save me. Save me, please.*

# Chapter Twelve

Thrilled he had a chance to catch up with one of Melanie's teachers, Wes sat engaged as Janice Yarber chattered and moved around the classroom with the energy of a much younger person. "She was an excellent student. I knew she could sing, but, oh, I was so proud of her on that show. Melanie should have won." The older woman picked up papers and placed books back on the shelf in the back of her classroom.

Wes smiled. He liked that Melanie's former English teacher had such fond memories of her former student and continued to keep up with her students after they left her classroom. Rick Jenkins, the cameraman on the shoot with him, was following Mrs. Yarber. They had arrived during her planning period to conduct the interview, and the teacher was wasting no time as she prepared for her next period of students. Finally, the silver-haired woman sat down and continued talking as she began organizing papers on her desk.

"The only thing that concerned me about Melanie was her home life."

Wes asked, "Why the concern?"

She looked at Wes and then looked over at Rick behind them. "Oh my! Maybe I shouldn't have said that."

"No. Hold on. Rick, let's stop rolling tape. Why don't you get some B-roll from around the school?"

"Sure, Wes!"

Wes turned to Mrs. Yarber. "We will continue off the record. Will that be okay with you?"

"Okay." Mrs. Yarber sat very still, in stark relief to the whirlwind of activity she'd engaged in, as she watched Rick grab his bag and camera.

Rick called over his shoulder, "Wes, I will see you outside in a bit."

"Thanks, Rick." Wes turned his attention back to Mrs. Yarber. "Now, you mentioned you had concerns about Melanie's home life."

She swallowed and fidgeted in her seat. "Well, neither of her parents ever came to support her. They missed teacher conferences all the time. One day I made a trip out to her home. Her mother was there taking care of some younger children. She seemed to be more interested in her other children and didn't seem to care that Melanie had been missing her classes."

Wes asked, "Melanie was skipping classes?"

"Yes. Now, I understand the mother had her hands full. I believe all the other children were under the age of four. The mother . . . Well, I should stop referring to her as the mother. She was really Melanie's stepmother." Mrs. Yarber shook her head. "She just kept saying, 'Melanie can take care of herself.' At the time, Melanie was only fourteen years old. Children still need guidance at that age. Teenagers need adult guidance even more so because they are learning about themselves and witnessing so many new experiences."

"Where was her father?"

"Now, that really disturbed me. I never met Melanie's father. I heard later that her dad was serving time in prison. Something about getting caught with drugs. That's terrible."

He looked down at his notes. Serena had spoken to the stepmother; in fact, they had some clips of her talking to the media. There was no footage of Melanie's father, even with his daughter missing and showing up on the news each night. Larry Stowe had to have been released from prison in the last year, though. Melanie's father had found a way to see his daughter on *American Voices*. Wes wondered if Larry might have worked out something with his parole officer that allowed him to leave the state.

Wes planned to head out to Melanie's home after the interview. "Mrs. Yarber, I have one more question. Do you remember any of Melanie's friends or boyfriends?"

"In my class, Melanie was especially chummy with a girl named Lisa Sloan. I don't think she was involved with any boys when I had her, but I do remember the boy they talk about on the news."

"Jay. Jay Strong."

"Yes. He wasn't in any of my classes, but he was a young man who had quite a reputation with the staff. Jay was a least a few years ahead of Melanie. I think he eventually dropped out of school. He stayed in trouble all the time. It's a shame that she got caught up with him. Do you think he has something to do with her being missing?"

"I don't know. He's a person of interest right now with the police." Wes stood and held out his hand. "Thank you, Ms. Yarber. I appreciate your time."

"Not a problem. I do hope they find her. She was such a talented girl."

Wes headed out into the high school hallway. It was in between classes, but a few students were still walking around, giggling and talking. He remembered his high school days. While he enjoyed some recognition as a reporter, in high school he was "church boy." No matter her hours at the hospital, Wanda had made sure they were in church during the week and on Sunday.

It didn't help that he liked the idea of dressing professionally when he went to school. This usually meant one his favorite vests and a bow tie. Good grades were expected of him, and he liked the challenge. A chick magnet, he was not.

He headed into the parking lot, toward the car, memories following him. Rick was standing at the back of the car, packing up the gear. He turned toward Wes. "Hey, did you get what you needed here?"

"Yes, I did. Do you know how far Melanie's family home is from here?" Rick was the driver and had been assigned to Serena for the previous interviews.

Rick answered, "About two miles. You want to head there next? Do you think they will want to do another interview?"

Rick had a point. Due to Melanie's fame from being on *American Voices,* there was national media hanging out all the time at the Stowes' house. "I'd like to try. I want to see if we can find out where the father is hiding. Don't you think it's odd that he hasn't shown his face at all?"

"Yeah! If it was my kid, I would be out there searching for her. You know it's crazy that she was snatched up just like that and no one saw a thing."

Wes pondered out loud. "I know. She had to be heading toward her car. Somebody must have been watching her all night."

When Melanie's friends finally came out of the club, they noticed her car was still in the parking lot, but there was no sign of Melanie. They didn't waste any time calling the police, which was a good thing. Did Melanie have some kind of stalker? With her being on a national television show, who knows what overzealous fan had fixated on her.

Wes often wondered what happened later to people who had the infamous fifteen minutes of fame from being on reality shows and in talent contests. Melanie was talented. Did offers come in for her even though she wasn't a winner? She had made it to being the fourth finalist. Really, if she had had more votes, Wes gathered, like others, she could have won the competition that season.

Both men finished loading the car. While Rick drove to the Stowes' home, Wes looked at his notes. Melanie had had her own apartment up until a month before she disappeared. Maybe for financial reasons, she'd moved back home. A home where, according to Mrs. Yarber, Melanie was at odds with or not really cared for by her stepmother. The more he read about Mrs. Gladys Stowe, the more he wanted to meet her for himself. After her husband had gone to prison, Gladys had raised his daughter until she graduated. Melanie had moved out right after her high school graduation. Why did she return? Had the relationship between the two women improved?

Wes could tell as they drew closer to the Stowes' home that there was a crowd of reporters staked out around the house. It had been almost a week since the twenty-one-year-old went missing. If Melanie had been an average woman of color, one without the national spotlight, the news story would have been reported locally, but not nationally, and certainly not almost a week later.

Rick asked, "What do you want to do?"

"Let's regroup. It might be better to focus on the boyfriend, Jay Strong." Wes had a few contacts that used to work with Pops. They might be willing to share some details. In the case of a missing person, it was important to relay any clues or details to the public.

Wes pulled out his phone and clicked through a few e-mails. One message caught his attention. Mainly because it was a notification e-mail from Facebook. He had received some great tips from social media and always anticipated coming across something good. To his surprise, the message was from Angel Roberts. She wanted to meet with him tomorrow for lunch at Southern Soul Café. Well, this was good. At least he hoped it was. He was certainly looking forward to seeing her again.

# Chapter Thirteen

Angel had spent the morning with her grandmother. Hard to believe it had been almost a week since Fredricka had her stroke. She still was having trouble talking, but Angel thanked the Lord for every sign of improvement. To see some of the spark back in Grams's eyes gave Angel hope. *She is going to be okay.*

A bundle of nerves, Angel entered Southern Soul Café. She still couldn't believe she'd invited Wes to lunch. The Wes Cade. Showing up at the Cades' house on Sunday and now this . . . She'd had a surge of forwardness that she couldn't explain. She just hoped she didn't embarrass herself in front of the reporter.

Last night Angel had found herself back on his Facebook profile page, checking out his posts. As she'd scanned some of Wes's wall posts, she discovered he had been featured in a local magazine as one of the top ten bachelors in Charlotte. That might be why she saw that some women had posted comments and photos that were not very ladylike. She'd surfed away from the Web site in disgust at the way some of the women were throwing themselves at the man. Wes came off as very friendly and charming. She hoped he would remain that way.

She had purposely arrived early at the café. There was a line, as usual, for lunch. This place stayed busy throughout the lunch hour and started back up again for the dinner crowd. If one wanted good old-fashioned soul food and music from an era that ushered in soulful melodies like no other, this was the place to be. It occurred to Angel that she should have chosen another place, but really, Wes would be recognizable anywhere.

Angel walked up to the hostess. The woman was shorter than Angel and had a big, toothy smile. The young woman squeaked out, "Welcome. How many?"

"I'm here to see Eddie," Angel answered.

"Okay. Wait just one moment." The hostess leaned over and picked up a phone from behind the desk. "Eddie, someone is here to see you."

Eddie had left her a voice mail yesterday. She hoped he didn't want to talk to her about his daughter's upcoming nuptials. Angel still hadn't sent the e-mail to Lenora. What she was waiting for, she didn't know.

Angel moved out of the way as other guests streamed into the restaurant for lunch. She'd seen the framed photos on the wall a number of times, but she admired them again. Southern Soul Café was owned and founded by Eddie, as a tribute to the band Southern Soul, which had started back in 1961. There were photos of the band from performances, some with well-known celebrities. She picked out her granddaddy in a few of the photos. Nick Roberts was a handsome man. Angel came from good stock indeed.

There was a photo of her mother on the wall, toward the back. Angel sat in that booth every time she ate at Southern Soul Café. Elisa had sung on and off with the band ever since she was a little girl. As a birthday present to her father, Elisa had sung with the band in 1991. By then Granddad had long since stopped playing due to arthritis, which robbed him of time with his beloved guitar. Elisa had disappeared a few months later, and so that birthday present was a bittersweet memory, one that, Angel saw, had often brought Nick to tears.

"Would you prefer a booth, Miss Roberts?"

Angel smiled. "Hey, Uncle Eddie."

Eddie was without the cowboy boots and hat today. His white shirt was tucked into black denim jeans. He straightened his black tie and held out his arms. "Well, I'll be. I can't believe I have the great pleasure of seeing Miss Angel Roberts quite so soon. How's Fredericka doing?"

"Grams still has a long way to go, but she is much better than she was last week."

"Good to hear!"

"Thanks for coming out in the dining room to see me. I wanted to make sure I talked to you."

"Well, I'm glad to know I still can be a part of your life. Plus, I love to mingle with the customers, make sure they are enjoying the food. Saves someone in the kitchen from getting yelled at by me. Come on back. I will show you to your table."

Angel laughed. She knew it was strange that she felt so at ease with a man she had always affectionately called uncle, but she couldn't bear to talk to his daughter. Maybe she would finally get past the betrayal. As she followed Eddie toward the back of the restaurant, she hoped trying to rekindle a broken friendship wasn't what had motivated Eddie to call her last night. She'd hate to disappoint him with her true feelings, which she felt ashamed of.

It took them a while to reach the booth as Eddie stopped and talked to patrons along the way. Angel realized how hungry she was when she peeked at the plates. Southern Soul Café was known for its fried chicken and macaroni and cheese dish. She hadn't eaten a decent meal since her grandmother went into the hospital. She and Grams cooked together. Finally, without having to tell him, Eddie led her straight to her favorite booth.

As she drew closer, Angel eyed the photo on the wall. Elisa was about three months pregnant, barely showing in the green dress. Something about knowing she was in her mother's womb in the photo made Angel feel close to her mother, who had been invisible to her for so many years. She should ask Eddie for the photo.

"Lots of memories in here, huh? You look just like her. Sure do miss that voice," Eddie commented. He slid into the booth, admiring the photo. Then he turned to her and asked, "You know, I may have asked you this before, but do you have her pipes?"

Eddie's memory must have been getting bad. He'd asked her all her life if she could sing like her mother. Angel preferred not to sing in front of people. Even her granddad couldn't get her to sing publicly. She would do anything for him but sing. "Singing was my mother's dream. Not mine."

"Oh, yeah. You are into the tech stuff. Probably why you are so good at video. Speaking of video, remember I had a project for you?"

"Granddaddy! Granddaddy!"

Angel observed as a young boy came running toward them, almost colliding with a server holding a tray. Like a little athlete, the boy leaped into the booth and into Eddie's arms.

Eddie laughed. "Boy, where did you come from? You can't just be running in my restaurant like that. What's wrong with you?" The whole time he scolded, Eddie tickled the little boy. The child turned and grinned at Angel.

She sucked in her breath. He was the mirror image of Kenneth, with dimples just like his dad. He was a little cutie. Swept up in the bundle of cuteness, Angel turned to see her former best friend approaching the table. Angel tensed and leaned back. This was a mistake!

Today was an unusually warm April day, but Denise looked ready to head to the beach. She was dressed in a flowing skirt and a tank top. To her surprise, Angel noticed Denise wasn't sporting her usual long tresses, but instead had a short Afro.

Denise walked up to the table and placed her hands on her hips. She was still slim and didn't look like she'd carried a child at all. "Kenny, I told you not to run."

Eddie said, "He's fine. It's good for somebody to be glad to see me. How come he's not in day care, anyway?"

Denise answered, "Well, I wasn't planning to come in today. I decided to keep him home." She turned toward Angel. The two women locked stares until Denise said, "Hello, Angel. It's been a long time."

Angel looked away. "Yes, it has been. You look different." Angel wondered what Kenneth thought of Denise's look. She remembered that Kenneth had always put down her tendency to dress like a tomboy. Angel liked to keep her curly hair in a ponytail and loved her jeans and Converse. She knew she looked like a college student, but she had her own style.

Denise reached up and ran her hand across her short hair. "I'm trying out a new look."

Angel wasn't sure she wanted to continue the small talk. She smiled. "It suits you." She actually meant that. Denise had model looks. The gold hoops against her mocha skin were perfect. She looked almost queenly.

Angel turned her attention back to little Kenny. He was smiling at her. A few years ago, when she had heard about his birth, she didn't think she would ever want to see him, but here he was in the flesh. *So cute*. She smiled back at him. He was a child. How he came into the world was certainly no choice of his.

"Kenny, come on back to the office with me. I have work to do."

"No!" Kenny yelled.

Denise glared at her father. "Dad. You could *try* to help me."

Angel watched the exchange. Denise had always butted heads with her dad. Like most musicians, Eddie had been on the road most of the time and had been more of an absentee father.

Eddie responded by holding little Kenny up to his face. "Little man, you need to go with your momma. Me and you will play together later."

The little boy said, "Okay."

Denise reached down and grabbed Kenny by the hand and pulled him away from Eddie. "Come on." Kenny kept looking back as his mother pulled him toward the office area of the restaurant.

"That is a handful, you hear." Eddie shook his head. "Hold off having one of those as long as you can."

Angel hadn't had a boyfriend for so long, motherhood was far from her mind. For some reason, she felt a bit sorry for Denise. When they used to talk about getting married and having families, Denise had always said she wasn't sure if she wanted kids. Angel said to Eddie, "I didn't know Denise worked at the restaurant."

Eddie explained, "I talked her into coming to work for me a few months ago. I know you girls don't talk much, but she had been out of work for a while. Both her and Kenneth had been struggling. I told her to come take care of my paperwork since she's always been good at organizing. She finally did it. When bills need to be paid, sometimes you can't be picky about a paycheck."

She had really been out of the loop. There was a time when she and Denise confided everything to each other. But that was where Angel went wrong. She had complained way too much about Kenneth to Denise. How he would go hang out with the guys and not want to do anything with her. Not until it was too late did she realize Kenneth had been hanging out with Denise during those times she was looking for him.

Wes would be here soon, so she needed to find out what Eddie needed from her. "Eddie, what type of job did you have in mind?"

"Oh yeah, I was talking to this young cat the other day. He was telling me how that youngster, the Canadian boy, Justin B . . . How you say his name?"

"Justin Bieber?"

"He was discovered on the Internet. I'm not on the Internet that much, but I was blown away."

"These days if you have talent, there are a lot of opportunities to get discovered. I'm sure you heard of the *American Voices* show."

Eddie shook his head. "Oh yeah! That young girl that's missing, she was on that show. That's a shame. You know, back in the day it was a lot more hard work to get a record deal."

Angel prodded him, saying, "So what are you interested in me helping you film?"

Eddie pointed to an area in the restaurant that was covered with curtains now but was the staging area at night for musicians and occasionally comedians. "I have young people sing on the stage all the time. I want to give some of these young people an opportunity."

"You want to put them on YouTube?"

"Yeah, I'd like to start a talent show. A Southern Soul talent show. Let people vote on who they think is the best soul singer."

"That's sounds like a cool idea, Eddie. But these days people will be looking for something."

"Not a problem. I have a few contacts in the music business still. Maybe we can work out something for the winner. So what you say? Can you help me get these performances online? I thought it would be great attention for the restaurant. Who knows? I may get a reality show."

Angel laughed. She wasn't so sure about the reality show rage. Although she could picture the drama Denise and Eddie could generate to bring in ratings. "Okay. You tell me when, and I will be here."

"Great! I will get a date and get back with you. So what you having to eat?"

"I will just have some water for now."

"Water?" Eddie said incredulously. "Girl, you know you can have any plate on the house."

She waved her hand. "You don't have to do that." Angel didn't wear a watch, so she pulled her phone from her bag. Wes was due any moment. "I'm waiting on someone, and I think I should order when he gets here."

Eddie raised an eyebrow. "He?" Then he grinned. "So who is he? You are being awfully secretive."

She shook her head. "You will see soon enough. No secret."

"All right. Well, I will take care of you before he arrives so he won't have a skeleton waiting on him."

She rolled her eyes. *Really?* She'd gained weight over the past few years. After Eddie walked away, Angel turned back to the wall and looked at the photo of her mother. It was like Elisa was looking right at her, her mouth open, belting out a song. She looked so happy. How come in the remaining memories Angel had of her mother, she seemed sad? *What happened, Mom?* she thought.

Eddie came back to the table with a glass of water and a basket. "There you go, young lady." There were packets of butter peeking out from under the red cloth. "Enjoy!"

"Thank you, Eddie." Angel pulled the cloth back to find piping hot corn bread muffins. She grabbed a muffin and sliced it open with her butter knife. Then she rubbed a dab of butter across the corn bread. As she placed the warm, moist corn bread in her mouth, memories of long ago wrapped around her mind. A time when her mother was happy. Her entire family was whole, laughing and enjoying good food and each other.

That was what she longed for.

# Chapter Fourteen

Wes looked at the clock on the car's dashboard. He hoped Angel was still there. The interview with Jay Strong had run longer than he intended. When there was an opportunity he could not miss, Wes struggled with decisions. With Alan breathing down his neck to get an interview, Wes had decided this morning to drive to Strong's Auto Body Shop.

He didn't need to have his Honda checked, but Wes handed over his keys and sat in the waiting room, enduring a competitor's news stories. He had no idea if the service person recognized him, but he was concerned only with whether Jay was working today. After fifteen minutes, he went outside, looked around, and then slipped into the garage. Sure enough, his Honda had been pulled in and the hood was raised.

Jay looked at him with suspicion. "I know you. You're a reporter. What do you want, man? I don't need no more reporters trying to ask me questions."

This man was working on his car, so Wes switched gears. "Man, I just want to hear your side. I know you must really love Melanie, and her disappearance must be killing you." Wes was pushing it. He doubted Jay knew how to really love a woman.

He was about Wes's height, but Jay had to have been considered for or offered the wide receiver position on the high school football team. Maybe if Jay had gone the sports route, the discipline would have kept him out of the trouble that eventually led to him being a high school dropout and working at this garage.

The man scowled and then put his head back under the hood. A few seconds later, he spoke. "Melanie was a good woman. I hope they find her."

*Do you want them to find her?* Wes had to calm some of his thoughts and suspend some of his judgments so he could keep the impromptu interview going. He asked, "So how did you feel about her being on *American Voices?*"

Jay stuck his head out from under the hood and threw a tool in a box. "I was excited for my girl. She could sing. I hoped she would get a record deal out of the whole thing."

"Did she?"

Jay sniffed. "People were knocking on her door, but no one was coming through for her. The offers would fizzle and go nowhere. She was starting to be a drag about the whole thing. It was like that show was a waste of her time."

"So she was depressed? Do you think maybe she left on her own, you know, just to get away?"

"Where would she go? I'm sure she was feeling low. Anybody would. She was broke. Me and her hadn't talked much in the past few months. She came to me for money a few weeks ago. I found out she moved back in with her dad's old lady. She couldn't stand that woman. I guess she was pretty messed up."

"You cared about her. She trusted you. How long had you been a couple?"

"We'd been together since high school. On and off. Yeah, we cared about each other."

"But you had one of those relationships where you weren't really good for each other. Maybe you argued a bit too much."

Jay eyed him. He finally responded, "I'm sure we argued like any couple. Things got heated, and we yelled at each other. No big deal." He held up his finger. "I never put a hand on her, though. People trying to make me out to be something I'm not."

"Yeah, but you were arrested for a brawl at a club a year ago."

"The guy deserved to be put in his place. He was drunk and in my face. Look, you want me to finish your car or what? I don't have anything else to say."

Wes was hoping to push more but realized after looking at his watch, he needed to leave soon. "Thanks, man. That's all the questions I have. I appreciate your time. I hope you and Melanie can be reunited."

Jay hunched back over under the car's hood. Wes thought he looked deflated, but one could never tell what people would do in a fit of rage. He hoped that Jay Strong wouldn't be accused of foul play.

After his car was ready, Wes zipped in and out down I-77 toward the exit that would lead to Southern Soul Café. He had been there only a few times, mostly with Pops. He liked to see the part of Pops's life that he rarely talked about. The fact that he'd played in a popular band had always fascinated Wes. It was hard to imagine that the quiet, thoughtful man could set an audience on fire on the piano. Wes had never seen him play except on old VHS tapes his mother kept. He often wondered why Pops gave up the band to go to the police academy and then work his way up to detective.

Wes arrived at the parking lot of Southern Soul Café as a line of cars was leaving. He was able to park near the door. Hopping out, he headed inside.

A cute young hostess greeted him. "I know you. You are on TV."

He smiled. "Yes. Thanks." Wes didn't mind the recognition, but sometimes it felt a bit awkward, such as now, as the young lady was staring at him. He cleared his throat.

She smacked herself across the forehead. "Oh, I'm sorry. How many in your party?"

Since he was about fifteen minutes late, Wes realized that Angel might have gone. Great way to make an impression on a woman after the awkward episode on Sunday. He told the grinning woman, "I'm meeting someone. She is a little taller than you, has dark curly hair, fair skin."

The hostess's grin drooped. "I think I know who you are talking about. Eddie was talking to her. Follow me."

*Eddie? Who is Eddie?* Wes followed the hostess. He caught sight of Angel and tapped the hostess on the shoulder. "I see her. Thanks." As he approached, Wes noticed an older man sitting across from Angel. He looked familiar to Wes. Angel was laughing.

"Hello, Angel." She turned to him and smiled. There was a twinkle of joy in her eyes today, and not the deep sadness he'd seen on Sunday.

"Hello, Wes."

"Sorry I'm late." Wes pulled his eyes from Angel to look over at the older man.

Angel introduced her tablemate. "Wes, this is Eddie Gowins, the owner of Southern Soul Café. He also used to be the drummer in the band."

"Oh yeah. Now I know why you look familiar. You should know my pops."

Eddie narrowed his eyes. "Your pops was a musician?"

"Yes, well, he's my grandfather. Lenny Cade. He played the piano along with Angel's granddad."

"Oh yeah." Eddie rubbed his cheek. "I remember Lenny. He left the group not too long after I joined. I haven't seen him in years. How's he doing?"

"Not too good. Age stuff."

"Sorry to hear. We are all getting up in age." Eddie was looking at him like he was sizing him up. "Aren't you a reporter?"

Angel answered, "Yes, he is, and I need his help with something." She looked pointedly at Eddie.

"Okay, I can catch a hint. I will leave you two to have lunch." Eddie slid from the booth. "I tried to keep Angel from starving while she waited on you to arrive."

Angel laughed. "I was not starving."

Eddie winked. "If you say so. Looks like you wiped out them corn muffins pretty good." He pointed at Wes. "You be good to her, young man. She's like a daughter to me. Talk to you later."

"Thanks, Uncle Eddie."

As he sat down, Wes noticed the basket and the yellow crumbs on a plate. "I would say you must have been pretty hungry."

Angel rolled her eyes and smiled at him. "Well, you were running late."

He grinned. "Sorry I'm late. Are you related to him? You called him uncle."

She shook her head. "No. He's been a family friend for so long. I have always called him uncle. Not that my real uncle cared for me doing that. I used to be friends with Eddie's daughter."

"Used to be?"

"Long story." Angel then said, "I'm glad you could make it. I know you must be busy."

Wes was finding Angel quite intriguing. She had some mystery about her that he wanted to dig into. Maybe they would become friends. "I got caught up in an interview, but I didn't want to miss out on talking to you," he responded. "This used to be a popular place to eat with my pops. I was surprised you suggested it, because it's been a while since I've eaten here." Wes looked at the wall. "Wow, would you look there." He pointed. "That's Pops right there. He's so young."

Angel commented, "You look like him."

"Yeah. The same could be said about you and your mother." He'd recognized Elisa in the framed photo above Angel's head. "I'm sure a lot of people have told you, you are the splitting image of her."

"I've been told."

"Do you sing?"

She stared at Wes.

"I'm sorry. I didn't mean to ask that question."

"Yes, you did," she answered. "You are a reporter, and I'm sure that's what your inquiring mind wanted to know. And I sing a little. It's never been an aspiration of mine."

A waitress came to take their orders before Wes could ask more questions. He would've loved to hear her sing. They both ordered the make-your-own lunch meal, which included a choice of meat and two sides. Wes chose fried chicken, mashed potatoes and gravy, and macaroni and cheese. Angel ordered pork chops, greens, and macaroni and cheese. Wes couldn't wait to dig in. It had been a long morning.

After the waitress left, he decided to ask Angel a safe question. "I had a chance to look at your Web site. You do beautiful work."

"Thank you. I'm in the midst of the wedding season now."

"How did you get into doing the wedding videos?"

"A good friend introduced me to Lenora Freeman."

"First lady of Victory Gospel?"

"Yes, and the best wedding planner in Charlotte. I'm contracted to work with her to produce videos. Helps me fund my documentary."

It seemed like they had just ordered when the waitress appeared again, this time with steaming plates of food. After the waitress left, Wes asked, "Would you mind if I said grace?" He held his hand out.

"Please." Angel placed her small hand in his and held her head down.

He prayed, "Father, God, thank you for this opportunity to fellowship and get to know each other. I pray for the nourishment of this food to help provide the strength we need. In Jesus's name."

They both said, "Amen."

While they dug into their food, Wes commented, "So you attend Victory Gospel Church? I love going to service there. A lot of members. You can't beat the energy level."

"It's a huge church. Yes, I usually attend the eight o'clock service with my grandparents, or, well, just my grams now. I started going to Bible study because a friend encouraged me to try it out. After going to Bible study for a few months, I became a Christian."

*Mmmm, so she is a new Christian. A babe in Christ.* "That's awesome. I grew up going to church. Became a Christian around twelve, but I hate to admit that in college, I kind of went a bit on the wild side for a while."

Angel laughed. "Really? I bet you have some stories to tell."

"Not anything I want to report on the local news. Tell me more about the documentary you are working on."

"It's about my mother's life. I was hoping it was a way to find out what happened to her. I have footage of my mother singing in talent shows as a little girl. Singing was all she dreamed of doing. I wanted to show how talented she was before she disappeared."

"So you will be talking to the people who were with her that day?"

"That's a goal."

"Does your list include your father?"

Angel put her fork down and carefully wiped her mouth. "I don't know. He's somewhere on the West Coast. I'm not trying to find him."

"He's not anymore."

She looked at him. "What?"

"I'm sorry! I guess you didn't know. He moved back to Charlotte about six months ago. Not too long after your grandfather passed away."

She shook her head. "That's crazy! How do you know this? I mean, not that I care. We haven't spoken since I was a little girl."

Wes didn't want to give away that he had been learning as much as he could about Angelino Mancini. He wanted to know if the man had gotten away with a crime all these years. Pops had tried so hard to find some evidence of foul play. What he had found was that Angelino's boxing career had ended just as prematurely as Elisa's singing career. He'd packed up one day and left, not looking back at a town where many thought he took Elisa's life and hid her body.

Angel placed her napkin on the table and reached inside her pocketbook. "I'm sorry. I have to go." Her face had grown visibly red.

*Ah, Wes!* They were really having a great conversation. Why did he bring up her father now? "Are you okay? Did I say something wrong?"

"No. I just . . . I'm in shock, I guess. It's been easier not to think about my dad, but you're saying he's here. I don't know. He's a sore subject for me." She reached into her wallet and pulled out her debit card.

"Don't. I will take care of the bill. Besides, I was late and made you wait."

Thanks." Angel scooted out from the booth. The sadness had returned to her eyes.

He didn't want her to leave like this. This was bad, maybe worse than Sunday. "Hey, Angel, I'm really sorry. Look, if there is any way I can help you with the documentary about your mother, let me know. I do want to help you."

She nodded. As he watched her walk away, he saw the old guy, Eddie, approach her. Angel waved to him and headed out the door. Eddie looked back to where he sat. Wes turned away. Maybe he ought to have paid more attention to Eddie's words when he said, "You be good to her."

There was something fragile about Angel Roberts, and it tugged at his heart. He looked over at the photo of Elisa on the wall. Wes realized that getting close to Angel would be impossible if her past continued to cling to her. *What happened to you, Elisa Roberts? Your daughter deserves the truth. Pops needs to be set free of his guilt.*

# Chapter Fifteen

Angel was in a funky mood most of Wednesday and decided not to go to Bible study, then changed her mind. She was still a bit shook up after talking to Wes yesterday. The sad part was she had been enjoying their conversation right up until Wes mentioned her father being in Charlotte. It had weighed heavily on her the rest of day and last night. Wes was a reporter, and he had obviously been digging into her past, even before she showed up at the Cades' home on Sunday. No wonder he was okay with inviting her inside. Maybe Detective Cade had shared something with Wes and he'd been investigating ever since. What bothered her was that if he was trying to help her, he could share what he knew. She wasn't some story.

Angel tuned back into the group and noticed everyone was paying attention to Candace, who was speaking. "This week's lesson was a hard one for me, as I'm sure it was for you too. How many of you have ever felt betrayed?"

Angel raised her hand and noticed most of the group members did too. As Candace asked more questions, Angel observed the number of hands that went up each time. She felt better that she'd come tonight. By no means was she alone in her feelings.

Candace continued, "Well, amen. I hope all of you will walk away tonight with a new mind-set about how to handle people when they have done something to lose your trust or have abandoned or even rejected you. Turn with me to the Gospel of John and then to chapter twenty-one."

The classroom was filled with the sound of flipping pages. Angel was still getting used to finding things in the Bible, but tonight she turned right to John. The four Gospels were where she had started reading and learning about Jesus.

Candace waited until everyone was in the proper place and then said, "A few weeks ago, we celebrated Easter. Let's go back a bit to the night before Jesus was crucified. What happened to Jesus's disciples?"

A woman named Lily Owens answered, "They left him. Just scattered."

Another woman, Clara Miles, said, "Yes, Peter, who was supposed to be the rock, denied him three times."

Angel spoke up. "Judas sold him out too. He led the soldiers right to Jesus with a kiss."

Candace shook her head. "You are all right. Jesus was betrayed by those he had gathered and prepared for ministry for three years. How do you think he felt? Especially after he was beaten, the crown of thorns was placed on his head, and then having to walk up to Golgotha. The nails in his hands and feet."

The room was quiet as Candace described the scene of Jesus's death. Angel found herself imagining it, but also thinking about people in her life. Kenneth. Denise. Her father.

Candace asked the group, "Does anyone want to share a time when you felt betrayed? How did you react? What has changed, if anything, for you today?"

Several hands went up, but Angel chose not to share. As she listened to the other women share, she couldn't help but think back to the day she saw Kenneth and Denise together. She had been so excited about getting her first film project and had wanted to get Kenneth involved. She'd figured they could enjoy the day together.

His car was outside. She had a key to his apartment and didn't think to knock or ring the bell. It seemed weird that the blinds were closed and the lights were off, but Kenneth wasn't the cleanest person in the world. It was best that his messy apartment stayed in the dark. She heard noises but didn't even stop to consider what she might walk into as she opened the bedroom door.

Angel placed her head in her hand and rubbed her forehead. This wasn't the place to have that memory. She fought to find memories of the mother and father she'd lived most of her life without knowing, and then she had an awful realization: For a while, Kenneth and Denise had been her world, and then they were gone. Maybe that was why their betrayal hurt even more.

Angel looked up and saw that Candace was observing her. She tried to smile, but she knew Candace had seen her go off to another place. Right there in the middle of Bible study. *Lord, help me.*

Candace said to the group, "As I sat during the trial of the person who murdered my loved ones, I needed to find a way to get past my feelings of betrayal and pain. If I hadn't, the door that needed to be open for me to share my story and for us to come together each Wednesday to share our stories of overcoming might have stayed shut. That hurt really does not stay with you forever as long as you are willing to forgive and let it go. Once you do forgive that person or persons, you can truly move forward into a place where you can tell others about the goodness of the Lord. He knows about pain and betrayal. And He rose in victory over all of it."

Angel sat and listened thoughtfully to Candace. She understood where Candace was coming from, but wasn't fully sure if it was something she could do.

"Let's pray." Candace's voice rolled out smooth and sweet. "Father God, we thank you for watching over us and our families, keeping us all from harm and danger. We want you to take care of those who have family members who have fallen ill. By your stripes they are healed. Please free our minds of troubles, worry, and most of all, allow us to be able to forgive others as you have forgiven us. In Jesus's name."

After they prayed, the women in the group started talking and hugging each other. Angel made her way over to Candace in between the hugs and good-byes to ask, "You mind if I walk out with you?"

"Of course not. How are you holding up? Fredricka doing okay?"

"Yes. She should be moving to the rehabilitation place tomorrow. She is still having trouble speaking, and her right side isn't cooperating, but they say she is improving."

Candace swung her bag over her shoulder. "It's going to be a process. Your grandmother was relatively healthy for her age, though. She could recover fully."

"I hope so. The doctor said that it's different for everyone with a stroke. They don't really understand how the brain works and rebuilds."

The two women walked out into the hallway. Angel grew quiet.

Candace asked, "You have something else on your mind, don't you? I noticed you were a little preoccupied."

"Yes, but my mind was on this lesson." Angel smiled, but then she stopped walking and looked at Candace. "Yesterday I met the little boy that Kenneth and Denise had together."

"Oh! How did you feel?"

"He was so cute. A ball of energy. And he looks so much like Kenneth. I remembered how I couldn't get over the fact that the two people that were closest to me not only betrayed me, but also brought this child into the world as a reminder. How can I forget that, Candace?"

Candace hooked her arm through Angel's arm so they could keep walking. "Forgiveness is not about forgetting. It's about helping you to move forward. Have you ever thought this through? You told me often how you always felt like you couldn't be yourself around Kenneth. What if God saved you from a relationship destined for heartache? You are young and doing your thing and running your own business at your age. At twenty-five, I had two babies, a cop for a husband, and was struggling to find something that I could do outside of the home."

Angel grinned. "I guess. Who knows who God has for me?"

"Well, I'm glad that you recognize my wisdom, missy."

They laughed as they walked out the door into the parking lot.

"You know, we can so easily get wrapped up in our past and our pain that we miss out on what God has for our future," Candace added. "Believe me, I never imagined meeting anyone else after losing my Frank."

"And look at you now, with Detective Darnell Jackson by your side. He's pretty hot for an old guy."

Candace stepped back and looked at her. "Old? Girl, who are you calling old? He is seasoned. We are both seasoned. Now I just need to get my last child out of the house."

Angel said, "Oh, watch out, Daniel." Candace's oldest daughter, Rachel, was a freshman at UNC Chapel Hill. Daniel was a junior in high school.

After she hugged Candace, Angel climbed in her car. She felt hopeful. Maybe she would get to a place where she could shake the past. One step at a time.

# Chapter Sixteen

This was the hard part of the interview. Wes watched Lisa Sloan choke out her words. "I should have gone with her. I can't believe I let her leave alone."

He looked over at Rick, who gave him a sympathetic nod from behind the camera. Wes wanted to give Melanie's best friend time to compose herself. "I'm so sorry. I know this must be really hard."

"She didn't even want to go." Lisa sniffled and wiped her eyes with the crushed tissue in her hand. "I wanted to get out of the house so bad. The kids had been driving me crazy." Lisa took a deep breath and looked straight at Wes. "It's been over a week."

"I know. She could be out there somewhere."

"Where?" Lisa's face crumpled again. "When I saw her car was still in the parking lot, I just freaked out. If she had come back into the club, she would have come over to me. I can't believe someone would harm her. But after *American Voices* she had become pretty popular. We joked that she was more popular now than we had ever been in school."

Wes asked, "Was there anyone you can recall who harassed her?"

"Melanie has always been pretty. She would get crazy e-mails and posts on her Facebook profile from guys."

Wes made a note to check Melanie's profile page. "Was she still with Jay Strong? I imagine he probably wouldn't have been happy with that type of attention."

Lisa rolled her eyes. "Yeah. I never understood what she saw in him. He's a complete loser. No, Melanie was through with Jay long before she auditioned for the show. He started to remind her too much of her dad."

"Abuse?"

Lisa shook her head. "Her dad drank a lot and ended up in jail. Jay drank too much, and his friends were not exactly role models. He could also be real mean. If Jay ever hit her, Melanie would have told me."

"Okay. By the way, where is Melanie's dad? I've only seen her stepmom."

"I don't know. He's been out of prison. He was always trying to be young."

"What does that mean?" Wes asked.

"You know, he was one of those cool dads when we were all younger. He threw parties, and all the kids loved to go to Melanie's house. Then her mom died, and he remarried. He still tried to be cool, but no one wants to hang around their parents."

"Didn't he try to come back into Melanie's life while she was on *American Voices?*"

"Oh yeah! It was the second-to-last show Melanie was on. She did so well the week before. I begged my boss to let me take the time off from work. My mom was so mad, but as soon as she said she would watch the kids, I was on a plane to Los Angeles." Lisa sighed. "Melanie and I had a blast. Anyway, that night after the show Melanie seemed really upset for some reason. I couldn't figure out why, because my girl *sang* that Christina Aguilera song." Lisa bobbed her head and snapped her fingers in the air. "I was finally able to get her to tell me her dad had tried to contact her. She didn't want to talk to him. Who could blame her?"

"So he did show up? Did you see him?"

"Oh no, no. I never saw him. I guess he called her or sent her something. I can't recall, but I do remember her saying over and over again, 'He's going to ruin everything.' I told her, 'Girl, you just go out there and sing. Don't worry about your dad.' The following week I thought she did good, but something was off in her voice." Lisa waved her hands to fan away the tears that had sprung in her eyes. "She just didn't get the votes she needed. I felt so bad for her."

"I know that was probably devastating. Have you seen Mr. Stowe since Melanie's been missing?"

Lisa shook her head. "No. Why do you ask?"

"I mainly want to get a better picture of Melanie's life. I just realized I have never seen him."

Two small children burst into the room, with an older woman behind them, carrying a baby. Lisa called out, "Hey, Mom, you were supposed to keep the kids outside for a while."

The older woman looked at Wes and then at Rick. "I'm tired. You can take your children back." She walked over and handed the baby to Lisa.

"Thanks a lot," Lisa yelled. "Chris, Maurice, stop running around here like you lost your mind." She turned back to Wes. "I'm sorry. I hope I was able to help you."

Wes stood. "Yes, you did." He waved to Rick to stop rolling the tape. Then he turned around. "Lisa, I do have one more question for you."

The baby in Lisa's arms started squalling. Lisa rocked back and forth. "What else?"

"Was Melanie happy after the show? Did any offers come in for her?"

Lisa stood and held the baby close. "She waited a lot to hear back from people. There was an offer that came in a few days before she disappeared, but she wasn't really hopeful about it."

"Why is that?"

The baby's cries quieted as Lisa began pacing. "She wouldn't admit it, but I knew Melanie. I think she was embarrassed by the attention during and after the show. A lot of people were asking her when she would have an album out. She kept saying soon, so this time I think she wanted it to be a sure deal."

A crash was heard in the other room. Lisa looked at him with panic in her eyes. "I really have to go." She headed toward the back. "Boys, what are you doing in there?"

"Thank you for your time." Wes didn't know if she heard him.

He helped Rick with his equipment, and they left the house. Behind him he could hear Lisa yelling. As Rick packed the station car, Wes pulled out his phone. He'd sent a few messages to Angel, but she hadn't responded yet. Wes hoped he hadn't alienated her. He really wanted to talk to her again.

Rick interrupted his thoughts. "You ready to go?"

"Yeah, let's head back to the newsroom."

After Rick started the car, he asked, "You got big plans for the weekend?"

Wes let out a sigh. "I don't know if I call being in a wedding party big plans, but it's a favor to a childhood friend."

"Well, is he having a bachelor party?"

"Of course! It's tonight."

Rick grinned. "Then have fun tonight. It will make tomorrow bearable. Be glad you aren't the one getting tied down."

Wes looked forward to the day when he would be waiting for his bride to walk down the aisle. One day it would be his turn.

# Chapter Seventeen

Angel had had fun filming Tommy and Sharise yesterday. The couple had been lovebirds since college, and during the shoot they both pointed out special places on campus and were affectionate. She was glad to be able to capture their memories with her camera and looked forward to the ceremony tomorrow.

Angel pushed her chair back and rubbed her eyes. Being in the house by herself, she'd decided to get started on editing the footage from yesterday. Her eyes were blurry from sitting at the computer too long. She walked down the hall from the office space, which her grandparents had allowed her to use. If it wasn't for them helping her out, she would have never gotten her business off the ground. It was probably one of the reasons why her uncle Jacob seemed irritated with her career choice. Angel could have moved out, but she saw how Grams struggled to take care of Granddad, and she knew she had to stick around and lend a hand. Her uncle lived too far away to help out. Now Angel wasn't sure how the living arrangements would work since Grams still did not have complete mobility back on her right side.

When she entered her bedroom, her eyes fell on the music box on her dresser. She forgot she'd taken it down a few nights ago. The music box had been placed at the top of her closet, along with other childhood favorites. It was the last birthday gift her father gave her.

She walked over and lifted the lid. Then she wound up the ballerina to watch it turn around and around. Inside the box, she had kept old jewelry, movie tickets, and photos. Most of the trinkets were from when she was a small girl. She reached in for the one and only photo she had of her parents together.

Angel had always thought she looked funny with her fair skin and unruly black curls. Her parents must have really loved each other at one time. At least that was what she liked to think as she stared at the photo. Her mother, with her chocolate complexion, sat on her father's lap. Her father was a very handsome man. He wore a polo shirt that showed off his large, tanned muscles. Her parents had held their heads together, cheek to cheek, for whoever was behind the camera.

She had always wondered if they had considered getting married. From what she understood, her mother broke off the relationship. Was it because of race? Did her father's family accept her mother? Her grandparents had never talked about her father, but they must have accepted him at one time. Despite all that had happened, she had still had a decent childhood. She knew she was loved for being Elisa's daughter.

There was a knock at her door, jarring her thoughts. She turned around to find Jacob standing at the door. They hadn't spoken since their argument the other day. He still looked worn out and so much older. Maybe she should give him a break. He had lost his father and was probably really worried about his mom.

He said, "Hey, I wanted to let you know I have talked to a friend about getting a visiting nurse whenever Mom comes home."

Angel sat down and placed the music box next to her on the bed. "Great. So when will they release Grams?"

"Well, she is going to be in rehab probably for the next few weeks, so I'm not sure. It depends on how she continues to improve. We will figure it out when I get back."

Angel frowned. "You are leaving?"

"Yes, I still have to work." He looked over at her video equipment on the floor. "Are you keeping busy?"

"I'm working a wedding tomorrow." She expected him to say something smart, but his attention had turned to something else.

Jacob frowned. "You still have that old thing?"

"What?" She picked up the music box. "It's the only thing I have from my dad."

Jacob stared at the music box. "I didn't realize you still had it. Your mother loved him."

She wasn't sure she wanted to go down this path, but since Jacob was in a sharing mood, she said, "I guess that's good for me. Did you like him?"

Jacob shrugged. "I didn't know him that well."

Angel shifted on the bed. "What do you mean?"

"She loved to sing. It's all she wanted to do." He looked thoughtful. "She loved you. She was a good mom, if that's what you are wondering."

"What about my dad? He hasn't been in my life since she . . . went missing. Did you think he had something to do with her going missing?"

"I don't know."

"You had to have your thoughts on what happened. This is the most I have ever heard you talk about her."

Jacob fidgeted in the doorway like he had someplace to go. He finally answered. "It's hard to talk about her."

"I don't have that many memories. I feel like I didn't get to know her. I want to know what happened."

"Angel—"

"He's back, you know."

Jacob stared at her. "Who?"

"My dad is back in Charlotte."

"How do you know this? Have you been trying to get in touch with him?"

She ignored his questions. "I want to ask him for myself what happened that night my mother disappeared, and I want him to look me in the eye when he answers." She wanted to know even if she didn't like what she heard.

Jacob stepped into the room. "Look, I don't know why your father came back here after all this time, but don't dig up the past."

"Don't you really want to know what happened? She was your sister. Granddad was the only one who really tried to find her."

"And it killed him in the process."

"What? Granddad died from complications of diabetes, Jacob."

"He died a long time before that, Angel. At least to me he did."

Angel knew Jacob and Granddad had had an awkward relationship, but still she knew how proud Granddad was of him. "I think you are just talking crazy talk. Granddad loved you."

"Your mom was the favorite. She was the center of everything. When my parents lost her, you became the favorite."

Angel was stunned. If she didn't know any better, she'd think Jacob was sounding like a jealous little boy. "Jacob, you had the perfect childhood. Perfect wife. Perfect career. What is your problem?"

"Nothing is ever perfect. It's those things that seem so perfect that you most have to watch out for. Do yourself a favor. If your dad hasn't reached out to you in all these years, why bother?" Jacob walked out, his words stinging Angel conscience with their bitterness.

*If he hasn't reached out to you in all these years, why bother?*

In the midst of the thoughts pummeling her, the music box started to play by itself. She picked it up with the intent of throwing it across the room, but instead Angel pulled it toward her body and wrapped her arms around it. Why was it that when she felt some sense of hope, it was like someone toyed with her emotions and snatched it away?

# Chapter Eighteen

Angel prayed for a long time before crawling into bed. She prayed for her uncle Jacob. It had occurred to her, after her tears had dried, how negative her uncle could be. She didn't understand what his source of anger was, but realized everyone in her family had handled her mother going missing differently. Grams was hopeful for her return, while Granddad had been determined to find her, even if it was to bury her. She wasn't sure what Jacob was really feeling, but his obvious resentment was something he would have to deal with.

She opened the door to the sanctuary and was immediately taken by the transition. Lenora had transformed the sanctuary into a beautiful place for holy matrimony. Angel called over her shoulder while she carried her camera and her tablet. "Thanks. I appreciate your help today."

Daniel, Candace's teenage son, followed with more bags. "Not a problem. This is cool!"

Angel grinned. Not only had she gained a surrogate sister with Candace, but she also felt like she had another family. She enjoyed spending time with the Johnsons. While Daniel was sixteen, he was pretty mature, and he was a tech geek. Without his help, she wouldn't have been able to get her Web portfolio online.

She had stopped by the Crown of Beauty Salon early this morning, as Candace and her staff worked on the bride and her wedding party. She had shared with Candace what she needed to do. Candace had responded, "Well, I can get you some help. That boy of mine is probably just stuck in front of a video game. This is perfect to get him out of the house, and he loves working with video too."

So here they were, lugging her camera equipment to the front of Victory Gospel Church.

She told Daniel, "Set that camera up front, and I will place this one here in the back."

"All right." Daniel walked down the aisle and put the bags on the floor.

Angel was excited about using multiple cameras. In the midst of what seemed like one long week, her new camera had arrived. With the camera Daniel was setting up, she would be able to get close-up footage. The camera in the back would capture the bride's walk down the aisle and the couple from the back. It might be just a wedding, but she intended to capture this beautiful moment with all her cinematic skills.

She looked around Victory Gospel Church. The sanctuary was huge, with plenty of space for the large number of wedding guests expected to attend. A few people had arrived early. They were at least an hour away from the ceremony. She set the camera on the tripod and looked through the lens.

"Are you ready to go?"

Angel peeked from behind her camera to find Lenora dressed perfectly in a pale peach suit and a matching wide brim hat. "Yes, we are set to go. Wow! You are looking fabulous."

"Honey, I have to look the part of wedding planner extraordinaire and first lady today. I see you have some help. That's good business sense to get an assistant."

"Thanks, but I can't take too much credit. Candace was looking for something for her son to do, and I happen to need help with this one. I'm excited about all this footage we will have for the final video."

Lenora laughed. "Good! You know, with two boys of my own, I know exactly where Candace is coming from. She did a wonderful job on the girls' hair. They are all just beautiful."

Angel nodded toward the tall urns at the front of the church. White flowers and greenery spilled over the tops of them. "The front of the church is gorgeous!" The whole sanctuary was magical and romantic. There were white ribbons with white flowers attached hanging on the ends of each pew. All the way down the aisle, it looked like a secret garden. "Everything is beautiful. I hope to use your services one day."

Lenora beamed. "Well, I will be delighted to help plan your wedding. You know, we don't talk much personally, but is there a young man in your life?"

Angel shook her head. "No, but I've been there before. You know, dreaming about the dress, the ring, everything."

"What happened?" Lenora inquired.

Angela looked away. "Well, the one I thought was my Prince Charming found someone else." Angel remembered she still had the draft e-mail about Kenneth and Denise that she was going to send to Lenora. Now wasn't the time to say anything.

"Oh, Angel. I'm sorry."

"I don't mean to be a bummer."

"No, honey." Lenora patted her on the shoulder. "It was his loss. You hear me? God has someone even better. You just wait and see."

"Thank you, Lenora." Angel couldn't help but smile. Candace had said the same thing to her about three days ago. She hoped these ladies were right. For some reason, maybe because she was in the middle of wedding season, she wondered if she would be a bride one day.

"We will talk more later. I need to check to make sure everyone is dressed." Lenora moved past guests as they flowed in.

Angel walked to the front of the sanctuary toward Daniel to check the camera's focus. "Looks great! Let's start filming the guests as they come in."

"Gotcha." Daniel stood behind the camera.

Angel made her way to the camera in back. As they entered the sanctuary, she asked a few guests if they had any well wishes or words of wisdom for the young couple. One guest after the other wished the couple the best, and some gave words of advice, saying such things as "Keep the communication open," "Be honest," "Remember to have date night," and "Take your time having kids." The advice went on and on. Angel heard the organist start up and thanked the final guest for her advice.

She adjusted the camera to make sure it was focused on the wedding party as they entered. Then she sprinted down the side aisle toward the front to make sure Daniel had the camera focused tighter on where the couple would accept their vows soon. As she returned to the camera in the back, she twisted her hands together and forced herself to take deep breaths. It was important to get everything right. It wasn't like she would get this chance again.

As Angel positioned herself in front of the camera lens, she noticed that the groom had stepped out from a side door at the front. Tommy was looking dapper but was definitely more nervous than he was when she saw him on Thursday. She wondered how Sharise was doing as she waited to walk down the aisle. Before she moved from the camera, Angel caught sight of Tommy's best man. She stepped from behind the camera. Was that . . . ? She looked back through the lens again.

Wes Cade was the best man. Okay, she was floored. How in the world did she keep running into this guy?

She had figured after meeting with him earlier this week at Southern Soul Café that maybe she had overreacted, as she usually did. She was the one who had reached out to him for his help. What did she expect? Since she would be here into the night, filming the reception, she knew avoiding him would be impossible.

The wedding was beautiful. An hour later Angel and Daniel had the cameras set up for the reception. Like the sanctuary, the Victory Gospel Center had been transformed into an elegant, romantic place. The lights were low, and candles and white flowers were at the center of each table. Instead of a deejay, the couple had opted to have a live band. As the band played soft jazz in the background, Angel watched as the guests arrived.

"Angel." A familiar deep voice startled her.

*No. No. No.* Angel turned around to look into the face of the man who had broken her heart, the one for whom she'd hoped to walk down the aisle and say "I do." She quickly looked around. "Kenneth?"

Kenneth was even more handsome than before. His hair was closely cut, and he wore a goatee. "Hey, it's good to see you. You look wonderful." He looked at her face, which was full of questions. "I work with Tommy."

"Okay. Where is Denise? Is she here?" Angel looked around.

"Little Kenny is sick, so she stayed home. You know, I remember you used to carry a camera around all the time. So you make money with this now. Nice!"

She could not believe she was having this conversation. God must be testing her. She was feeling a big, fat "F" coming on, because she did not want to be talking to Kenneth. She took a breath and realized he had been asking her something while she was trying to tune him out.

"I'm sorry. Did you say something?"

"I said, I'm glad to see you. Are you doing okay?" he replied.

She narrowed her eyes. "What's that supposed to mean?'

"You know . . ." Kenneth stared at her with puppy dog eyes. "I'm so sorry."

*Oh no, he is not!* She held her hand up. "Don't. This is not the time. I'm over all of that. Just enjoy your friend's wedding. I'm working." Angel turned her back to Kenneth, biting her lip. If she was really over him, why was his presence making her feel like a heat wave had just washed over the room? Her ears were probably red from the steam rising. *This is just perfect!*

# Chapter Nineteen

Wes was happy for Tommy and Sharise, but he was exhausted. He wanted to head home, but being the best man didn't give him that luxury. It had been a hard week, and he didn't feel like he had accomplished much. He had his suspicions, but he didn't have anything new on Melanie Stowe to bring back to his producer. He knew that first thing on Monday morning, Alan would be on him to dig deeper.

"Hey, man, you're not supposed to be looking glum. I'm the one who just got married." Tommy came up beside him and sat down.

Wes looked at him. "You should be the happiest man in here. What are you doing over here? Where's Sharise?"

"She went to talk to her best friend. So, I decided to see mine."

"Okay, y'all are going to have to do a little bit better."

"Oh, we will as soon as we get out of here. I'm happy to be married, but planning this wedding has been one big ordeal. I'm happy everything turned out great."

"Sharise was a beautiful bride, and I'm sure you two are going to be great. So, when are the kids coming?"

Tommy widened his eyes. "What? No. No. Don't start talking about that yet. Let us get to the honeymoon first."

Wes laughed. "I can't wait to see the first little versions of you and Sharise."

"Okay, now you are scaring me. That's coming just no time soon. Hey, there is my lovely bride. I'm going to get her away from her friend, and I will catch you later."

Wes nodded. "All right." As Tommy walked away, Wes turned his attention to the corner of the room. He had noticed Angel earlier but didn't know what to say or do. She hadn't returned any of his messages. Right now she appeared to be upset with the guy standing next to her. Wes couldn't remember his name, but he was at the bachelor party last night. The guy was a real jerk. He was the kind of guy who demanded attention, despite the evening not being about him.

Wes got up from his seat and weaved his way around tables toward Angel. He figured he might do a bit better than this guy with getting a conversation going. As he approached, Angel looked up. Was that relief in her eyes, or maybe it was his imagination?

"Hello, Angel."

She was definitely smiling at him with her mouth and her eyes. Once again he was reminded how much he loved her eyes.

Angel stepped away from the guy. "Hello, Wes. I didn't realize you were in the wedding party."

"Oh yeah, I've known Tommy and Sharise for years. Tommy since high school. Sharise and I met in college. They met each other and have been a couple ever since." He turned to the man. "You were at the bachelor party last night. Looked like you were having a good time. What was your name again?"

Kenneth looked from Angel to Wes. "Kenneth. Kenneth Morgan. It was a great party. So, you and Angel are friends?"

Seeing the question in Kenneth's eyes, Wes couldn't resist. "Yes, we have become fast friends." Wes was happy to be rewarded with a smile from Angel. He had done something right for a change.

"I will leave you two. Good to see you again, Angel."

As Kenneth walked off, Wes turned to Angel. "I'm sorry. I didn't mean to interrupt."

Angel shook her head. "Believe me, you saved me."

"Boyfriend?"

"Ex-boyfriend. Long time ago."

"Weddings bring out the romantic side of people."

"Not. He's going to be getting married this summer. To my ex–best friend."

She smiled, but Wes could tell the attempted humor didn't reach her eyes. "I'm surprised you said he's going to be getting married soon. He didn't appear to be tied down to anyone last night. I would say he was the life of the party."

"Kenneth likes attention. So you said you went to high school with the groom?"

"Yes, we both had the honor of being church boys."

She raised her eyebrow. "Church boys?"

"Let's just say that Wanda and Tommy's mom enjoyed keeping us in church and out of trouble. We, of course, would find a way to cut up and get into foolishness, anyway."

Angel giggled. "I bet."

To keep the conversation going, he asked, "How's your grandmother doing?"

"She's been transferred to a rehabilitation facility. It's hard to see her, but she is trying hard. It can be really frustrating for her. She was so energetic before."

"I can imagine."

She asked, "How's Detective Cade doing?"

"Last I talked to my mom, he seemed in good spirits. It's kind of sad to be around him. We used to hang out all the time, and then . . . some days he doesn't know me or Mom. It's like we don't exist. In his mind he could be back thirty or forty years."

Angel said, "That must be difficult. I read a bit about Alzheimer's. It affects the short-term memory first."

"Yes, it's hard. Mom is a nurse, and she mainly takes care of him. Lately, I think it's taken a toll on her, though. She seems older, and I don't mean age-wise. She is just tired. She would have attended the wedding today, but someone has to watch him. She doesn't want to put him in a nursing home, but he has run away a couple of times. It's just scary when he goes missing." He looked at Angel's face. "Oh, I shouldn't have brought that up."

Angel frowned. "What do you mean? You were saying he can get lost. It can happen when he gets confused."

"Sorry. I just thought about . . . Well, I have been working on the Melanie Stowe case and . . . you know, your mother."

"It's fine. Do you know if the police have any clues about what happened to Melanie? It's been a week and a half now. I've been trying to follow her case a little."

"No. It's pretty cut and dry. Someone snatched her up in the parking lot on the way to her car, and no one saw it. It could be a crazed fan that became obsessed with her on *American Voices*. There are not a lot of clues."

Angel responded, "When I saw the story on the news, it reminded me of my mother's disappearance. I guess because they both had these singing careers they were pursuing."

Something about what Angel said struck a chord somewhere in Wes. Possibly because he was investigating both cases at the same time, he, too, thought the similarity was interesting. Still, the missing person cases were twenty years apart.

Wes noticed the band had started to play a slow number. The conversation between him and Angel, along with the other conversations at the reception, came to a halt as all eyes were on Tommy and Sharise on the dance floor. Wes wondered what that felt like. To stare into the eyes of the woman you would spend the rest of your life with. He looked over at Angel, who had directed her attention to the camera on the tripod.

She turned to look at him, and they just stared at each other for a brief moment, until Angel looked away to focus on the camera with a slight smile on her face. Wes forgot that only about twenty minutes ago he had felt exhausted and had been ready to call it a night. Now staying for a little while longer was a bit more appealing. He just needed to keep the reporter's hat off so he wouldn't spoil the growing friendship he had with Angel Roberts.

# Chapter Twenty

A noise from behind the door startled her from sleep. Melanie slept all the time, but it was more like dozing off in a car or on a plane. Her head nodded and jerked at any odd sound. This time she knew she had heard something for sure. She focused on a sliver of light under the door. Then she saw a shadow at the threshold. *He's back!* She turned her back to the door and shut her eyes tight. Her heart felt like it was trying to beat its way out of her chest.

As light pushed away the darkness, she told herself, *Don't move.* This was the second time he'd come. The first time, she'd stood and faced him. Melanie's questions had caught in her throat as she noticed the flicker of steel emerge from the switchblade in his hand. Against the light of the door, she hadn't been able to see his face clearly. It hadn't mattered; she knew he'd come to end her exile and send her away for eternity. She had curled up on the bed, pleading with him not to hurt her.

He hadn't touched her. Instead he had brought her more food, this time including a banana and two apples. She wasn't sure if she should be grateful or alarmed. How long was he planning to keep her here?

Now he was back. He always smelled like he'd just taken a shower. Though she was scared of his presence, the scent of his cologne was a pleasant alternative to the constant mustiness of the room. The floorboards crackled as he drew near her. A few seconds later, she felt his breath across the side of her face.

Her gut instinct told her to reach toward him and fight for her life, but knowing his switchblade was nearby, she didn't dare. It was best to attack him upon his arrival, catch him off guard. If only she knew when he would come.

Melanie heard him walk over to the wall across from the bed. She slowly opened her eyes while his back was turned, and watched him pull out more water and food from a bag. He took his time arranging the items on the table. When he turned back around, she closed her eyes. She had yet to get a good look at him. He wasn't young. That was all she could tell. The man moved very deliberately, like he was thinking with every move-ment. Then, as stealthily as he'd come in, he was gone, the door locked. She kept her eyes closed awhile longer.

Melanie scooted off the bed and walked over to the table. She stared at the assortment of food. Water, peanuts, and more fruit. She amused herself by saying, "Well, most of the food groups are represented."

Her humor died when she noticed he had left her something else.

Not many people knew how much she loved this candy bar. Maybe it was a coincidence. She knew it wasn't.

# Chapter Twenty-one

Angel followed Jennifer into her office at the Bring Them Home Foundation. The offices were in a house. When Angel entered, she was enamored of the cozy living room that served as a waiting area. Jennifer's office was a former bedroom and was filled with filing cabinets. There was a large couch with a blanket on one side of the room. Angel had a feeling Jennifer was really dedicated to her nonprofit, so much so that she pulled all-nighters. On Jennifer's desk were flyers with a photo of Melanie Stowe from a performance on *American Voices.*

"Jennifer, thank you for letting me interview you for my film. We can shoot a segment for a PSA if you would like, but are you sure this is still a good time?"

Jennifer was dressed in jeans and a T-shirt. She had been out early with a group of searchers looking for Melanie. She pulled her hat off and ran her hands across her short red hair. "This works for me. Please no formalities here. I'm so excited that you are going to document your mother's life. So many adults go missing each year, whether it's foul play, mental illness, or circumstances that have led to homelessness. I think what you are doing will garner attention for other missing people."

As Angel pulled her camera and tripod out of the bag, she responded, "I thought the film could be a way to help other families with missing persons." She shrugged her shoulders. "Maybe they don't know about your organization." Angel had determined that she wanted to tell Elisa's story whether or not she was ever found.

"We do appreciate it. This week we have workshops going on with law enforcement. We are excited about agencies working together toward a common goal."

Angel sat the camera on the tripod and then turned it on. She asked, "Law enforcement workshops? That sounds like a perfect place to start. Hold on just one moment." Angel looked into her camera to check the lighting. Since there was a window on the left side of Jennifer, Angel took the time to adjust the light meter. Jennifer wore a bright green T-shirt, which provided great color balance.

Satisfied with her camera setting, Angel grabbed her notebook and turned to the questions she had prepared. "So, why are you doing workshops for law enforcement?"

Jennifer sighed. "Well, as you probably know, when an adult goes missing, it's not always taken quite as seriously as when a child disappears. When a person is eighteen, they can come and go as they please. Often-times these cases are not handled with care, especially when it comes to family members in search of their loved ones. So we train law enforcement and the inves-tigators on how to interact with families and also the media."

Angel scribbled in her notebook and then looked up at Jennifer. "You know, the investigator in my mom's case was also a family friend. I believe he tried his best, but my granddad didn't think he did enough."

Jennifer shook her head. "Yes, I'm aware of Nick's feelings. He came to us because he just couldn't wrap his head around the fact that your mother couldn't be found. He really just wanted to bring her home, even if it was just her body."

Angel swallowed.

"Are you okay? This is hard, and it's admirable that you are doing this."

Angel smiled and shook her head. "I'm fine. Let's continue. When did you start your foundation? Are you the only one devoted to missing persons?"

"Oh no, there are many foundations and organizations doing this work, but we are connected. Meaning we, along with law enforcement, forensic scientists, the families of missing loved ones, we all have access to and the ability to add information to NamUs. NamUs is the National Missing and Unidentified Persons System. It's the main database for missing persons and unidentified decedent records."

Angel responded, "It's an incredible database. I searched there last night and, of course, found my mother's profile."

"It's one of the most important tools we have. There is also The Doe Network, which provides information too. Many unidentified persons have been identified by family members who diligently searched for them."

"Thanks. I'd like to look into the Web sites more."

"I'm sure you will find it to be very helpful. Your grandfather was of an older generation, so he didn't seem to take to computers too well."

Angel laughed. "No, neither of my grandparents cared too much about computers. Anytime they wanted to see something, I was their Internet guide." Angel looked at her notes. "Jennifer, I just have a few more questions, and I will be out of your way. Now, tell me, is it true that you have to wait twenty-four hours, and sometimes up to seventy-two hours, to report a missing person?"

"Not necessarily true. If the missing person fits the Bring Them Home Foundation criteria, we like to report them missing as soon as possible. We have an investigator on staff who will immediately focus on the missing person. The sooner an adult is reported missing, the sooner the investigators can help find them. In fact, in many cases missing persons are found and returned home in a few days. It's sad, but sometimes a person is reported missing when he or she has simply chosen not to go to work and avoid friends and family."

"But the longer they are missing, the greater the chance that foul play is involved, right? I mean, in my mother's case, she walked out of the house and didn't tell anyone where she was going."

Jennifer shook her head. "Yes, your mother's case is a tricky one. Her car was never recovered. There is no evidence of her stopping by a bank or spending money. Back then there were no cell phones to be traced. No one has come forward with decent information. There were people who claimed to have seen her, but they were all over the place. Your mother couldn't be in so many places at once."

"Agreed." Angel wanted to be able to pick Detective Cade's memories about those call-ins. "Would you say if there is foul play involved in a missing persons case that the person responsible could easily have been someone the missing person knew?" she asked. "I mean, I can't imagine someone harming another person and just keeping it a secret."

"That's pretty scary, Angel." Jennifer clasped her hands. "Unfortunately, if there was an abduction or some type of foul play, the victim usually knows the person, but maybe not personally. But there was some interaction. Oftentimes family and close friends are looked at first."

That explained why everyone looked so hard at Angel's father. "Thanks, Jennifer. Is there anything you want to add to the interview?"

"Certainly, I want to stress the importance of immediately notifying the police when someone goes missing. You should dial nine-one-one. Be sure to note their physical features and what they were wearing. Having a recent photo really helps the process too."

"Awesome." Angel stood and shook Jennifer's hand. "I really appreciate your time. I can see why my grand-dad liked to keep in touch with you. I think he had some peace in knowing someone was still looking for my mother."

"That's what we are here for. Now, the police did all they could do as well. I remember Detective . . . um . . . What was his name?"

"Detective Cade."

"Yes. He never gave up looking. In fact, we kept in touch periodically. He had a wealth of details and information about Elisa's case. I don't think I had ever seen such compassion from an investigator. It sounds like your mother was well loved and dearly missed by many people."

"I see that now more as an adult. You know, speaking of missing persons, what are your thoughts about Melanie Stowe? She is getting a lot of coverage in the media. Do you think it will help?"

Jennifer picked up a flyer off her desk. "I hope so. Melanie is an unusual case with her celebrity status from *American Voices*. Many, many adults go missing with nowhere near the media attention locally, and certainly not nationally. You can't turn on the news these days without hearing about her. That's going to be good if she has been spotted."

A blond-haired girl peeked in the doorway. "Sorry to interrupt, but, Jennifer, we will need you in the conference room soon."

Jennifer answered, "I will be right there." She stood and stretched her arm out toward Angel. "Angel, it's been a pleasure. Let me know how the documentary goes, and if you can pull a PSA from the interview, that would be fantastic. I would love to include it with our workshop material."

"Certainly. I will be in touch."

As Angel packed up her camera and equipment, she thought about Melanie. It had been almost two weeks since she vanished. She wondered if the young singer would fare better than her mother had. Angel hoped so. She entered the hallway and headed out toward her car. The sunshine warmed her, but she wasn't thinking warm thoughts. In her heart, she knew she needed to conquer a fear that had been eating away at her the past few days.

Her interview with Jennifer was for a double purpose. Angel wanted to help spread the word about the foundation, but she also wanted to trace what happened to her mother twenty years ago. Jennifer's words haunted Angel. *Oftentimes family and close friends are looked at first.* Should she really try to reach out to her father? If he did have something to do with her mother going missing, how would he feel about his long-lost daughter showing up at his front door?

# Chapter Twenty-two

"Alan, you are not serious, are you?" Wes looked incredulously at his news producer. "If Serena had this assignment, you wouldn't hesitate to let her go through with *her* own story ideas."

"I'm not saying you aren't delivering, Wes. I just think with Melanie being a Charlotte native, we aren't doing her story justice. Look at what CNN is reporting. We need a different angle."

"I'm aware of the need to bring a unique angle. It was me who brought the exclusive interviews with Detective Darnell Jackson and Candace Johnson a few months ago." Of course, it didn't hurt that Wes had a connection. He coached basketball along with Darnell at the Victory Gospel Center. Since Darnell was dating the beauty salon owner, interviewing Candace had turned out to be a sweet deal.

"And we are proud of you for pulling off those stories. I need to see you do it again. I just think we need to throw around some ideas."

Wes looked away and then back at Alan, whose thick eyebrows were a unibrow. Sometimes Alan's obsession with getting ratings and an award-winning story was even too much for Wes. Not that he didn't strive for the same goals. "I told you I believe we need to locate Melanie's dad. No one knows what happened to him. It's like he disappeared too."

Alan waved his hand. "I don't know, Wes. Would he kidnap his daughter or harm her? Why?"

Wes looked back at his notes from Lisa. "Both Lisa and Jay mentioned that Melanie was having a difficult time securing a record deal. There was a deal on the table, but she wasn't talking to anyone about it."

"Why not?"

"I guess because she had been pushed into the spotlight from the *American Voices* show. Most of the people I have talked to thought she had been voted off too soon, that she should have made it all the way to the finals. Her fans want to see her get an album out there, since she wasn't a winner on the show. Melanie felt that pressure."

"So a girl with that kind of talent . . ." Alan leaned back in his seat and placed his hands behind his head. "Why didn't she have record companies knocking at her door?"

Wes shrugged. "I don't know. I'm not sure this has anything to do with her being missing."

Alan leaned forward. "I know you are going with your gut here on the father, but I think we need to look at this from another angle. Give her fans something to hang on to. Who offered Melanie record deals? Why were contracts never signed? What was the latest offer? Why such a secret?"

After getting pelted with Alan's questions, Wes thought for a moment. Finally, he answered, "Okay, you have a couple of points. I will focus on the record deals, but I still want to ask questions about the dad."

Alan threw up his hands. "Fine. Just make sure we deliver the news story that Charlotte wants to hear. That all her fans want to hear."

"I'm on it. By the way, where is Serena? I would love to know what her take would be on this story."

"Told you Matt sent her on a trip up to New York. Something is brewing, but no one is sharing with me."

"Must be a serious story for Matt to give her expenses." Then again, Wes knew Serena could get anything she wanted, including permission from the station's news director, Matt Lemon, to pursue a hot story.

"No telling what Serena has up her sleeve. In the meantime, Melanie Stowe is our biggest local and national story. Dig up some stuff."

Wes arose from the chair and left Alan's office. He wasn't sure pursuing Melanie's record deal failures would reveal anything about why she went missing, but he was intrigued. As he sat at his desk, he started to wonder if he wasn't mixing up the cases a bit. Really, the father he wanted to talk to was the man Pops had tried to investigate in the Elisa Roberts case.

Two different missing person cases, but something was odd. He thought about what Angel had said over the weekend. There were a few similarities in the cases, even though they were twenty years apart. They were both dynamic singers, and both disappeared in their early twenties. Despite the vocal talent both these women had, life wouldn't allow them to pursue the recognition they desired.

Wes tapped the keyboard to awaken the computer screen and logged into Facebook. He had made a note to check out Melanie Stowe's profile page. She had a public fan page that had over twenty thousand members. Those were pretty impressive numbers. Wes scrolled through the posts, looking for any odd postings. Most of the posts were from fans wanting the young singer to be found safely. Many prayers were going up for Melanie.

As he continued scrolling, he stopped on one post, mainly because the avatar represented a person who was older than some of the other members. He'd posted, Melanie, girl, I can't wait to work with you in the studio. You are going places, girl. World, watch out for your next big superstar. Was this related to the record deal? The message was posted about a week before Melanie went missing. Wes scribbled down the date and then clicked on the avatar to pull up the profile page. Minister J.D. Wes sat back. He knew this guy. In fact, Minister J.D. was the founder of the men's conference Wes had attended last year.

The minister had an unusual background. In the nineties, he had a brief stint as a hip-hop artist known simply as J.D. After one big album that sold a million copies, J.D. found himself pulled into the darker part of the business. He was seen publicly in a drunken state, was charged with a few DUIs, and then finally ended up in rehab. The former hip-hop artist lay low for years before opening a small church in South Charlotte. During the past five years Minister J.D. had acquired quite a flock at Kingdom Building Church. The congregation was not nearly as large as the one at Victory Gospel Church, but many young people liked Minister J.D.'s style of preaching. He was known to drop a rhyme or two.

Wes would definitely be visiting with the minister in the near future. In the meantime, he had a meeting with a friend who he hoped would help provide a better perspective on Melanie's case.

About two hours later, Wes found himself lifting his body off the ground to slam the ball into the net. He came down to the ground and shouted, "Yeah, baby! Detective, I believe I took care of business today."

Shaking his head, Darnell grinned and retrieved the bouncing ball. "Okay, you got game today. I will give it to you." He rubbed his goatee. "Although you might not want to try that jump again. An old man can get hurt off a jumper like that."

"Old man! Really, if I'm not mistaken, I believe you got a few years on me, Detective."

Both men laughed as they walked off the court.

"Thanks for letting me whip up on you. Great stress reliever," Wes commented.

"Mmm, enjoy, because that will be your last time."

"I doubt it. You see you have a problem."

Darnell stopped and looked at Wes. "I do?"

Wes continued walking and said over his shoulder, "Yeah, you are a man in love. Men in love can't concentrate on anything else."

Darnell threw his head back and laughed. He caught up to Wes. "Can't argue with you on that one."

Wes asked, "So, when are you going to pop the question?"

"Whoa, bro! Slow down. Candace and I are not walking down the aisle anytime soon. We have both been married before, so we are going take our time."

"That's smart."

"What about you? One of the most recognizable bachelors in Charlotte. I've heard about your groupies."

"Man, you need to stop. I don't know how my name ended up in that article. I just report the news. Although, I have found myself in the danger zone at work. You know who I'm talking about."

Darnell gave Wes a look. "Please don't tell me you are referring to Serena Manchester."

"For some reason that I haven't figured out yet, I've been on her radar. I know she wants something. Just don't know what yet."

"Well, it's good you are keeping an eye on her. She is one tricky woman. I do believe she will do anything to get a story."

Wes knew that Darnell was right. The detective was betrayed by Serena a few years back on a case, and it almost cost Darnell his job at the Charlotte-Mecklenburg Police Department. Wes was really concerned about why Serena was in New York, especially since she had had so many questions about Pops. His gut told him her questions related back to a cold case, but which one?

As they approached their cars, Wes remembered to ask Darnell the question that had been on his mind. "Hey, can I ask you about Melanie Stowe?"

"Sure. Technically, she is still a missing person case, though."

"Yeah, but it will be two weeks tomorrow. Do you think there is any chance of finding her alive now?"

Darnell shook his head. "I hate to say it, but it could be any day now, weeks, or even months when she could become a homicide case. And at that point, I would definitely be on it. I have been keeping up with the case when I can, though. There isn't much to work with."

"I know. I wish someone had witnessed something that night. It's crazy. So, what do you do with a case where there is no body? Like, there's this case Pops worked on years and years ago. They had this person of interest, but they had no body and no evidence of a crime scene. All they could do is let him go. What if he got away with it just because he was clever enough to cover his tracks?"

Darnell leaned against his car. "That's a hard one. There's not much you can do unless the person confesses. These days we could do a little more with DNA, but in the case of Melanie Stowe, her car was swept for prints and there was nothing. I will say this, though. Someone had to be watching her very carefully. They had to know she was going to be at the club that night, and once they saw her alone, they took the opportunity."

"A stalker. Maybe someone who was just a bit too much of a fan."

"Yeah, it's my understanding folks are looking into that now, but that's a wild-goose chase."

"There had to be some communication via e-mail, her social media, or a phone call."

"Yeah, there was a lot of it. Do you know how many people tried to contact this woman? She probably went on that show thinking she would achieve her dreams. I imagine it had become a bit of a nightmare for her." Darnell shook his head and held out his hand toward Wes. "All right, man. I have to head back. We have to do this again. Next time, it's on."

"You got it!"

Darnell and Wes exchanged a brotherly handshake. Wes got into his car. As Darnell drove off, Wes started thinking. He hadn't had a chance to speak to Melanie's stepmom himself, but now he wondered what the real reason was for Melanie moving back home. Before he could turn the car on, his phone rang.

Angel's number showed on the display.

# Chapter Twenty-three

Angel couldn't help but smile as she heard Wes ask, "Are you sure about this?"

She responded, "Not really, but it's too late to turn back now. I'm sitting outside his house. I figured I would let you know. You know, if things don't go well, I can blame you." She laughed nervously.

She had located her dad's house. It was actually pretty scary how much information about a person one could find online. After her dad left the Charlotte area, he had lived in several cities out west, but mainly Las Vegas and then San Diego. He seemed to start and lose businesses quite often. He'd finally hit it big with his latest business.

Wes said, "I wish you would have let me go with you. It might not be a good idea to do this by yourself."

"I have to, Wes. Besides, he's my father, and I need to know the truth."

"If you sense something isn't right, just leave. Okay?"

Angel heard the concern in Wes's voice but was preoccupied by a movement in the house. Someone was peeking at her from the bay window in front of the house.

"Angel?"

She became aware of the urgency in Wes's voice. "Yeah, yeah. Hey, I think someone is watching me from inside the house. I'm going to head to the door. Pray for me. Bye." She clicked the phone off. Angel wasn't sure why she'd called Wes. She couldn't bring herself to tell anyone else.

Before she went to bed last night, she had mapped out the route to the Mancini home. She had prayed to God during the entire thirty-minute drive that if this wasn't the right thing to do, He would stop her.

*Trust in the Lord with all your heart.*

When she'd left the house, the sun was shining bright, but at some point in her journey clouds had gathered, bringing raindrops. Through the short rainstorm, Angel had kept driving.

She looked at the house again and said to herself, "Okay, let's do this." As she walked toward the front door, she could smell wet grass and see raindrops lingering on the flowers. The clouds had pulled back, allowing the sun's rays to break through.

She took a deep breath and pressed the doorbell. A few minutes later she heard a woman's voice behind the door say, "If you are a reporter, go away."

Angel frowned and answered back. "I'm not a reporter. I'm here to see Angelino Mancini. Is he here?" Angel assumed the woman must be her dad's wife.

The door opened from inside, and Angel could see the shape of a woman through the screen door. The woman responded tartly, "Yes, can I help you . . . ?" The woman stopped talking and then opened the screen door. Angel stepped away from the door quickly as the woman stuck her head out. The woman stared at her. "You?"

Angel did a double take. She'd seen this woman before. It was the strange woman from Lenora's bridal shop. Angel said, "I saw you last week."

"Yes, I was there getting my daughter's dress fitted. Are you here about the dress?" the woman questioned her.

Angel felt really warm all of sudden, and it had nothing to do with the sun shining on her back. Why did she not think her father would have another family? A wife and a daughter? "Maybe I should come back." She turned around.

"Wait," the woman called out to her. "Your father would want to meet you."

Angel spun around and narrowed her eyes. "You know who I am?"

The woman shook her head. "I knew who you were when I saw you last week. You look so much like your mother. I'm Leslie. Why don't you come in? Your father will be back in a few minutes."

Angel stared at the woman, taking in her blond hair and blue eyes, which were so very different from those of her chocolate-skinned mother. She wondered again what had driven her parents together and ultimately apart.

Inside the house on the cul-de-sac, Angel took in the high ceiling and the staircase that led up to a second floor. Leslie showed her into the living room, which was off to the side. Angel followed her, her sneakers sinking into the plush white carpet. She had a feeling her father had indeed done very well and Leslie enjoyed decorating the home.

Before taking a seat, Angel glimpsed at photos of a young girl with tanned skin and brunet hair on a table behind the couch. She asked, "Your daughter?"

"That's Celeste." Leslie walked over to the other side of the room and picked up a framed photo of another child. "You recognize this little girl?"

Angel did a double take for a second time. Of all the scenarios she'd imagined, she clearly hadn't expected this. The little caramel-skinned girl with the curly ponytail was definitely a mini-version of her staring back at her from the photo. Her eyes blurred as she looked away from the image. This wasn't making sense. Her father had never reached out to her all these years. Why would his wife recognize Angel and have a photo of her in the living room?

"Would you like something to drink?" Leslie asked.

Angel shook her head, although it felt like something had found its way into her air passages and was lodged there. She cleared her throat. "Why did you think I was a reporter?"

Leslie clasped her hands. "Oh, there was a reporter here a few weeks ago. Sometimes it's best to leave the past alone."

Angel frowned and started to ask Leslie what she meant, but the front door opened, interrupting her. Leslie looked at her and then walked briskly out of the room.

*It's him. He's here.*

Angel rubbed her head, experiencing a swift feeling of coldness, then warmth, come over her. Her stomach churned as she faced the man who'd entered the room.

She recognized her father's face, despite his extra weight and graying temples. His eyes were locked on her and were brimming with emotion. Was he excited or horrified to see her? She couldn't tell.

After a few seconds, he spoke. "I always knew this day would come. It's good to finally see you again, Angel."

Leslie smiled and touched her husband on the shoulder. "I will leave you two alone."

She watched Leslie leave and stared at her father, still not quite sure what to say.

He asked, "Why don't we sit down?"

She waited for him to pass by and sit in a chair that must have been his chair. A large flat-screen TV stood in a tall cabinet with doors. She sat down on the couch, her eyes studying other parts of the room before landing on his face.

He said, "So, you are a videographer. I've seen your work. It's really good."

Her mouth felt cottony as words tumbled out. "How do you know about me? And how does your wife knows who I am?" She had more questions now that she was here.

He leaned forward. "I know you have many questions, but I've never forgotten you. I have sent you cards and gifts every year. Especially on your birthday and again at Christmas. At some point I hoped your family would understand we needed to have a relationship. It's one of the reasons I wanted to move back east. I was hoping we could meet again."

Angel shook her head. "I have never received anything from you."

Her father's shoulders sagged. "That figures. Even after the police cleared me as a person of interest, your grandparents forbade me from contacting you."

"Well, what happened that night? I remember you both were shouting at each other. Then you came into my room and brought me my birthday present. You said, 'Happy birthday, princess.' Then you were gone. I wound up the back of the music box and watched the ballerina go round and round until I grew sleepy. I must have fallen asleep, because I opened my eyes and felt my mother kiss me on my forehead, and then she was gone. It's like I lost both of you the same night."

"I'm so sorry, Angel."

"Tell me, what did you say to her?"

"I just talked to her. I wanted us to get back together."

"Why did you break up?"

"We were both young. She wanted her singing career. I was moving my way up in the boxing division. We were just on two different paths."

"So you came to beg her to come back to you? Why then?"

Angelino looked at her for a long time. "You look so much like her. Your mother wanted to be a star. The stage was where she loved to be the most. I loved her voice. She could move me to tears. After she had you, she waited a long time to get a record deal. She finally got an offer."

"And?"

"I told her not to take the deal. She was furious and accused me of trying to hold her back. I told her she just needed to be patient. The record company wasn't reputable. She wouldn't have the long career she had always wanted. I wasn't the only one who warned her. Her dad and Jacob told her the same thing."

"Really? What did you know about the company?"

"Royal Records was the company. They came up fast and heavy in about two years. There was some shadiness around some of the artists, not that they didn't have legitimate talent. I checked around with some friends in the industry and a lawyer. I knew Elisa wouldn't. She had gotten to a point where she wasn't listening to anyone."

Angelino rubbed his head much the way Angel had rubbed hers a while ago. He sat back in his chair and sighed. "One of their artists, a one-hit-wonder rapper, was killed a few weeks after Elisa was offered the deal. That should have set off all kinds of alarms for her. I told her she really should think this through. The music industry was hard on a person. You were young and needed your mother."

Angel watched her father's face. He seemed in pain, as if he had really wanted to save her mother. "Why would they suspect you did something to her?" she asked.

Angelino sighed. "I loved your mother, but we did fight. She knew what she wanted. I wanted what I had growing up. A family." He looked at her. "How is your family?"

"My granddad passed away a few months ago, complications of diabetes. Grams suffered a stroke a few weeks ago."

"Ah, kid! So sorry to hear. Your grandparents were beautiful people. They accepted me in Elisa's life. It always hurt me that they thought I did something to her. I would have never hurt her. I want you to believe me."

Angel wasn't sure what to believe.

"I hope you received the birthday card I sent recently. You turned twenty-five about two weeks ago. That's how old she was when . . ."

She looked at him. "I never saw it." She stood. "I need to go. Thanks for seeing me."

He stood with her. "I hope you will come back. Get to know Leslie and Celeste. Your sister."

She'd always wanted a sibling, but this was enough for today. Angel turned and headed out of the living room. When she reached the front door, her father opened it and said, "Anytime. You are welcome here anytime."

Angel gazed into her father's eyes, still stunned by the warmth she saw. She nodded and walked toward the car, not daring to look back. Tears blurred her vision. She was having a difficult time envisioning the man she had just met being the monster her family had painted him to be. Or was he the worse monster of all? The kind you couldn't see until it was too late?

# Chapter Twenty-four

Angel had said something to Wes that he couldn't recall ever hearing from a woman. *Pray for me.* All the anxiety he felt about her going to see her father and what could happen faded away as he prayed for Angel. He prayed for her safety and for her visit to be the first step toward her having a relationship with one of her parents. He was reminded of that one brief moment during the wedding when they looked at each other.

Was it just him, or did Angel feel something too? He was not a believer in love at first sight. Then again, ever since she showed up at the house to see Pops, Wes felt compelled to help Angel find closure about her mother.

Wes drove by himself today, instead of bringing Rick. He had something he wanted to do, and he didn't want to be obvious by driving the news station vehicle or bringing a cameraman. So he parked his personal car in a parking space about five houses down from the Stowes' home. With Melanie being gone for about two weeks now, the media attention around the house had subsided. He had gathered interviews with members of the search team, noting that some of them had also wondered why more of Melanie's family wasn't represented. Wes had decided to talk to Melanie's stepmother, which he hadn't done since Serena passed the assignment to him.

He rang the doorbell and waited. Finally, the door was opened. Wes looked down to see a young child looking back at him. He bent down and said hello to the little girl. She was a miniature, but chubbier version of Melanie. The girl was holding a purple Popsicle in her hand, and the juice had run down her arm, staining the front of her dingy white T-shirt.

"Get away from the door. I told you not to answer that door," a woman shrieked from the back. Snatching the child out of the doorway, the woman, whose hair was braided, looked at Wes. Her tiny braids were pulled back from her face to show weary, red-brimmed eyes. "What do you want? I don't want any more reporters here. Stay away from me and my children." The woman started to close the door.

Wes held his hand out and shouted, "Wait! I just want to know how you are doing."

She held the door open a crack and said, "What do you care?"

Wes kept talking. "It must be hard to feel like a prisoner in your own house. Do you need anything? Are the kids okay?"

"We're fine."

"I know the search team is exhausted. You have a lot of good people working to find Melanie. Do you want to share anything about your stepdaughter?"

The woman pulled the door open wider. Finally, she sighed deeply. "Come in. You have five minutes."

"Thank you. I appreciate it."

She shoved her finger at him. "I'm just letting you in because I've seen you on TV. You seem okay."

Wes smiled, thankful for being a familiar face. As he stepped inside, Wes was sure his eyes grew wide. There were toys everywhere. He gingerly stepped around Legos, toy cars, and dolls. Two children were asleep on one couch, while the child who had answered the door had plopped down cross-legged in front of the television.

The woman kept walking as Wes weaved his way behind her to a dining area off the living room. The dining room table seated six but didn't seem to be a place for eating, as a sewing machine, thread, yarn, and piles of children's clothes covered the top. Gladys sat down in a chair that had already been pulled away from the table. Wes pulled out the chair adjacent to where Gladys sat. He realized she probably had been sitting at the table when he arrived. She picked up a child's pair of pants and absently folded them, placing them on a neat stack of clothes in front of her.

A question crossed Wes's mind. *Why would Melanie move back here?* He hadn't seen any other parts of the house, but how would the twenty-one-year-old fit in this house physically and mentally? He couldn't tell Mrs. Stowe's age but was sure she was younger than she appeared.

"Mrs. Stowe, is it all right if I call you Gladys?" Wes interpreted the slight movement of her head as a nod. "Gladys, I know this must be a rough time for you, so I won't hold you long."

"Would you like some water?" she asked him.

"No, I'm fine." Wes looked over at the shelves. There were family photos. "Did Melanie stay here before she disappeared?"

"She stayed here for a while. She had found another apartment, but she still hadn't moved all her stuff out yet."

"Do you know what happened to the other apartment?"

The woman shook her head. "I have no idea. Look, I loved the girl like she was my own. After her father went to prison, I made sure she was cared for and she graduated. This was her home."

"That was admirable of you. Where is Mr. Stowe these days? I heard he had been released."

Gladys rolled her eyes. "Who knows? I certainly don't, and most days I don't care. He wasn't much help, other than making babies."

Wes decided to change the subject. "How did you feel about Melanie being on *American Voices?*"

"I was proud of her. She should have won. First time I met her, she was singing. She was a singing little girl." Gladys fiddled with the clothes on the table. "She'd been through a lot. Losing her mother when she was young. I tried to make it work, but her father was a different story."

"Have you seen him?"

She narrowed her eyes at him. "Why? He in some kind of trouble?"

Wes tried to keep the emotions from his face. Why would she ask that question? "Not that I know of. I just was wondering why he wasn't on the news. If I was a father, I would be talking to reporters and staying in the public's eye."

Gladys looked away. "I knew when I married Larry that he was something special. It wasn't until he managed to get caught with the drugs that I knew he was special in the head. All these kids and he cared more about himself. I wouldn't let him move back in here when he got out. The kids don't know him. I couldn't tell you if he is even aware Melanie is missing, especially if he's been drinking."

"Where would he go if he is still in town?" Wes hated to ask so many questions, but he wanted the opportunity to locate Larry Stowe.

Gladys said, "He was living in a run-down place, working odd jobs, but he didn't keep the place that long. I know a few places you can look. Good luck finding him. I sure could use the child support."

\*\*\*

An hour later, Wes opened the door to Charlie's Place. He personally was not a drinker, but as soon as Gladys mentioned the place, he knew where it was located. It was perfect because it would give him a chance to meet with Albert Langley, better known as Big Al. Big Al was destined to be a linebacker in the NFL, but an injury and falling on hard times had left him hanging out on the streets, and most of the time he could be found at Charlie's Place.

The bartender was wiping down the bar counter. Wes waved. "Hey, have you seen Big Al today?"

The bartender nodded. "He's in the back, playing pool, or trying to."

"Thanks, man." Wes headed toward the back. It wasn't quite happy hour yet, so the pool area was not terribly smoky, although the remnants of cigarette and cigar ash clung to the walls. It didn't take Wes long to spot Big Al since it was only him and three others in the room. Big Al lived up to his name. He appeared almost as broad as he was tall now, thanks to pounds of flesh versus the muscle that once was there.

Wes walked up behind him and said, "What's up, Big Al?"

The man turned around, his face menacing. The first time Wes met him, his first instinct was to run, but the more Wes talked to him, the more he realized the man was just a big teddy bear. Bouncer material he was not.

A big toothless grin broke across Big Al's face. "Wes Cade. How you doing, man?" He placed the pool stick on the table and picked up a mug. He gulped down the liquid before turning back to Wes. "I haven't seen you in some time, Mr. Reporter. What you need?"

"It's good to see you too. You doing well?"

"I survive. Tony up there lets me clean up the place for him. Not bad work, I would say."

Wes laughed. "Yeah, I guess, if you get to play pool. You know, I can still look into some other offers for you."

"Naw, I'm good. What can I do for you today?"

"Well, I was hoping you would be on the lookout for someone."

"That don't sound too hard."

Wes grinned. "Good." He pulled a photo out of his shirt pocket. "I'm looking for the guy in the photo." He didn't know if it was his charm or if Gladys really wanted her husband found, but she'd given him a photo of Larry. At first glance it had seemed dated, like it had been taken in the eighties. However, when Wes examined the date on the back, he realized it wasn't from quite that far back.

Big Al took the photo and squinted. "Mmm, seems like I've seen him before." Then Big Al laughed so hard, his belly shook. "Man, this cat look like he could be a member of Run DMC. I used to have a Kangol hat like this."

That was exactly what Wes thought. "Yeah, I agree. Do you think you have seen him lately?"

Big Al scrunched up his face. "It seems so. Maybe not in the last few days. But he has been in here."

"This is good to know. I heard he might hang out here. If you do see him, here is my card again." Wes handed Big Al one of his business cards. "My cell number is on there, so call me anytime."

"You got it, man!"

Wes drove back to the station. As he walked in, Lillian, one of the writers, came up to him. "Hey, Wes, you have someone waiting for you."

"Oh, yeah?"

"It's a woman." Lillian winked. "That bachelor article might make you a married man one day."

"Wow, lucky me." He grinned at Lillian, who grinned back at him.

He rounded the corner to find Angel sitting in the lobby. "Hey, Angel. Have you been waiting long?" As Wes drew closer, he couldn't read her eyes. "How did things go with your dad? I hope I'm not in trouble."

She stared at him and then laughed. "Is there some place we can talk?"

Laughing was a good sign, he hoped. Curious, he responded, "Sure. We can talk inside the conference room."

When they entered the conference room, Angel jumped right in by asking a question. "Do you know something that I should know?"

"No. I—I . . ." Wes stuttered.

"Did you go to see my father?"

"I have never met the man. Look, why don't we sit down and you tell me what happened?"

Angel placed her bag on the table and sat. "I'm sorry. The visit went better than I expected. I'm still soaking it all in. But as I was driving back, I remembered that when I knocked on the door, my . . . my dad's wife thought I was a reporter. I don't even know why that detail stuck with me, because I got hit with a whole lot yesterday."

Wes shook his head. "I promise you, it wasn't me. I've been aware of Pops's friendship with your grand-dad over the years. I thought if I helped you, maybe I could help Pops too. He really was passionate about finding your mother. Not that he didn't have other cases, but this one hit home for him."

Angel said, "Our granddads were close friends at one time. I think my mom's disappearance drove them apart."

Wes sat down beside her. "So visiting your father was a good thing. I think it's pretty awesome that you just did it."

She rewarded him with a smile. "Yeah, to be honest, I was ready to turn around when I called you." She giggled. "I guess that sounds crazy."

"No, not at all. You had me worried for a minute there. I prayed that everything worked out for you. What did you think of him?"

"Thank you for your prayers. He wasn't bad." Angel grew quiet. Then she added, "I found out I have a half sister."

"Wow. Did you get to meet her?"

"Not yet. It was enough to meet him. He was nice, and his wife knew who I was when I arrived. You know, the crazy thing was I ran into my dad's wife last week at Lenora's bridal shop. I had no idea. I remember wondering why she was staring at me.'"

"Really?"

"Apparently, my dad has been trying to contact me all these years, and I never knew. I have never seen his letters and cards."

"Your family was probably trying to protect you."

"I know, I know." Angel rose up from the chair. "It all just seems unfair. I mean, after I turned eighteen, it seems like they would have given me the chance as an adult to figure out what I wanted to do."

Wes stood too. "Well, I think God is trying to work it out for you now. To give you some peace and maybe closure."

She faced him, her eyes looking lost. "I hope you are right. Something is going on, and I can feel myself wanting to let go of the past. There is just one big piece of the puzzle. Maybe you can help me."

"Sure."

"I did talk to my dad about my mother. He said that night he came over to try to convince her not to take this record deal. He said he told the police over and over again that instead of concentrating on him, they should look at the guys who ran the record company."

Wes thought, *Record company. This has come up before.* "Do you remember the name of it?"

"Royal Records."

"Okay, I will see what I can find for you."

"Thanks, Wes." She looked at him and then smiled. "I need to go see my grams. She should be finished with her rehab for the day."

He shook his head, still looking at her. "Okay, well, I will be in touch."

After they walked out of the conference room, he watched Angel as she headed down the hallway. She turned and waved at him. He waved back.

"Don't tell me you went and got a girlfriend while I was gone."

Wes groaned and then turned around. "Serena, I see you are back."

"Just in time, I see." Serena peered around him. "So, who's my competition, and why does she look so familiar?"

Wes looked at Serena. "You think you've seen her before?"

"Yes. Who is she?"

Then it dawned on Wes. "Why don't you start by answering some questions?"

Serena crossed her arms. "Kiddo, I asked you a question first."

"Well, Serena, we have some serious talking to do."

# Chapter Twenty-five

Wes waited for Serena to answer his question, as they sat across from each other in the conference room. She flipped her hair across her shoulder and gazed back at him. Finally, she pointed her finger at him. "I passed a great story to you. I don't need you trying to get in on this story."

"I wouldn't do any such thing. Look, I've been in the middle of this since I was a kid. My family knew the Robertses."

"Okay, fine. Look, I just happened to come upon some interesting connections."

"Connections?"

Serena sighed. "You have to keep your word that you won't mess with my story."

"Of course I wouldn't, but if you have something that could point toward Elisa Roberts, please don't sit on it. You have a family who has been waiting decades to find out what happened."

"Wes, I don't know what happened, but I do have a theory that maybe your grandfather hadn't considered. Do you know about the rapper K-Dawg? You probably were a child when he was killed."

"Yes, I remember him. He's a Charlotte native, and he only had that one hit song, "We Down With It." It's a known favorite, right alongside "Electric Slide Boogie." I didn't think that was your kind of music."

"What? Please! How old do you think I am?" Serena eyed him. "That was the jam for me." Serena moved her shoulders as if the song were playing in the room. "I liked the dip to the side."

Wes smiled. He could imagine Serena was a hoot as a teenager.

Serena continued, "Anyway, K-Dawg's mother came to me a few months ago at this event where I was the speaker. He's been gone twenty years, and she asked if I was interested in pursuing his story, you know, to commemorate him." Serena sat up and smiled. "So I did some digging. Do you know who sang the background vocals on that song? Probably not."

"You're right. I have never paid attention to the female's voice." Wes stared at Serena. Then it dawned on him. "Elisa Roberts?"

"Yes. Apparently, Elisa's vocals on that song led her to getting the record deal at the same company where K-Dawg and a couple other Southern rappers were really blowing up."

"Let me guess. Royal Records?"

Serena frowned. "How do you know that?"

"Don't worry about that. Tell me what this has to do with Elisa going missing."

"I'm not sure. Like I told you, I'm pursuing a different story here. Her name came up. I can say my sources thought K-Dawg really liked her. She was a little bit older than him, but they went to the same high school. And it was rumored that a fight broke out that night over a woman, and it carried outside the club, where K-Dawg ultimately was shot."

Wes shook his head. "I'm still lost. How is Elisa going missing connected?"

"Are you not seeing this? Look at the timing. A few weeks after K-Dawg is killed, Elisa goes missing. What if she went missing because she saw something or, better yet, because she knew who was responsible for the shooting? Suppose she was the woman who was at the center of the fight."

Wes thought out loud. "Who was the other guy? Who said Elisa was the woman?" He sat up. "I mean, if she was the woman, this could still point back to Angelino Mancini. Pops could never find evidence pointing to Angelino, and he had an alibi for the night Elisa disappeared."

Serena shrugged. "How airtight was that alibi? Did anyone think to ask him where he was the night K-Dawg was shot?"

Wes tapped his fingers on the table. "So, you think he did it? You went to see Angelino?"

"Yes. No. I went to his house, but the wife wouldn't let me in once I told her who I was."

Wes said, "Mmm, I wonder why."

Serena stared daggers at him. "Whatever, kiddo. Look, someone shot K-Dawg that night and got away with murder. All those people outside that club, and nobody saw a thing. Really? I believe one of the witnesses could have been your girlfriend's mother."

Wes corrected her. "We're just friends. I'm helping her find some closure."

Serena stood and shook her head. "That may never happen."

"Aren't you basically trying to pursue a twenty-year-old murder case?" Wes asked. "Who's to say that the mystery behind Elisa's disappearance can't be solved too?"

"You really like her, don't you?"

"What?"

"Do yourself a favor. Separate work from your personal life. You have a young woman who's been missing for two weeks. Concentrate on her. That's your story."

Wes stared at her. "I am pursuing the story on Melanie. What difference is there in you and me both pursuing old cases?"

"The difference is that when I break my story, there is no emotional involvement for me. I cracked a story. When you bring your girlfriend this quote, closure, unquote, how do you think she will feel about you afterward? Especially if dear old dad did do something to mom." With that, Serena walked out of the conference room.

After Serena left, Wes held his head in his hand. He didn't want to admit Serena had a point. This had all started with him wanting to find closure for Pops. Now Wes was driven to help Angel find the truth. With Angel reuniting with her father, Wes hoped the truth wouldn't lead to her losing him again. If that was the case, would Angel be able to handle it?

There was another question he had to acknowledge. What was he really after? The story or the girl?

# Chapter Twenty-six

Last night at Bible study, Candace had continued the discussion on forgiveness. This time she'd focused on anger and bitterness. After her morning prayer, Angel read through the verses from the book of Ephesians again. *Get rid of all bitterness, rage and anger, brawling and slander, along with every form of malice. Be kind and compassionate to one another, forgiving each other, just as in Christ God forgave you* (Ephesians 4:31 New International Version).

She couldn't help but go back in time. Her past clung to her like an ill-fitting outfit. Walking into that bedroom four years ago had spun her already topsy-turvy world into a new dimension. It had taken her a few seconds to absorb what she had seen. *Kenneth and Denise.* She remembered hurling the nearest object she could find across the room, which happened to be one of Kenneth's coveted basketball trophies. Both Kenneth and Denise screamed and jumped from the bed. She was scared of her anger, and something drove her to leave the room. She peeled the rubber from her car's tires as she sped from the parking space. It was by God's grace that she didn't run over someone or drive off the road in her rage.

Weeks, months, and then well over a year went by before she stopped being the angry chick. That was until she found out that Denise had had a baby boy. Then Angel found herself spiraling back into a sea of anger and self-pity. She must have gained twenty pounds on her petite frame. Grams had tried to talk to her, telling her to let it go, or the bitterness would eat away at her and cause her to make ugly choices.

After the meeting with her father, Angel thought more about her mother. Angel didn't remember too many details, but she was aware of her mother's moods. That seemed to be what she remembered most about her. Angel could recall that the last kiss on her forehead from her mother was hurried, as if she had someplace to be. In the past week, she had heard her father and Jacob both talk about her mother's drive to get her singing career started. Could she have been so angry and bitter about being held back from her dreams that she stepped into a deal that led to her disappearance? There were so many questions. She hoped Wes would come through with some details about the record company.

Angel spent the rest of the morning cleaning the house. As she cleaned, she searched for any evidence that her father had been telling the truth. She still couldn't believe her father had sent her a birthday card a few weeks ago. Angel felt like she was intruding in her grandparents' bedroom as she opened drawers and shifted clothes. Many of Granddad's items were in the dresser. If there was any correspondence from her father, Angel had a feeling Grams wouldn't have thrown it away.

She jerked her hand from inside the drawer of her grams's desk, startled by the piercing ring of the phone on top of the desk. Angel looked at the caller ID, recognizing the phone number. She picked up the phone. "Hello, Jacob."

"Angel, I don't know if you received my voice mail, but I will be at the house in about thirty minutes."

"No, I didn't. Why? What's going on? Is something wrong with Grams?"

"No. She's fine. We need to meet at Trinity Home Health Care. I want to talk to them about care for Mom when she comes home from rehab in a few weeks."

"Okay, well, yeah, I will be ready. Did you just get back in town?"

"Uh . . . yeah. I'm on the move. I will see you in a bit."

Angel hung up the phone, but it rang immediately. She frowned and picked up the phone again. "Hello, Jacob. Is this you again? Is there something else you forgot to tell me?"

"Angel?"

Angel froze when she heard the female voice. Definitely not Jacob. "Yeah?"

"It's Liz. Do you know where your uncle is?"

"Aunt Liz, I'm sorry. I don't know why I didn't recognize your voice. He will be here in a little while. He just called. I guess he just arrived in Charlotte. "

Liz paused. "Arrived?" she finally said.

Angel said, "He left for New York last Friday. I just heard from him, so I assumed he just arrived back in Charlotte."

"He was here? In New York?"

Angel frowned. Liz's questions were confusing her. Then she remembered Jacob had moved out of their home. "He told me he had to return to work." Liz was so quiet, Angel thought she'd hung up. "Liz, are you still there?"

"Angel, your uncle lost his job last year."

Now Angel was floored. What was up with the family secrets? "I had no idea. Well, didn't you say he moved out? Suppose he found another job?"

"He hasn't. I only asked him to move out a few weeks ago. I don't know what he is doing, but he's not looking for a job."

"Of course he is. Jacob is, like, lost without working. I heard with the economy, it just takes a while to find what you are looking for."

"Yes, it's not that easy when you are Jacob's age, but your uncle has not been himself for a while," Liz revealed. "I can't even begin to explain to you what has happened and when it all began. Even before he lost the job, he was just . . . preoccupied."

"By what?" Angel inquired.

"I don't know. I just know after he lost his job, which I didn't find out about until I went looking for him one day, he was just not the same Jacob. I told him he needed to get himself together, seek counseling or something." Liz choked up.

Angel swallowed. She felt bad for Liz. "I'm sorry that Jacob is not acting right. I wish I knew what to tell you." Now Angel was wondering where Jacob had been all this time. What really alarmed her was how Grams was actually being taken care of. She didn't understand her grandparents' finances. "Liz, when Jacob gets here, I will tell him you called."

"Thank you, Angel. I still love your uncle. I just wish whatever is going on with him, that he would get some help. I gave him an ultimatum when he left. That he either get some help or this marriage was over. I know he has carried demons for years, and he's never one to talk. It's time. Past time."

Angel heard the front door open. "Liz, I have to go. Good-bye."

"Good-bye, Angel."

Angel hung up the phone and went out into the hallway to see her uncle. He was dressed just like he'd been when she saw him at the hospital a few weeks ago, his clothes rumpled and his beard fully grown in now. She remembered her uncle being such a handsome man.

The man who stared at her looked older and beaten down.

Jacob asked, "Are you ready?"

"Liz called," Angel responded and watched her uncle's face. As usual, he was stoic, his face void of emotion, but she could sense questions in his eyes.

Jacob answered, "What did she want?"

"I guess she was worried about you."

"Sure she is. Look, we need to go, or we will miss the appointment."

"Let me grab my bag."

They had to ride together, and Angel wasn't about to let the drive be in silence. She waited until Jacob backed his BMW, which was visibly unclean, out of the driveway. There were coffee cups on the floor, and she noticed clothes on the backseat. Her uncle was a workaholic, working out business deals even during family events. It wasn't unusual for him to be a walking office. He had worked hard toward having the American dream. He was a proud man. How was he carrying on day to day without his job?

She decided to ask him a question that she felt safe to ask. "How will Grams's medical bills be paid?"

Jacob looked straight ahead, not even giving Angel a glance. Knowing that she had talked to Liz, he probably already knew his secret was out. He cleared his throat. "Medicaid will take care of her bills. We just need to get her care set up for home. It's going to be hard for her, but we—or, rather, you—have been through this with Dad. She will probably be in a wheelchair until she hopefully can walk on her own."

With Granddad having been an amputee in a wheelchair, the house was pretty set up. There were ramps at the front door and the back door. It had been only three years ago when Angel watched as her grandparents' bedroom and bathroom were transformed to comfortably accommodate her granddad.

"Who knew that Granddad's needs would be suitable for Grams now? How long will she have to continue doing rehab?"

"Not sure how long. It all depends. She will continue to need to see the physical therapists and speech pathologist." Jacob braked for a light and finally looked at Angel. He said, "It will work out."

She thought for a split second about her next question and then asked, "Are you and Liz going to work things out?"

Jacob turned away and stared ahead. When the light turned green, he pushed the accelerator a bit too hard, making the car lurch forward. Angel didn't think he would answer, but he finally responded, "I'm concentrating on my mother right now. That's the best I can do."

With that Angel didn't ask any more questions, but her mind whirred with thoughts about what the future held. Before long they arrived at Trinity Home Health.

*Trust in the Lord with all your heart.*

Angel and Jacob met with Wilma Houston, the director of Trinity Home Health Care. Ms. Houston was pleasant enough, but a deep sense of sadness fell over Angel like a blanket as she listened to the services offered and nodded. She'd always felt different, but now it seemed she definitely wasn't living the typical life of a twenty-five-year-old. Her conversation with Jacob had left her more uncertain.

After they left the director's office, Angel thought she heard someone calling her name. She turned around to see Wanda Cade coming toward them.

Wanda came up to Angel and hugged her. "Angel, it's good to see you again." She looked over at Jacob and beamed. "Well, Jake, it's been a long time. You owe me a hug too."

Angel watched her uncle's face. For the first time in a while, he smiled and reached down to hug his old friend. "Long time no see, Wanda. You look good."

Wanda waved. "Oh, stop. It's been rough. As I imagine it has been for you. How's your mother? Angel told me about Fredricka's stroke."

Jacob nodded. "She has a road ahead of her. We were just talking to the director about hiring a nurse."

"Good plan," Wanda replied.

Angel asked Wanda, "How's Detective Cade doing?"

Wanda shook her head. "Well, I guess I may be in a similar situation. Wes has been telling me I should get some help. I'm just looking at my options. I'm so used to taking care of him myself, but it's getting hard."

Jacob and Wanda looked at each other for a minute. It felt like a long minute to Angel. She asked, "So, you two were really close at one time . . . friends, that is?"

Wanda laughed. "We were pretty tight. Jacob could be fun."

"My uncle?" Angel lifted an eyebrow. "For real?"

Jacob frowned. "Hey, I knew how to have fun." He smiled again. "Does seem like a long time ago, though."

Wanda agreed. "You used to be able to make me laugh so hard, my stomach would hurt for hours afterward."

So what happened to him? Angel wondered as she looked at Jacob. It was like the man who was considered the stable sibling, always taking care of things, was on the verge of falling apart, if he hadn't already. Despite the distance, she had known she could always count on her uncle. Lately, she wasn't sure whom to depend on anymore.

# Chapter Twenty-seven

"Please stop fretting. I can handle this okay. Don't you need to be going?" Wes rubbed his hand over his head and observed as his mother gripped the car keys in her hand.

"He's just had a really bad day. I really need to work this shift tonight. I've traded as many shifts as I can. Ms. Williams had to go out of town. She's been so good about helping me watch him." Wanda looked back into the bedroom where Pops lay resting. "As long as he is sleeping, he shouldn't be any trouble."

"We will be fine. Like you said, he's sleeping. He usually sleeps through the night, right?"

"I know you think this should be simple, but he could wake up disoriented, and he may not know you."

"Mom! He's sleeping. Now go. I got this."

Wanda stared at him for a long minute and then took a deep breath. "Okay." She kissed Wes on the cheek and went out the door.

He closed the door behind her, hoping to use the time to rest himself. Wes had been running and tracking down leads. He had finally set up a time to talk with Minister J.D. If he could find out what the minister knew about Melanie's secret record deal, surely this would make his producer, Alan, a happy man. Wes was interested in knowing what type of contacts Minister J.D. still had in the business to be able to help Melanie.

Wes sank down into his mother's chair. No wonder his mother loved this chair. He could feel the tension leaving his body as he jotted down notes for Minister J.D. Soon his eyes began to close. Seeing a losing battle coming, Wes tossed his pen and notebook on the coffee table and decided to let a catnap take over.

He was jarred awake by his ringing cell phone. Wes sat up as quickly as he could in the recliner, which seemed to be pulling his body backward. With one last lurch forward, he reached for the phone. "Hello." He rubbed his eyes and realized it was after ten o'clock.

"Hey, Wes. This is Big Al, man. I think I see your guy."

Wes shook his head. "What?"

"Your man, the one in the photo you showed me, with the Kangol hat. He's here, kind of creating a scene."

"You're kidding me. What's going on? What's he doing?" Wes grew warm with excitement. Melanie Stowe's dad had surfaced.

"Well, he seems upset. Is this guy the father of that missing singer?"

"Yes, he is. Is he talking about her?" Big Al didn't answer him back. "Al? Al, are you still there?"

"Yeah, man. Hey, look, brother man just broke down. I don't think he knew she was missing. Isn't that crazy?"

*Yeah, real crazy!* Wes thought he heard something in the back. He got up and walked toward the hallway but didn't see anything.

Big Al continued. "Drunk as a skunk. What do you want me to do with him?"

Wes asked, "How long do you think you can keep him? Has anyone come up to him to ask questions?"

"I don't know. He has been talking to a lot of people."

"Hey, Al, hold on a minute. I got to check something."

Wes looked at his watch. He walked to Pops's room and peeked inside. He could make out Pops's body in the bed. He walked into the room to listen. Pops was breathing regularly and sleeping soundly. Wanda would kill him if he did what he was thinking about doing, but he had to do this. It would take him all of fifteen minutes to drive downtown, ask questions, and come right back. He could return in an hour. Even as he thought about it, Wes felt uneasy.

"Al, try to distract him and hold him. I will be there soon."

Wes peeked in on Pops one more time. *He's sleeping. He will be fine.* Wes drove the whole way, willing Pops to remain asleep and hoping this wasn't a wasted trip. If Melanie's dad slipped through his fingers, this could be one of the stupidest stunts he had done in a long time to get a story.

He arrived at the bar and looked around. He didn't see Big Al anywhere at first. He nodded to the bartender he'd seen the other day and walked toward the back. Wes saw Melanie's dad before seeing Big Al. He glanced around the room and slipped into the chair across from the man. He looked much thinner and grayer than in the photo, but sure enough, he was wearing a Kangol hat. The hat could've been the same one in the photo.

Larry squinted at him. "Who are you?"

"Just here to be supportive. I heard about your daughter."

The man rubbed his head. "It's my fault. Sins of the father have come back to haunt me."

Wes leaned in farther. "Sir, what do you mean?"

"Somebody took my girl to get at me." Larry picked up his glass and drained the rest of the liquid. He looked at Wes. "You going to give a brother a refill?

There was a big cat around here helping me out." Larry searched around the bar.

"Probably Big Al. He should be back soon. Why would someone take your daughter to get back at you?"

Larry looked back at him; his bloodshot eyes were watery. "I've done some bad things."

"If you think you know who has your daughter, why don't you tell the police? People have been searching all over for her."

"No! I told you, I did some bad things."

"Your daughter has been missing for weeks. Don't you want to save her?"

"It's too late."

Wes looked at the man across from him. Whatever had happened to Melanie, his gut had been telling him this man had to have something to do with it or knew who did. This was out of Wes's league, though. It was time to get some backup, but he needed to be sure not to let Larry disappear again. "You look like you could use some rest. Can I take you home?"

"I don't have a place to stay. Got kicked out of the last place I stayed."

"I can get you a room for the night. Get you a good night's sleep. Maybe we can talk more tomorrow." Wes looked at his watch. He'd been there almost an hour, and he really needed to get back to the house. "So, what do you say I get you a place for the night?"

Larry must have been ready for a bed, because it didn't take too much convincing from Wes for him to get in the car. Wes drove to a nearby motel, paid for a room, and made sure Larry entered the room. Then he dialed Darnell's cell number.

Detective Jackson came on the phone. "Wes, this better be good, man. I just got in the bed."

"Man, I'm so sorry, but I thought you might want to know I found Melanie Stowe's dad. He was pretty wasted, but he confessed he knew who took his daughter."

"Are you sure?" Darnell asked.

"Yeah, he was spouting stuff like 'sins of the father.' Look, I got him a room at the Wren Motel. His room number is two-twenty-three. Can you get someone down here pretty early? I don't want him to slip away, and I've got to get back to the house." It was now over an hour and a half since he had left Pops alone.

"All right, man. I'll be there to pick him up."

"Great. Keep me updated. Don't forget I helped you find him."

Wes drove like a madman back to his mom's house. As he approached the front door, he froze. The front door was cracked open. *No!* Either the house was broken into or . . . Wes pushed the door open and called out, "Pops." He ran into the house. Nothing seemed to have been disturbed in the living room. The lamps were still on, and the television was showing an old black-and-white *Twilight Zone*. Wes rushed to Pops's bedroom. He turned the light switch on.

*He's gone. Where would he go?* It was after midnight. There was no way he could explain this to his mother. Wes ran toward the kitchen and checked the side door that led into the backyard. It was locked, but he opened it and ran down the steps. "Pops!" he yelled. Wes turned and unlatched the gate in the fence, headed to the street, and sprinted down the sidewalk. "Pops!" If there was any time in his life when he wished he could turn back time and reverse a decision he'd made, it would be right now.

# Chapter Twenty-eight

Melanie rocked back and forth on the bed, humming, "What a friend we have in Jesus, all our sins and griefs to bear!" She hadn't thought of this song in years. It was one of her mother's favorites. Mary Stowe would sing or hum the song in the morning or at night. When her mother was alive, they went to church almost every Sunday. Her daddy went on occasion, usually on a holiday like Easter. Most of the time, it was just her and Mom.

Her mom could have sung in the choir, but she preferred to sit on the pew. Melanie could remember hearing her mother's soulful and smooth singing along with the choir. *What a privilege to carry everything to God in prayer!* Oftentimes people would turn around and look at her mother, smiling. Her mother would smile back and keep on singing. It was the joy on her face that had always struck Melanie. She never looked that peaceful when they were home, especially when Daddy was around.

Melanie stopped rocking and looked over at the table. She'd rationed what the man had brought her to eat. It seemed it took him longer and longer to come. Was this a part of his game? Why did she have to be his game piece? She still hadn't touched the candy bar he'd left. It was tucked away. Her mind still spun with questions about how he knew.

*Does it matter?* Melanie rocked again. She was almost sure she would go crazy from being cooped up in this place. Today, for the first time in a long while, she could vividly see her mother's face. Not the face that was thin from the cancer that tore at her body, but a fuller version, smiling and singing.

Melanie started to hum again. She hummed along as she heard her mother's voice and then opened her mouth. In her mind, she sang alongside her mother. *O what peace we often forfeit, O what needless pain we bear, all because we do not carry everything to God in prayer.*

As she rocked, she prayed. "God, if you save me, I will sing for you. I will sing for you."

# Chapter Twenty-nine

Wes prayed. His mother would be home in a few hours. He had been up and down the neighborhood, driving around and around. His body was so tense with worry, Wes thought he would explode. Then he remembered where, a few weeks back, his mother had found Dad. It was worth a shot. He drove a few blocks down to the park. Surely, Pops didn't really walk this far. Wes drove by the park and at first glance saw no one there.

He parked the car and walked around. From a distance, he could see a figure sitting on a bench. *Please let that be him.* Wes walked up slowly and said, "Hello."

Pops turned around and looked at him. "Hello. What are you doing out here, young man?"

Wes exhaled, not realizing he'd been holding his breath. "Pops, I have never been so glad to see you. We've got to get you back. Mom is going to walk in the door soon, and I already will be toast when I have to tell her I lost you."

"Who are you?"

"I'm Wes, your grandson."

"I don't have a grandson."

Wes nearly lost it, curling his hands into fists. This was a nightmare. *Okay, keep your cool.* Pops had wandered away because he was confused. Wes needed to be smart to figure out how he was going to get him back home. Wes decided to try a different tactic.

"Why don't I take you home?" Wes looked down, observing that his grandfather had on shoes, but he was still dressed in pajamas. "We should get you back so you don't get sick."

"I can't. I'm waiting on my friend."

Wes pleaded. "Well, maybe I can take you to your friend's house. We can save him the trouble, and I can give you a ride."

"No, Nick will be here soon. He is always on time."

"Nick?" Wes asked. "Nick Roberts?"

"Yeah, we are going to practice. Got a gig tonight. How do you know Nick?"

"No, the gig is another night. You mixed up the night." Wes was trying to think of whatever he could to get his pops out of this park. His phone rang. Wes pulled his phone from his pocket.

"Wes, where are you? Where's Pops? I have been calling the house. Do I need to leave the hospital?"

He closed his eyes as he heard his mother's frantic voice. He should have known his mother would try to call to check on Pops. "Don't panic. Pops and I are at the park. We will be home shortly."

"Wes! How did he get there? Did you watch him?"

"Mom, I messed up. Let's not get into that now. I will have him home soon."

"I'm going to try to get off earlier. I knew this wasn't a good idea. You don't know how it is with him."

Wes pleaded with his mother. "No, Mom, just finish your shift. I will have him home. Please let me do this." He pressed the button on the phone to end the call.

*I can handle this.* His broken promise to his mother dangled before him. He could only pray that both the Jesus in her and the fact that he was her son would keep her from wanting to kill him. He sat down on the bench next to Pops.

Pops said, "You sound like you have some trouble, young man."

Before he knew it, laughter had bubbled up in Wes. His laughter bounced around the park, and then Wes fell silent as tears of gratefulness flooded his eyes. Wes looked over at his granddad. "I'm in pretty big trouble, but I believe God is helping to save me in my foolishness."

"God is good like that, son. You should come out tonight to hear us play."

Wes went along with the conversation. He needed his pops to trust him enough to get him out of this park. "I would love to hear you play." Pops had stopped playing with Southern Soul before Wes was born. Wes asked, "So is there something special about tonight?"

Pops looked at him. "Yes, it will be the last time I play with the band."

"Why would you stop playing? Don't you love the band?"

"I do. Love playing with the fellows. Things have changed. I have a family that needs me. Plus, it's time to move on. When Nick comes, I'm going to tell him."

Wes realized that Pops had reached way back into his memory bank. Why was Pops focusing on this particular memory? Wes would have to ask his mother, if she would even talk to him, why Pops continued to return to the park.

He said to his grandfather, "Let me get this straight. Tonight is your last night playing with the band, but you haven't told your friend Nick yet. Won't he be upset with you springing this on him?"

"Nick? No, he won't be upset. We talked about it before. I told him I was thinking about it. I warned him that things were changing too fast."

Wes was totally confused by the conversation. "What was changing? The music?"

Pops stared off into space.

Wes tried to prompt him. "Pops, what was changing?" He touched his grandfather's shoulder. "Why don't you let me drive you? Nick wants me to take you to him."

Pops nodded. Wes stood and took his grandfather by the hand. The conversation had stopped. He didn't know where Pops was now, but he was able to get him inside the car. Ten minutes later, he drove into the driveway to find his mother's car was there.

Wes guided Pops into the house. Wanda jumped up from the couch. "I was ready to call the police if you hadn't gotten back here."

"I'm sorry. I will get him back in the bed."

"No, you've done enough."

"Mom."

"Go home, Wes. I can handle it from here."

Wes watched his mother take Pops back to his bedroom. He did the only thing he could do. He left, feeling the weight of his choice on his shoulders.

# Chapter Thirty

Southern Soul Café was not yet open, but Angel could hear the bustle of cooks and servers getting ready for the Saturday lunch crowd. Angel walked to the back, toward Eddie's office. She was looking forward to working with Eddie on the talent show this weekend. There were flyers posted in several areas around town, and last night Angel noticed a Facebook page had been dedicated to the event. Eddie had a talented marketing crew.

Angel was walking up to the office door to knock when she heard a voice from inside the room. A very familiar female voice wailed from behind the door, "How could you do this?" Angel stepped away from the door. It was Denise in the office. "I don't care. I can't take it anymore. You are never going to grow up!" Was Denise talking on the phone to her father? When she didn't hear another voice, Angel knew for sure that Denise was alone, on the phone and Kenneth was on the other end of the line.

She had wondered how long it would take Denise to find out what Angel had always complained about. Kenneth, with all his good looks and charm, was as selfish as a person could be.

Angel really wanted to see Eddie now so she could spend time with Grams this afternoon. She had no intentions of returning to this side of town until next weekend, so she knocked on the door and called out, "Hello? Eddie?"

She waited for a few seconds and then started down the hallway. The door opened behind her.

"Wait, Angel."

Angel turned around to see Denise's tearstained face. She told Denise, "I can come back."

Denise shook her head and wiped her eyes with her fingers. "No, my dad told me to make sure you stayed. He had to run and pick up some supplies. Why don't you wait in here?"

"Okay." Angel stepped into the office.

"Have a seat. I will be out of the way in a minute." Denise went behind the big oak desk and shuffled papers. It had been a long time since they'd been in a room together, just the two of them. Angel sat down in one of the leather chairs across from the desk. She remembered that when Southern Soul Café opened, both of them would spend a lot of time in this same office after school. Later they worked in the restaurant to make a little extra money. She and Denise took turns being servers and hostesses.

Angel cleared her throat. "Nothing much has changed in here."

Denise replied, "Yeah, Dad isn't much on change."

"Change can be hard." Then Angel added, "Congratulations on your upcoming wedding."

Denise stopped rearranging the papers and stared at her. "Do you mean that? I always hoped you wouldn't hate me forever."

Angel replied, "I don't hate you."

"I don't blame you if you do."

"You were my best friend, like a sister I never had. I would have never thought you would cause me that much pain, but it's history now. You have little Kenny, and there are no mistakes. He's precious."

Denise blinked. "I wasn't expecting that from you."

Neither was Angel. She noted the sadness in Denise's eyes. The deep weariness in her former friend's eyes did not conform with what Angel usually saw on the faces of the brides she filmed. "Are you happy?"

"Would you gloat if I said I wasn't?"

"It wouldn't do me any good to gloat, and I'm sorry to hear that."

Denise sat down in the chair. "You know, I used to get so upset with you when you complained about how Kenneth treated you. I used to think in my head, 'Poor Angel. She just doesn't know how to handle the man.'"

Angel frowned. "Really? You used to agree with me that Kenneth was just putting me down for no reason."

"I know. He was, and you probably will not believe me, but I didn't set out to steal him."

Angel shook her head. "We don't need to dig up history." She had had enough of doing all that all on her own.

"But I have wanted you to know. That day was the first time."

"You expect me to believe that?"

"I was upset and was looking for you. I figured you were at Kenneth's place. He was there, and he didn't have a shirt on. I was a mess! He was so sensitive and told me it was okay."

Angel stood. "I told you I don't need to hear this."

Denise slammed her hands on the desk. "Well, I need you to because I made the worst mistake ever. I got pregnant, I missed out on finishing school, and I lost my best friend all because I wanted to feel loved and secure that day."

Angel looked away from Denise. She really hadn't come here for this.

She didn't have long to wait as Eddie came into the room with a box. "Hey, you are here. Thank you for coming by, Angel." Eddie sat the box down on the floor and walked in between them. "It's good to see you girls talking again."

Denise responded, "We were just catching up. Don't hold your breath on anything more, Dad." Denise grabbed papers off the desk and stuffed them in her bag. "I need to get home. Kenneth will have to go to work soon, so I need to be there for little Kenny." As she walked out the door, Denise turned around and said, "I hope you have asked Angel to sing for the talent show. She probably could blow the competition away."

Angel's ears burned, making her encounter with Denise even more awkward.

Eddie laughed and pointed his finger. "I knew you've been holding out on me. No way your momma could have a kid that couldn't sing. So what do you say?"

"Conflict of interest. I'm here to help you videotape the contestants and get the entries online."

"Well, wait a minute now. I didn't tell you about my surprise." Eddie sat back in his chair and leaned back.

"What surprise?" Angel asked.

"You could make your granddad and mom proud by joining Southern Soul on the stage."

"Eddie, I don't sing in front of people."

"Girl, you can't waste that talent. Besides, it will just be one number. The band will perform at the end of the talent show."

Angel still wasn't sure.

"Come on. It will be fun, and you will be a part of some history. Did you know Southern Soul is celebrating fifty years?"

"Fifty years? Wow. Has it been that long?"

"Oh yeah. The older members started the band in nineteen sixty-one. Now a lot of the older members are not around, but you know I've kept the band going with new members over the years. Got to keep the name out there. I hope you will at least think about it."

"I can't make promises, but yes, I will think about it." Angel had really made her mind up. She just didn't have the heart to tell Eddie there was no way she was singing in front of an audience.

# Chapter Thirty-one

Wes stared at the screen, not really paying attention to what he was typing. He stopped and pushed his chair back from the desk. He wanted to call his mother and express his apologies for not sticking to his promise. Pops was okay, and Wes was grateful he found him, but his mother's face and anger haunted him. She had been through so much, and he'd just added to the weight on her shoulders.

He picked up the phone to call Darnell. Hopefully, his efforts and his sacrifice would be worth it. Wes greeted his detective friend and then listened to his news. With each word, Wes felt more deflated.

"What? You couldn't hold him?"

Darnell answered, "Sorry, man. The man was intoxicated. Once people sober up, they are going to change their story. Plus, he really seemed genuinely broken up about his daughter being missing."

Wes fumed, "Did he explain where he was all this time? I know he is a drunk, but I find it hard to believe he doesn't know who was responsible. Suppose she was snatched up because of him."

"Wes, I really can't look into it. Unless Melanie Stowe's body shows up or there is some evidence that a homicide took place, I can't hold the man."

Wes sat back. "But something isn't right. I mean, you follow your gut on cases, right?"

"Yeah, man, but—"

"Listen, he found his way out to California for the *American Voices* show."

"There is no way that guy last night was allowed out of the state at that time. Wes, he was still on parole."

Wes sighed. "I wondered about that. Man, I'm sorry I led you on a wild-goose chase."

"Don't worry about it. Everyone wants to find the girl. You are doing your part. Look, if it will help, I will keep my eye on him. If he knows something, maybe he will drop some clues or lead us to her."

"Thanks, man."

Wes hung up the phone. He pulled up his notes. Melanie's best friend, Lisa, had said something about Melanie's dad showing up at the show. Did either of them really see him? If Larry wasn't there, then who was the guy at the show? Just when he thought he was close, more questions arose. He checked his watch. There was still some ground to cover on Melanie's life. Alan wanted information on the mystery record deal, so that was where Wes had decided to focus his efforts this afternoon.

Charlotte traffic was fast and heavy, as usual. Most people were heading back to the office from lunch. Wes drove into the Kingdom Building Church parking lot. Minister J.D. had founded the growing church and served as its pastor. The first thing Wes thought was how different the church seemed from Victory Gospel Church. Whereas Victory was a big, expansive modern building, Kingdom used to be a strip mall, which was converted to the Kingdom Building Church campus.

Victory had grown in size in the past year, after Reverend Jonathan Freeman officially took over as pastor. With a younger minister and family heading up the church, even more young families and young professionals flocked to the pews on Sunday. Where Reverend Freeman was known as a smooth and down-to-earth teacher, Minister J.D. was known to be charismatic and animated in the pulpit. He had a growing congregation of young people, especially young men. Minister J.D. founded the Be a Man Conference, which had been held annually every year for the past five years.

Last year, when Wes attended the men's conference, he walked out having committed himself to celibacy along with several hundred men. He'd largely kept to his commitment by choosing not to date. Wes had avoided walking into temptation until a few weeks ago. He now knew to keep his guard up around his co-worker Serena.

As Wes entered the building, children ran by him. A young woman followed behind them, asking them to stop running in church. The woman noticed Wes and said, "Hello. How are you? You are from television. The news."

He smiled. "Yes. I'm Wes Cade. Is Minister J.D. around?"

She nodded. "Oh yeah, he's downstairs in the studio." The woman looked down the hall, where most of the children had entered a classroom. "Come on. I will show you."

The woman guided him down a hallway. As they walked farther, Wes could hear a deep, thumping hum in the building. His guide stopped and said, "At the end of this hallway, make a right. You will find Minister J.D. inside. Have fun."

Wes expressed his thanks and followed the directions. When he turned the corner and stared at the door, what struck Wes was the sign above it, which read Royal Records. He thought, *Is this the same Royal Records I talked about with Angel?*

He knocked on the door and then tried the doorknob. When he opened the door, a deep thumping sound and rhythmic music greeted him. Wes went inside and closed the door behind him. To his amazement, it really was a studio, a full-fledged music studio. Two men were at the audio controls, while others were standing in the background, rocking their head to the beat. On the other side of the studio, behind glass, a young man with a baseball hat was rapping into the microphone.

Wes listened. The young man was rapping about how Christ had saved him from the streets. Before he knew it, Wes found himself rocking his head back and forth. The young man was really talented with his rhymes.

"You like?"

Wes hadn't noticed, but a tall, heavyset man had come to stand beside him. Minister J.D. in the flesh. He held out his hand. "How are you doing, Minister? I appreciate you seeing me."

"Not a problem. I'm really proud of these guys. They're using their skills to glorify the Lord. Shadrach here especially warms my heart. He's come a long way. Why don't we head to my office?"

"Sure." Wes looked back at the young man, Shadrach, and then followed the minister. As they walked back to where Wes had come in, he asked the minister, "So the hip-hop hasn't left you?"

Minister J.D. laughed. "I'm a messenger for God. He allows us to deliver his good news in many ways. I don't believe I spent all those years in the hip-hop world for no reason."

When they arrived at the church office, the minister's secretary waved to Minister J.D. as he walked by and handed him a folder. He nodded and went into his office. Wes followed.

Minister J.D. said, "Have a seat, young man. What brings a WYNN news reporter to the church? Are you a man of God yourself, Mr. Cade?"

Wes said, "Oh yeah, ever since I was a kid. I strayed a bit in college but came back around probably right before I became a reporter. I would love to do a piece on the church. There are a lot of growing churches in Charlotte, and you are one of them."

"Yes, we are. We really love this community and want to be a spiritual hospital for those in need. I would appreciate it if you would do some features. I would like the community to know about our food bank, after-school program, and all the other ministries we offer."

"I will definitely plan to do a feature. Now, I hope this is okay, but today I wanted to talk to you a bit about the music part."

Minister J.D. raised his eyebrow. "I'm intrigued and honored."

"I have been reporting updates on Melanie Stowe, and I understand she was coming to see you about a recording session maybe."

The minister bowed his head. "Yes, yes. Melanie was a special young lady. *Is* a special young lady. I hate that she has been taken from our sight for so long and do hope she can be returned to us. I've known Melanie all her life. I watched her sing as a little girl, and for her to be on *American Voices,* well, that was a proud moment."

"She had some problems with really making it after the show. I imagine it was hard for her to see her dreams dry up a bit."

"Yes. We never know what plans God has for us, but I felt that God had a plan for Melanie. My goal was to support her and give her the encouragement she really needed."

"Are you aware of any record companies approaching her?"

"You know, today is different. Lots of independent record labels out there. I have one myself."

"Yes, I noticed. Royal Records. You are a busy man."

"Like I said earlier, you deliver the good news in a way the audience needs. Music is a powerful tool. Melanie had the voice. She also wrote songs. I told her to meet with me and let us sit down and work out a plan for her. Unfortunately, that meeting has never taken place."

Wes saw an opportunity to dig a bit deeper. "You said you knew her all her life. So, you knew her dad?"

Minister J.D. laughed. "Yes, I did. Larry, better known as El back in the day, was a good friend of mine. We were young and stupid. We had skills and loved making music. All of that went south, so to speak, after we lost K-Dawg."

Wes stared at Minister J.D. Questions were whirling in his mind so fast, he didn't know what to ask first. He wasn't sure where this was going, but Melanie and Elisa seemed to keep connecting in some way in his mind. He just couldn't figure out how. "You all hung around K-Dawg?"

"We grew up together. Got signed together at the former Royal Records. We were his posse." Minister J.D. sat back in his big leather chair. "K-Dawg has been gone twenty years. Kelvin Dentin was his name. He was my cousin. I decided to bring the label back under new management, hoping to bring something good back to Charlotte musically."

"I'm so sorry. I didn't realize he was family. You don't have any ideas who may have shot K-Dawg that night?"

"I had ideas, but everyone had their alibis. I eventually got out of the whole music game. For so long we

just wanted to make music, and then he was gone."
Minister J.D. sighed. "But God had another plan for
me. I was to not sit in pity over my friend, but let young
people know the kind of lives they need to lead."

"What about the old Royal Records?"

"What about it?"

"Well, I heard the former company wasn't the best
place to be for artists."

Minister J.D. let out another belly laugh. "No! It
wasn't. Back then Royal Records was run by thugs.
Greedy thugs. They wanted to get the money and the
fame. We should have had legal counsel look at those
contracts. Did you know for many years, none of us
saw a dime from 'We Down With It'? Years ago I finally
got a lawyer. I didn't need the money, but K-Dawg's
momma, she suffered so much. The least they could do
was take care of his mother after he was killed. He was
at the club that night, promoting the upcoming album
release."

Wes asked, "Do you remember the woman who sang
background on the song?"

Minister J.D. leaned forward. "Yes, I remember her.
She had a great voice, really pretty too. I think she went
to the same high school we did. She was a couple of
grades ahead of us. K-Dawg was kind of sweet on her,
but she wasn't really interested. I think she had a kid."

"Yes, her kid is a friend of mine. The woman was
Elisa Roberts, and she went missing a month after K-
Dawg died."

"Really? I didn't know that. I mean, I remember her
going missing. I just didn't realize it was around that
time. I was probably still torn up over losing K-Dawg."

"The night K-Dawg was shot, do you remember if
Elisa was there?"

"K-Dawg had a lot of women around him. My memory ain't what it used to be. I couldn't tell you. Why the interest?"

"Just looking for connections," Wes answered.

"You think she saw or knew what happened? That someone came back to get her? Lord, have mercy."

"I don't know. It just seems funny. I came to talk to you about Melanie, and I had no idea about the connection. So was Larry Stowe an artist too?"

Minister J.D. laughed. "El, Larry, was the hype man. Like the Flavor Flav of the group. He knew how to get the crowd going. He was close to K-Dawg too."

That explained why Larry always seemed to be dressed like an old-school rapper. The man had never given up the identity. Wes looked at his watch and realized he needed to get back to meet with Alan. At least he would have something to present to the producer this time. He stood.

"Minister J.D., I need to run back to the station. This was a very interesting conversation. Thanks for your time."

The minister stood and extended his hand to Wes. "Not a problem. You need to come out and visit us sometime. Where is your church home?"

"I attend Victory Gospel."

"I see. One of Reverend Freeman's members. I like him. He's a good man. I know it's been hard on him, taking over the church for his dad. I hear it's growing over there."

"Yes, but I will be looking forward to your Be a Man Conference this summer."

"You been before?"

"First time last year. Still hanging on to my finding a wife commitment."

"Well, all right now." Minister J.D. grinned. "That's what I want to hear. I imagine God is going to lead you to your future wife real soon too."

Wes smiled. "I hope so. Seems like all my friends are getting married or thinking about getting married."

"Well, you want to find the right one. Don't just settle. Be sure the woman is the one God sent you."

"Thanks." Wes left Minister J.D.'s office, still smiling about the minister's advice. As he headed back to his car, his mind went to Angel. He had a couple of things to share with her, but his mind was more on what the minister had said. *Be sure the woman is the one God sent you.* Wes wondered if God might have sent her already. He shook his head. Angel was definitely an interest and had been ever since she'd showed up that Sunday. Still, he needed to rein himself in and not jump ahead.

He glided the car from the parking space. Before Wes drove off, he caught sight of a man who looked vaguely familiar walking down the church sidewalk. Wes slowed the car down and watched as Larry Stowe entered Kingdom Building Church. So, Larry had come to visit an old friend today. Wes wondered why. If he didn't need to get back to the station, Wes would've parked the car and headed right back inside the church.

He knew his gut was right. Melanie's father knew something about why his daughter had gone missing. Now, where Elisa Roberts fit into the scenario, Wes didn't know. But there was a connection from the past to the present. That Wes was sure of.

# Chapter Thirty-two

Angel liked Ella Mae Jenkins. The nurse from Trinity Home Health Care was sweet and joyful, despite Grams's fussing. She heard Ella Mae say to Grams, "Now, sugar, it's going to be all right. You sit back and let me get you dressed." Angel was glad her uncle had hired the nurse to help look after Grams. While she had improved some, her mobility had not come back fully on her right side. She needed to be bathed, dressed, and helped with meals. This wasn't too foreign to Angel due to the fact that her granddad had had to be cared for in a similar way.

She knew her fiercely independent Grams must be feeling even more depressed since she was not the one in the caregiver role. Angel could mostly understand what she said, but oftentimes she felt the heat of Grams's frustration when it took a bit too long for Angel to catch on.

She showed Ella Mae to the kitchen, where they kept the medicine.

Ella Mae said, "Oh, you have quite a few medicine bottles up there."

"I know. I've been meaning to get rid of most of those, which were for my granddad." Angel looked at the bottles, remembering the night Grams had had the stroke. The doorbell rang, interrupting her thoughts. "That's my grams's hairstylist. Do you mind if I get her situated and then come back?"

"Not a problem, honey. I will get rid of the bottles that are not needed so we can start fresh with the new regimen for your grandmother."

"Thank you." Angel sprinted to answer the door. It was beautiful of Candace to take the time to bring Crown of Beauty Salon services to Grams. She had called ten minutes ago to let Angel know she would arrive shortly.

Angel opened the door. Grateful to see her friend, she hugged her. "You need any help?"

Candace answered, "Nope, I have everything I need in this bag. How are you feeling?"

Angel replied, "Overwhelmed. I'm praying a lot."

"That's a good thing. When we are weak, God is strong. You've been through a lot in a few months and in the past few weeks alone. After I finish Fredricka's hair, I want you to tell me more about your visit with your father. That had to be incredible."

"Yes. Wes said the same thing. I'm still soaking it all in, but it is an opportunity to get to know one of my parents."

Candace stopped in her tracks. "Wes? Is this a young man? I haven't heard you mention him before, and you said his name so endearingly." Her friend eyed her.

Angel blushed. "What? I have mentioned him. Wes Cade, the news reporter. His grandfather was the detective who looked for my mom. He's been trying to help me."

"Is that all?" Candace winked. "You know he's friends with Darnell. They play and coach the basketball team together at Victory Gospel Church. If I'm not mistaken, he is one of the most eligible bachelors in Charlotte."

"Where did you get that?" Angel led Candace down the hall to Grams's bedroom.

"Darnell showed me this Charlotte area magazine that comes out monthly. Your guy had a half page."

"I didn't know," Angel said quietly. "And wait a minute. We are just friends. He's not my guy."

"Mmm, by the look on your face, I would say you have more than just friendly feelings."

Angel couldn't disagree with Candace. She was pretty surprised with how quickly she and Wes had grown to be friends. She wasn't really looking for more. And if he was known as an eligible bachelor, Angel doubted Wes would even be interested. He probably had all types of offers.

Candace went into Gram's bedroom. "Hey, foxy lady. You ready to get that hair done?"

Angel watched as Grams's face lit up at seeing Candace. Grams held her good arm in the air and pulled on her hair.

Candace leaned over and hugged her. "I know you do. All the girls miss seeing you at the salon. I'm going to get this hair looking fabulous." Candace ran her fingers through Fredricka's hair. "Angel, you don't know how I love this woman. She has been like a mother to me. Can you help roll Fredricka into the bathroom?"

Candace pulled items out of her bag, while Angel pushed her grandmother's wheelchair into the bathroom. Candace followed behind and set up bottles around the sink.

"You are a pro at this. Do you do this often?" Angle asked.

Candace smiled. "Well, you know my aunt Maggie stays with us. She has good days and bad days from the cancer. Something about having nice clean hair always lifts her spirits, so I looked online and researched the best way to help someone who has a hard time standing at a sink or in a shower."

Angel watched as Candace set up the hair-washing tray on the back of Grams's chair and leaned the tray into the sink. Then she connected the hose to the faucet.

Candace winked at Angel. "Almost like the beauty salon experience."

"This is great. I'm going to go check with the nurse. I left her in the kitchen." Angel patted her grandmother on the knee. "I will see you in a bit, Grams. After Candace has hooked you up."

Angel entered the kitchen and gasped. Then she shook her head in amazement. Ella Mae had removed most of the old bottles and had placed new bottles on the shelf. "Wow, you've already taken care of everything." Angel pointed to the shelf. "This has to be above and beyond your duties."

Ella Mae waved her hand. "No, not a problem. I threw away a lot of the bottles in there and have added your grandmother's on the shelf here. On this door, I taped a chart of what medicines are here and the times they should be administered."

"Thank you. That is a big help." Angel took a look at the chart Ella Mae had created.

The nurse said, "One more thing. I found this stack of mail in the cabinet."

Angel noticed a large white envelope in the stack. Before she saw the return address, Angel knew who had mailed it. She tore open the envelope and pulled out the card. She read the message inside. *You turn twenty-five today. May all your dreams come true. Love, Dad.* He *had* sent her the card. Her dad was telling the truth.

"Honey, are you okay?" the nurse asked.

Angel didn't realize her hands were visibly shaking. "Yes, yes. I'm fine."

Angel knew her Grams would lay down her life to protect her daughter's only child. But Angel couldn't really understand why Grams would continue to shield her granddaughter from the only living parent she had. She left the kitchen and sat down in the living room. Angel read the card over and over again. She wasn't sure how long she had been sitting there when she heard her name.

Angel looked up and saw Candace at the living room threshold. "Hey, young lady, your grandmother has a fresh do and a smile on her face." Candace entered the room and walked up to her. "Are you okay?"

Angel held up the card. "I found a birthday card from my father."

Candace placed her bag on the floor and sat down next to Angel on the couch. She took the card from Angel. "You said you found it?"

"The nurse did. It was hidden in the kitchen cabinet. When I went to see my father, he told me he'd sent me cards and letters every year. I've never seem them. He sent this birthday card recently."

Candace handed the card back to Angel and grabbed her hand. "I can't begin to know how you are feeling, but remember the circumstances in which your grandparents lost their daughter, your mother."

Angel tried to pull her hand away, but Candace held it tighter.

"Your grandmother loves you. She has always been there for you."

"I know, I know." Angel shook her head. "I love her. I just wish she and Granddad had given me a chance to find out things for myself. I mean, I met my dad, and I don't know if he did or didn't do something to my mom. I'm confused."

"Trust God. Pray and let him lead you to where this all goes. In the meantime, treasure the card and the opportunity to know your father. Even more importantly, treasure your grandmother right now. Why don't we pray together?"

Angel nodded and bowed her head.

Candace prayed, "Father God, thank you for blessing this young woman. Thank you for opening the doors for her to begin to deal with her past. This is a confusing time for her, but, God, we know you are not the author of confusion. Help Angel to trust in you and lean not on her own understanding about things that have been revealed to her. Bless her relationship with her grandmother and her uncle, the family that is her connection to the mother she has missed in her life. Bless her reunion with her father that they may be able to get to know one another. Finally, Lord, bless Angel as she forges ahead with new friendships. We ask this in Jesus's name. Amen."

Candace reached out to her. Angel hugged her friend and wept. After a few moments she lifted her head and wiped her tears.

"You okay?" Candace asked.

"Yes. Thanks for being here."

"Hey, that's what friends are for, to be there when we need support. When I needed support, Fredricka was there for me."

Angel looked at her phone on the coffee table and noticed there was a text. She picked up the phone. "Wes sent me a text."

"He did. Wow. Look at the smile on that face," Candace commented.

"You need to stop." Angel knew she was grinning.

Wes wanted to meet to tell her what information he'd found out. She was looking forward to seeing him again.

# Chapter Thirty-three

Wes rubbed his hands together before ringing the doorbell. There was an unusual chill in the air after a thunderstorm last night. The low temperatures would have been comfortable except for the dampness that lingered. Some of Wes's goose bumps were from excitement.

Angel opened the door. "Hello, Wes. Thank you for accepting my invitation."

He grinned. "How can I say no to having lunch with you and your grandmother?"

Angel grinned back. "She will be thrilled to see you. When I told her about you, she kept saying, 'I remember that little boy.'"

He laughed and followed Angel into the house. After the week he'd had, Wes was delighted by Angel's invitation to lunch. He wanted to catch up with her to tell her what he had learned from Minister J.D. Angel led him through the living room, which looked vaguely familiar to him.

"You grew up in this house, right?" he asked.

"Yes. So did my mom. My grandparents have been here a long time," she responded over her shoulder.

Angel's grandmother sat in a wheelchair at the dining room table. Angel introduced him to her grandmother and then excused herself. Despite her condition, Fredricka Roberts looked regal, her eyes sparkling. Wes saw that beauty indeed ran in the Roberts family. He walked over and shook Fredricka's extended hand. Her handshake was quite firm, despite her recent frailties.

She said very slowly, "It's good to see you all grown up."

"Yes, ma'am. Now that I'm here, I do remember coming over here with my grandfather when I was younger."

Fredricka smiled and held her hands together. "Yes, yes. Nick and Lenny. Best friends."

Angel returned with glasses of iced tea on a tray. She added a straw to one and placed it in front of her grandmother. Wes liked seeing Angel in this role with her grandmother. He could tell she really loved her and doted on her. Angel turned to him. "Have a seat. I will bring out the sandwiches."

Wes pulled out a chair on the other side of Fredricka.

Fredricka asked, "How's Lenny?"

"Not too good. He has Alzheimer's. He has some good days, but some days he's confused."

Fredricka shook her head. "We are all getting old. Lots of problems. But . . ." She held up her finger. "God is good."

Wes leaned forward. "Yes, ma'am. God is good. All the time."

Angel brought out two plates with sandwiches. He noticed that she had brought her grandmother a plate that had cut-up grilled chicken alongside a helping of leafy greens and carrots.

She turned to him and asked, "Would you mind saying grace?"

He agreed. After he said grace, they dug into their food quietly. Wes was impressed with the club sandwich, which included grilled chicken, bacon, lettuce, tomato and Monterey Jack cheese.

"Are you a chef as well as a videographer?" he asked Angel.

Angel waved her hand. "Stop. It's just a sandwich. I did work at Southern Soul Café for a summer. Eddie let Denise and me work in all the areas, but we both liked to be hostess best. Anyway, I learned a thing or two in the kitchen and, of course, from Grams." Angel grinned at her grandmother, who winked back. "Anyway, this is pretty healthy compared to the Southern fried food from Southern Soul Café."

Wes appreciated the lunch and the healthy food. He felt pretty comfortable with Angel and her grandmother. The lunch reminded him that he missed seeing his mother and Pops. He hoped his mother had cooled down a bit so he could stop by and visit without feeling terribly guilty. They had finished their meal when the doorbell rang.

"Oh excuse me." Angel wiped her mouth with her napkin. "That's Ella Mae, the nurse."

Angel returned with a round-figured woman with her hair pulled back in a bun.

Ella Mae said, "Good afternoon, Ms. Fredricka. You almost finished with lunch so I can work with you this afternoon?" Ella Mae looked over at Wes. "Hey, I know you. You are on television."

Wes nodded. "Yes." He wiped his hands and stood to shake Ella Mae's hand. "Good to meet you."

"You too! Angel, you didn't tell me you snagged one of Charlotte's most eligible bachelors. You go, girl." Ella Mae grabbed Fredricka's wheelchair. "You two, behave and don't forget we are in here."

Fredricka winked as the nurse pushed her wheelchair out of the dining room.

Wes looked over at Angel, who had turned red around the ears, as she picked up the plates in front of her. He asked, "Can I help you with the plates?"

She peered at him. "No, I will add these to the dishwasher. You can wait for me in the living room. I'm anxious to hear what you have to share."

As Wes entered the living room, he was drawn to the photos of Angel as a little girl, which were displayed chronologically from grade to grade on the wall above the couch.

Angel came up behind him. "I can't believe you are looking at those photos."

"You were cute." Wes looked at her and added, "You are still cute."

Angel grinned. "Thanks. Oh, and I'm sorry about Ms. Ella Mae. Do you get recognized like that all the time from that article?"

Wes arched his eyebrow. "You know about the article too?"

"Yes, my friend Candace told me."

"Candace Johnson? She dates Detective Darnell Jackson. So you know each other? Small world."

"I know, right? She has become like the big sister I never had. Speaking of a small world, do you remember being at this house when you were younger? Your mom said we played together."

He laughed. "I kind of remember now. Funny how memories work."

Angel sat on the couch. "Tell me, what have you found out?"

Wes joined her on the couch. "Well, let me ask you a question first. Were you aware that your mother sang background vocals for a very popular song?"

"Yeah, I was. My granddad couldn't stand the song. Of course, he wasn't a fan of rap. I remember that song playing at my birthday party."

Wes made a note of that and asked, "Are you familiar with the rap artist who sang that song? He was killed not too long after the song came out."

"I forget his name."

"K-Dawg. His real name was Kelvin Dentin, and he grew up here in Charlotte. That night . . ." Wes tried to carefully word what he was going to say. "There are theories he had a beef with another guy and he was killed over a woman."

Angel looked at him, her eyes full of questions. "How does this relate to my mother?"

"K-Dawg was on the same record label, Royal Records. I had sources confirm that K-Dawg liked your mother. Now, hear me out. This is just a theory, but it's possible your mother could have witnessed K-Dawg's shooting and may have known who was responsible."

Angel jumped up from the couch, her eyes wide and alarmed. "Are you serious?"

Wes held his hands up to calm her down. "It's just a theory. She went missing a few weeks after the shooting."

Angel slowly sat down on the couch and began to rub her forehead. Wes could see she was trying to process what he'd told her. Finally, she said, "This is pointing back to my father if you are saying some jealous guy killed K-Dawg."

Wes remained silent.

"I'm not buying it." Angel shook her head. "Now that you bring this up, I should tell you that I looked more into my dad. He was a boxer. If he had had any beef with a guy, he would have fought him, not pulled a gun on him."

Wes nodded. "You are right. That's a good point. Plus, your dad wasn't anywhere near the club."

Angel said, "I know my mother was focused on her singing career, but if she was there and she saw something, I don't think she would have let the person get away with murder."

"She could have been scared, Angel. There were lots of people outside that club. No one came forward."

Angel looked at him. "Okay. Let me get this straight. You're saying if my mom did see what happened and she was scared, she must have told someone. That someone probably did something to shut her up."

"It's just a theory, but there's a bit more."

"Yeah?"

"I talked to Minister J.D., the pastor of Kingdom Building Church. K-Dawg was his cousin. They all were a part of the same group, grew up together. K-Dawg was, like, the first one of the group to come out with an album. Get this. Melanie Stowe's dad, Larry Stowe, better known as El, he was the group's hype man."

Angel dropped her mouth open and sat up straight. "What are you saying?"

Wes threw his hands up. "I don't know. Maybe there's a coincidence here, but I have had this gut feeling about Melanie's dad. When I found out all these guys were connected, I just . . ." Wes expressed his frustration by groaning.

Angel said, "Maybe you are trying to make too many connections. These are two different women that went missing twenty years apart."

"But . . ." Wes didn't get to finish his answer. A man came through the front door.

Angel called out, "Uncle Jacob?"

Jacob stood at the living room threshold and stared at both of them. He seemed to be disoriented. "Hey. Sorry. I didn't know you had company." Her uncle blinked and focused his eyes on Wes. "Do I know you?"

Angel answered, "You should. This is Wanda's son."

Jacob stared and broke out into a grin. "Wesley. Wow, I haven't seen you since you were a kid."

The phone rang. Angel reached over to pick up the receiver. "Hello." Wes watched Angel's face. She said to the person on the other end, "Can you hold for one moment?" She held her hand over the receiver and said, "I will be right back."

Wes watched her take the cordless telephone to the other room. He turned his attention back to her uncle, who had sunk down into one of the chairs. The man looked like he could use some sleep. "I heard you and my mom were good friends."

Jacob responded, "Yes, we had become buddies from when our dads played in Southern Soul. Still stayed friends even after your grandfather left the band."

Wes was reminded of the topic of conversation Pops had brought up the other night. "Yeah, I've always wondered why Pops left the band."

Jacob shook his head. "You know, people change. I think some of the band members were having issues. They were like a family, and they could get on each other's nerves. But mostly your grandfather wanted a more normal life. He wanted to be home with his family. I admire your grandfather for doing that. My dad wouldn't sit down from the band until the diabetes got to him. If he was alive today and was in good health, Nick Roberts would still be playing."

Jacob looked in the direction Angel had gone and then turned back to Wes. "We saw Wanda at Trinity Home Health Care the other day. I guess she is in the same boat as us. Taking care of a loved one is hard. How is she doing?"

Wes nodded. "It has been hard on her, taking care of Pops." He didn't know his mom had gone through with seeking outside care for Pops. Given all that had happened, he'd hoped she would follow through. As much as he loved Pops, he wanted his mother to enjoy her life again.

Angel returned to the living room. She smiled, but her eyes betrayed that she was troubled. "Hey, you two catching up?"

Jacob said, "Yes, we were catching up." He stood. "It's good to see you and your mother again. I will leave the two of you. Glad to see you have touched base again."

"Thanks, Jacob," Angel said softly, but she didn't look at her uncle.

Wes also stood and said, "Well, I hate to run, but I need to head back to the newsroom. I have to finish a story and submit it to my producer. I appreciate the lunch."

Angel smiled. "You're welcome."

He leaned over closer to her and lowered his voice. "Is everything okay?"

Angel looked over her shoulder and then back at him. "Why don't I walk you to your car?"

Outside, Angel closed the door behind them.

"What's up? You seem upset by that phone call," Wes prompted.

"The call was from Jennifer, from the Bring Them Home Foundation. My granddad kept in touch with them over the years. Every so often they will send updates if something comes up."

"You mean if they found some information about your mother."

"Yes. Well, mainly if a Jane Doe or an unidentified body has been found in the area. Jennifer said at some construction site—she didn't say where—they found parts of a skeleton. DNA has to be processed, entered into this big database, but they believe it's a woman." Angel swallowed. "Suppose it's her?"

Without thinking Wes reached over and placed his arm around Angel. "Let's just wait and see. I will be right here. I know how important it is to you to get to the truth."

Angel leaned into him. For a brief moment, Wes forgot his surroundings and enjoyed being so close to her. It felt right to him. Until he noticed that Angel's uncle was watching them through the living room window.

# Chapter Thirty-four

Angel guzzled down the water from her bottle. It was very hot today, despite it being only May. She looked over at the couple she was filming today, who were clowning around. Angel still couldn't believe they had met on Facebook a year ago and were now getting married. They were the first couple Angel had worked with that had met online. John and Maria were like any other couple, in love and into each other. Angel still wondered how well you could really get to know someone via the computer.

John was tall, with blond hair and startling blue eyes, while Maria was a vibrant redhead with freckles. Most of her wedding video packages were ordered through Lenora, but this couple had contacted her directly through her Web site. Another first for her. It made her feel good to see her business grow by being online, but she wasn't feeling being out in nature, traipsing around in the woods with this couple.

She wasn't really gung ho about being outside, but Angel had put on her mosquito repellent and had dressed accordingly for the adventure. *Me, bugs, and nature don't mix. Not to mention snakes.* Angel had got some great B-roll of the couple but was constantly looking on the ground for any creepy crawlies. If she saw one, this video shoot was so over.

Her overactive imagination was in full force despite it being morning and despite the sun shining through the trees. Still, some areas were so shaded, it felt like they were in a different world. John and Maria were in a carefree mood, running and chasing each other through the trees as Angel let the camera roll. She prayed she didn't catch something on film that would scar her for life. She'd watched her share of "young people in the woods" slasher movies.

As Angel stopped and examined what she'd shot today, her mind was excited and weary. This was going to be a long week too. The Southern Soul Talent Show was on Friday night, just a few days away. Thankfully, she would have Daniel's assistance on Saturday morning with editing and uploading the contestant videos to VidTube. Last night, while they went over the details at Candace's house, Daniel had added a photo that Angel had taken of Southern Soul Café. The photo made a beautiful background for the talent show page. People would have the following week to vote for their favorite performer. Eddie was offering a pretty generous prize of two thousand dollars to the winner to pay for studio time to record a demo. Angel hoped someone's dreams would come true.

Right now she was ready to call it a day. She couldn't remember sweating this much on a video shoot. Her T-shirt was stuck to her back. Plus, she noticed her camera's battery was running low. She held her head up from the camera. *Wait a minute!* Angel had been so engrossed in the camera, John and Maria had disappeared around the trees ahead. Not sure how she'd ended up so far behind them, Angel sped up. She felt a twig snap under her feet.

A woman's scream from up ahead jolted Angel, causing her to stumble. She caught herself, stood still, and clutched her camera. Sweat poured down her brow, and an insect buzzed close to her ear, almost touching her skin. Her heart felt like it would jump out of her chest.

Angel yelled to the couple, "John. Maria. Is everything okay?" *Okay,* she thought, *the online psycho isn't supposed to come out until after the wedding. Certainly not with the videographer present.*

Angel moved forward on her toes to catch up with the couple. When she peered around a tree, she saw John leaning down over Maria, who was sitting on the ground, grimacing. She appeared to be holding her leg.

Angel sprinted toward the couple and stopped in front of them. Maria's leg was bleeding. Angel asked, "Oh no, are you okay? What happened?"

John looked up at her. "We were playing around a bit too much. Maria stumbled over these rocks, I guess. They were covered up by leaves." He reached for Maria's arm and said, "Babe, can you stand?"

Angel stepped back as John helped Maria stand to her feet. Maria gingerly stepped forward. She looked at John and then at Angel. "I think I can walk. It's probably just a scrape."

"Are you sure?" Angel asked.

Maria nodded.

Angel said, "Okay, well, I guess you guys don't want any more footage today for the video." She was sorry Maria had got hurt, but she was so ready to get out of these woods.

John grinned. "No, we're good. Thanks for doing this for us. I know this was a bit of a workout. Did you get her stumbling on video?"

"What! I hope you didn't!" Maria shrieked. "If you did, please don't include that in the video. I'm so embarrassed!"

Angel held up her hand. "I promise I didn't see a thing, and there is no history on my camera." Through the trees the sun's rays were sharp, and they pierced her skin like laser beams. She was glad she'd had sense enough to put some sunscreen on too. Between the sunscreen and the mosquito repellent, Angel thought she would have a meltdown if she didn't get to a shower soon. She asked, "Can we head back to the cars?"

To her dismay, John and Maria walked a lot slower than before. Maria appeared to be limping. Angel thought Maria probably didn't feel anything now, but those types of injuries could hurt a lot later. The couple's wedding ceremony was two weeks away, so hopefully, Maria would have her injuries behind her before she walked down the aisle.

Angel looked through the woods and saw a cabin. It didn't look as well kept as the other cabins she'd seen this morning. They hadn't traveled far outside of the city limits, but it felt like they were in another world.

She asked John, "Hey, what is the reason this place is so special to you?"

John said, "My family owned a cabin up here. I loved to come up here during the summers. Maria and I talked about renting a cabin for the honeymoon. It's not far, and it's a great getaway, being near Lake Wylie."

Angel pointed to the cabin. "So do many people stay up here at this one?"

John answered, "No, this place actually isn't open as much. I guess they have a few people who still own cabins, but the guy who owned all this property disappeared a few years ago. It's rumored he was killed because he owed a lot of money to some interesting people."

She wasn't sure if it was the uncomfortable state of her skin, but Angel felt like something had just crawled up her back. "Are you for real?" Angel asked as she pulled her T-shirt away from her back.

"Yes. I remember that my dad used to talk to the owner all the time. Really nice guy. His family wasn't really into keeping this place up. I don't really know who owns it now. Anyhow, it's not the way it was when I was a kid."

They had finally reached the parking lot. Angel was grateful that civilization was about twenty minutes away.

Maria said, "We really appreciate your willingness to come up here."

"Not a problem. It's really beautiful up here. I guess I always thought being out in the woods meant camping, but the inside of the one cabin we went into was really nice."

"Oh yeah," John replied. "Most of these cabins these days have saunas, Jacuzzis, Wi-Fi, and flat-screen televisions." He laughed. "Believe me, it's like going away for a while, but you have all the amenities that you need."

"Cool," Angel responded. "Well, it was great hanging out with you two today. I will see you in about two weeks. I know the ceremony will be beautiful." Thankfully, the couple was having an indoor wedding. When they'd e-mailed their original request, they were thinking about an outdoor wedding. Maybe if it was on a beach, Angel would love to film an outdoor wedding, but after today she had no intentions of heading back to the woods.

She packed up her gear and loaded it into the car. John and Maria had walked to the other side of the parking space, to John's SUV. Despite her body's stickiness, Angel kind of liked the peacefulness of the surroundings. It was just so hot. The sun was really burning now. They had arrived around nine o'clock this morning to get started, but all that crazy hiking up the trail with her camera seemed to take forever. All she wanted was a shower and lunch. She closed the trunk of her car and waved to the couple as they drove by her.

As she opened the car door, Angel noted the map on her passenger seat. She scolded herself because she would have to figure out the way back. Angel always forgot to get the reverse directions when she printed out the maps. She had tried her phone earlier and knew the 3G wasn't working out in the woods.

A bird burst from the left side of her vision, startling her. She looked at the bird, but then another movement caught her eye. Angel stared into the trees. She had this creepy feeling that she wasn't alone. There was no one else out here that she could see. For some reason, Melanie Stowe's face came to mind. Angel stared for a second longer into the trees and then jumped into her car, slamming the door shut and locking it. *Okay, you are freaking yourself out, girl.* Then she laughed. There was probably some animal looking back at her, wondering what she was doing out there.

If she hadn't been moving so slowly, she could have followed John and Maria out. Angel turned the key in the ignition, observing the trees again. Something still felt off. Maybe she had watched too many horror movies when she was younger. All of them had some "crazy in the woods" scene, which might explain why she really didn't like being in the woods. Still, in her case it was broad daylight, and she had no reason to let her imagination run wild.

Angel placed the car in reverse and backed up. It took her a few minutes to find her way back to I-85, but soon she was on her way home. Her weird "cabin in the woods" moment was behind her.

About thirty minutes later, Angel pulled into the driveway. Inside she found Grams at the window in her wheelchair. The nurse, Ella Mae, was sitting on the couch.

"Hey. How's it going?" Angel placed her camera bag on the floor and walked over to Grams. She leaned down and kissed her on the cheek.

Grams said, "I'm good."

Her grandmother still slurred her words a bit, but Angel could understand her better now. "Well, you look good. I need to take a shower. I've been out in the woods today. Can you believe that?"

Ella Mae stood and walked over to pat and adjust Grams's pillow. She asked, "What were you doing, sugar?"

"Did I tell you what I do? I'm a videographer. I make videos for a living. Today I shot some footage that will be included in the wedding video package a couple purchased. Most of my business this time of the year comes from weddings."

"Oh, well, that must be fun. I love weddings." Ella Mae clasped her hands together. "Never had one of my own weddings."

"No?" Angel inquired.

"Child, the man I hooked up with was not the marrying kind. You would've thought by the time I got to child number three, I would have realized that. I can be slow. You make sure you find the marrying kind of man, you hear?"

Angel laughed and headed down the hallway to peel off her clothes and take a shower. About a half hour later, feeling fresh and clean, she came back into the living room with her laptop under her arm.

"Thanks for your help today. I know you didn't have to stay longer," she told Ella Mae.

"Not a problem." Ella Mae reached for her big purse and swung it on her shoulder. "Well, you two have a good rest of the afternoon, and I will see you both tomorrow."

"Thanks, Ella Mae. We appreciate all that you do." Angel closed the door behind her. "Grams, you want to sit here for a while longer?" she asked.

Her grandmother nodded and looked back out the window.

Angel started to grab her laptop but then thought she was being rude by not spending time with Grams. She could ingest the video she took later. There was plenty of time to edit. Angel asked, "Hey, Grams, you want your hair brushed? Candace did a great job with your hair. Maybe we can get her to come back."

Her grandmother smiled. Angel went to get Grams's brush from her bedroom. When she was younger, Grams would gently brush her hair and then let Angel do the same. Angel had always enjoyed that time. Angel pulled a chair from the dining room into the living room and set it down beside Grams's wheelchair. She sat down and glided the brush gently through her grandmother's silver hair.

Her grandmother began humming. Angel smiled. She always knew Grams was happy or working her way toward finding a peaceful spot when she hummed. She listened. Angel knew the hymn Grams was humming. Soon she was humming with her. *Pass me not, O gentle Savior, hear my humble cry.*

Angel surprised herself and opened her mouth to sing, "While on others thou art calling, do not pass me by." She hadn't sung out loud for her grandmother since she was a little girl. Angel wasn't sure why.

Grams smiled at her and said, "My Angel, my sweet Angel."

Angel reached down and wrapped her arms around her grandmother, feeling the boniness of her age and enjoying the warmth of her spirit. This was peace.

# Chapter Thrity-five

Melanie banged as hard as she could again and again on the thick glass window. She knew someone was out there or had been out there. There was a scream. She had fallen into another fitful sleep. Her body was feeling the pain of hunger. Her eyes had shot open to a woman's scream.

She'd run to the bathroom window and held her ear against the glass. If only she had something she could use to break the stupid glass. She had checked all corners of the room for anything sharp. Melanie had even tried digging around the seal with her fingernails to loosen the window frame, which was pretty useless. One day as she was digging, Mister—that was what she called him—had come in the room. She had stood still for a split second, had flushed the toilet, and then had ventured out into the bedroom.

Their eyes had connected. For the first time, she'd seen his face. He was an older man, and she felt like she'd seen him before. Not saying one word, he'd pulled out the usual food items from a bag.

"How long are you going to keep me here? What are you planning to do?" she had asked.

"That's up to your father," he had answered and then had left.

*Her father.* This was all about her father. The man didn't care anything about her. She didn't even know where he was, only that he'd shown up at the *Ameri-*

*can Voices* show. At least someone had told her he was there. He must have thought he could get something from her being on the show. She had refused to acknowledge his presence.

What had he done to get her in this mess?

Her dad was fun when she was a little girl. Later he always smelled like alcohol and could never keep a job. Mom had grown sick of him, and then, finally, she was really sick. Even as her mother was in and out of the hospital, Melanie couldn't depend on her father to be there for her.

She still couldn't figure out why Gladys had married her dad, but she was grateful that Gladys had tried to look after her when her dad went to prison. There was no one else. Her father's family was certainly not going to help. One of them had been killed when she was in high school, and the other was in prison. Both grandparents were gone. Her mother's sister had offered to help, but she wanted Melanie to move to Oklahoma. There was no way Melanie was going to leave her friends.

Melanie waited at the window a while longer. She knew what she'd heard. Someone was out there. She listened and heard another noise. It came from inside this place. He was back! She walked out into the bedroom and sat on the bed.

Maybe he did something to the woman, and that was why she screamed.

Melanie waited for the door to open. What was he going to do to her?

# Chapter Thirty-six

After talking to Angel, Wes was a bit anxious to learn more about that unidentified body. He couldn't seem to turn his thoughts away from the possibilities of the story aspect, so he looked up more information about the Bring Them Home Foundation. He also started to expand on his theory about the missing women a bit more. Suppose the two cases, though twenty years apart, were connected. It was probably one of the crazier angles he had ever conceived of for a story, but the what-if was too enticing not to look into it further.

He didn't want to ask any direct questions about the information Angel had given him, knowing she had confided in him as a friend, but he decided to contact Jennifer.

The woman was warm and friendly on the phone. "How can we help you, Mr. Cade? I enjoy your reports on WYNN."

"I'm working on a story about Melanie Stowe. It's been over three weeks since she went missing. I understand your organization has helped with coordinating the search efforts. What's next? Say her body was found somewhere without ID on it, how would she be identified?"

"Well, we certainly hope that isn't the case. The process starts with the medical examiner's office. If they are not able to identify a body, they will extract DNA samples. The samples are then entered into the Combined DNA Index System, or CODIS, database, which is managed by the FBI. This database can run matches against anyone who has been reported missing."

"How are DNA samples obtained for the database?" Wes asked.

"Well, our organization helps inform family members on how to provide items. A toothbrush is a very good item to provide. A hairbrush, as long as it hasn't been used by anyone else in the household, often provides good DNA samples. Then there are dental records in cases where the body has become decomposed."

"How would I be able to find out about any missing persons that may fit similar demographics?"

"You may be able to find some information in the NamUs database, but keep in mind many people go missing that are not reported."

"Thanks. I appreciate your time."

For the next few hours, Wes pulled up profiles and made notes. It did surprise him to see the sheer number of adults that went missing every year. It was like they just vanished. No clues, no body. Just nothing.

He'd printed out information on two African American women who were similar in age, early twenties, and who had gone missing between the time Elisa disappeared and now Melanie. Wes wasn't sure if he would discover any further connections, but finding out the truth had become important to him. He looked at the clock on his computer and realized he needed to get going if he wanted to get a seat at Southern Soul Café.


An hour later, Wes recognized the song playing as he walked into Southern Soul Café. Tonight the restaurant had been transformed into an event venue. The stage, which was normally filled with tables and chairs for patrons, had been cleared. The current members of the band were on the stage, but they weren't playing. The artist on the stage who was performing had a DJ accompanying him. It was the same young man he'd seen at Minister J.D.'s recording studio earlier this week. Shadrach had the crowd up and moving as he spoke his lyrics in rapid-fire fashion over the hypnotic beat.

Wes thought, *Nice!* Shadrach certainly had his vote for tonight's talent show. He looked around the room. The first person he laid his eyes on was Angel. She was behind the camera, capturing the stage and the crowd's reaction. Wes couldn't remember the last time he'd been out just to have fun on a Friday night. He was always so focused on a story. When Angel had mentioned the talent show, he'd figured it would be another opportunity to spend time with her. He didn't want to disturb her right now.

He scanned the crowd and saw Darnell sitting at a table with Candace. Wes started to head toward them but was tapped on the shoulder. He turned to see Minister J.D. Wes held out his hand and shook hands with him.

"Hey, Minister J.D."

"Good to see you. I hope you are paying attention to Shadrach up there. He's spitting fire tonight."

Wes responded, "He sure is. The crowd loves him, and he's spreading the gospel in his own way. I hope he gets far."

The minister nodded. "Yes, he's God's messenger. That's going to be the title of his album, by the way."

"You have a lot of plans for him."

"I do. He's like a son. Plus, I remember how I was at his age. Just wanting to get into the game and be out there on the stage. Shadrach is doing it right. Using his skills to glorify the Lord. I just want him to always keep that at the front of everything he does. The music business can be brutal."

"I can imagine." Wes wasn't planning to do any more work tonight, but he asked, anyway. "So, I thought I saw Larry Stowe the other day, when I left you. How's he doing?"

Minister J.D. turned his attention from the stage to Wes. "Larry, he's doing as well as he can. He's sober, which is good, but now he is really depressed, now that he knows Melanie is missing."

"He really didn't know his daughter was missing?" Wes shook his head.

"Hey, don't judge. Some people have demons that ride them hard, and they don't know how to deal with them or who to go to. Larry was and still is a good guy. He was always clowning around. After we all lost K-Dawg, it just changed the dynamics for all of us. We all reacted to his death in different ways. Larry would never really drink, but after K-Dawg's death, he started drinking heavily. He would get into all kinds of get-rich schemes, trying to get cash flow. It catches up with you."

Wes nodded his head. "You are right. All of us can walk down the wrong path."

"We have free will, so we can at any time step out and make the wrong choices. The awesome thing is God is always there, whispering in our ear to turn around, to come to Him, and let Him direct our paths. Boy, you about to have me preach up in here."

Wes laughed. "It was good talking to you again, Minister. I hope Shadrach does well tonight."

Wes headed toward the table where Darnell and Candace sat. "You two lovebirds mind if I take a seat?"

"Hey, man, come on and grab a chair." Darnell had his arm casually around the chair on which Candace sat.

Wes sat down and looked toward the back of the café again.

Candace asked, "You checking out my girl, Angel?"

"Oh, you know he is." Darnell winked.

Wes rubbed his forehead, knowing the grin on his face spoke volumes about his feelings for Angel. "I didn't want to disturb her. She's working tonight."

Candace said, "I'm sure she will be happy to see you. Did you know she was going to sing tonight?"

"Really? She's going to be a contestant in the talent show?"

"No. She's going to sing with Southern Soul at the end of the show. I did her hair today, and she was so nervous about it. Never sang in front of an audience before. I told her, 'Just do your thing, girl.'"

"Wow." Wes was really glad he'd come tonight. Angel hadn't mentioned she would be singing. He'd always wondered if she had inherited her mother's gift of voice.

He turned his attention to the stage, where Eddie was introducing the next contestant. A young woman, Janet Bruce, came up onstage with a guitar and sat down on the stool.

Before she started to sing, Janet said to the audience, "This song is dedicated to a friend of mine. Some of you may know she's been missing for a few weeks now. I went to high school with Melanie Stowe, and we miss her so much."

While Janet sang a ballad, Wes noticed that in the middle of the table where he sat, there was a postcard with Melanie's face on it. Wes took the postcard and read the bottom, where the Bring Them Home Foundation was listed as a contact. He looked at Melanie's photo. This was a different photo from the ones that had been circulating, possibly taken before she was on *American Voices*. A younger Melanie had looked into the camera, her face free of any makeup and her hair pulled up into a ponytail.

What happened to you? he thought. Wes wondered if it was even possible that she could still be alive. *If so, who in the world has you?*

# Chapter Thirty-seven

Angel panned the camera around to the audience. It almost felt like they were live on *American Voices* in Southern Soul Café. Eddie had implemented a superb marketing campaign in such a short period of time, because they really drew a crowd tonight. Latecomers were standing against the wall now to see the live performances.

She saw Wes come in and sit down at Candace and Darnell's table. Angel thought, *No telling what they are talking about.* She was sure Candace would make it known that she was aware of their growing friendship. Angel smiled. She was so happy that Wes took the time to have lunch with her and Grams the other day. Even her uncle Jacob, who was always in an odd mood, had commented that Wes was a good kid. Of course, Wes was clearly no kid.

Angel turned the camera back to the stage to focus on Eddie. Someone came to stand beside her. "You are everywhere with that camera." Angel closed her eyes. *Why is he here?*

She needed to focus on what she was doing, but she turned her attention to Kenneth and pointed to the camera. "I'm a little busy right now."

Kenneth jumped further into the conversation, as if he didn't hear her. "The competition is pretty stiff here tonight. So who do you think will win?"

"I don't know." Angel didn't want to admit it, but Kenneth was looking good tonight, which made her want him to get away from her even more. Kenneth had always been a careful dresser, and tonight he had chosen a snug pair of jeans and a button-down shirt, which probably could have been buttoned up more. *Why won't he just go away?* Here she was, finally thinking of moving on and happy about getting to know Wes, and her past was standing next to her, being annoying. She didn't need this right now.

"And how do people vote?"

Angel frowned at him. "Didn't you hear the rules? Eddie has said them several times already from the stage. We will upload the contestants on the YouTube page. People will be able to vote as many times as they want. Whoever has the most views wins the talent show. The winner will be announced next Friday." Angel looked around and asked, "Where's Denise?"

"Why aren't you singing?"

"What?"

"Come on. You can sing. Why aren't you up there?"

"I'm videotaping the event, Kenneth."

"I can take over the camera while you go up there."

"No thanks. It's too late, anyway, not that I'm interested." She wasn't going to tell him that she had finally caved in and agreed to Eddie's request that she sing with Southern Soul at the end of the show. For most of the week, Angel hadn't been sure what she would sing, but a song came to her when she woke up this morning. She had been singing the song throughout the day.

Angel looked to her right and saw Denise was a few feet away. Denise was watching Kenneth, who at that moment had decided to step uncomfortably close to Angel.

"Denise is looking for you." Angel pointed in the direction where Denise stood and turned back to the camera. She sensed Kenneth leave her side. A minute later, Angel observed Kenneth approach Denise, who was glaring at him. Denise jabbed Kenneth in the chest with her finger and walked away.

Angel felt a slight pang for Denise. Kenneth had always been a flirt. He wanted what he wanted no matter who got hurt in the process. Angel had learned the hard way, and it appeared Denise was getting a dose of the same medicine.

Angel wanted someone she could trust, someone who was always a gentleman and respected her. Even more importantly, he had to be a man of God. A man who sought God for guidance was going to think long and hard about how he treated a woman. Angel liked how Candace and Darnell interacted. Now, that was a couple who'd been through a lot together, and they really supported each other.

She kept an eye on the stage so she could make adjustments to the camera, but she also watched Wes, who seemed to be deep in thought instead of focusing on the stage. He was always dressed so preppy, but tonight he was a little more casual. Angel thought it was the first time she had seen him in jeans.

As if he felt her stare, Wes turned in her direction. He smiled and winked at her. That made her feel much better after having Kenneth interfere in her zone.

Angel caught sight of Eddie, who was weaving his way through the crowd toward her. "How's everything going?" he asked when he reached her.

"Everything is going good. I can't wait to get the videos online."

"Good! I'm happy about the turnout, and we have some great talent, but I know they haven't seen the best yet." Eddie grinned.

Angel stared at him. Then it dawned on her. "Oh yeah, when do you want me onstage to sing with Southern Soul?"

"I would say in the next twenty minutes. Can you find someone to help with the camera?"

Angel looked over at Wes. "I think so."

"Good! I can't wait to hear you. Make Nick and your momma proud."

Angel tried to figure out how she could get Wes's attention without leaving the camera. She pulled her phone out and sent him a text. A few minutes later, he was by her side.

"Thanks. I appreciate you doing this for me," she told him.

"Not a problem. I'm excited that you are going to sing tonight."

"I'm actually pretty nervous now. Will you pray for me?"

Wes grabbed her hand. "You will be fine, and yes, I will be praying for you. Now, go show them how singing should be done."

She laughed, liking the fact that Wes was holding her hand. Angel didn't want to let go, but she did and walked through the crowd.

This was crazy. What in the world was she thinking? Her mind locked in on how the crowd seemed to have grown more. The last contestant was a male singer, and he was belting out the final lyrics of the song "I Believe I Can Fly." She heard a round of applause from the audience as she entered the back of the café. To get to the stage, Angel walked through the kitchen. She thought she heard someone down the hallway, near the offices. Angel peeked around the corner. Kenneth and Denise were leaning against the wall. Was Denise crying? Angel stepped back. That was their business.

She continued to the stage from the back as the music grew louder. Angel observed the members of the band. The Southern Soul band members onstage were from a very different generation than her granddad's. Angel recognized only Eddie. Angel stepped closer to the opening to view the crowd from where she stood. She specifically looked for Wes, Candace, and Darnell. *Good*. She could see all of them. She wished Grams could have been there.

Angel stepped back and bowed her head. Her stomach was in knots. She prayed for that same peace she'd felt when she sang earlier this week with Grams. Angel also prayed for the song to touch someone who needed to be encouraged. It was one of her favorite songs by Nicole C. Mullen.

She opened her eyes to see Eddie beckoning her to come on the stage. Angel inhaled a deep breath and exhaled as she walked out onto the stage. She heard Eddie say, "Now, this here young lady comes from generations of Southern Soul singers and musicians. Her granddad, Nick Roberts, was one of the founders of the band. Tonight, as we close out, I ask Angel to share her voice with us. She hasn't done this before, so give her a round of applause and show your support."

Angel hugged Eddie and then stepped to the microphone that the other performers had used throughout the night. There were so many people in the audience. She focused on where Candace was sitting, beaming like a proud big sister. And then Wes. His smile was all for her.

It seemed like so much had happened to her in just the past few weeks. Some days she didn't know whether she was coming or going. She didn't know if she would find out the truth about her mother. *Focus!* Angel turned to the band members and nodded. As they began to play, she became one with the music and opened her mouth. Her focus shifted to the one who she was really singing to tonight. By the time she got to the chorus, all the knots in her stomach were gone. "Well, I know my Redeemer lives, I know my Redeemer lives, all of creation testifies, this life within me cries, I know my Redeemer lives." Whatever lay ahead for her, she knew God would be there.

# Chapter Thirty-eight

Standing outside the Victory Gospel Church sanctuary, Wes looked for Angel in the midst of the crowd entering the church this morning. He felt a tap on his shoulder and turned around. Angel was looking angelic this morning in a white dress and white heels. Her curly hair was pulled back in the ponytail, the same way it was when he saw her for the first time a few weeks ago.

"Are you looking for me?" She grinned.

He smiled back. "You look great this morning. Let's grab a seat."

They took a seat in the fifth row and joined the worship experience. He'd never attended church with any woman other than his mother. He had to admit he liked it. Wes tried to keep his eyes off Angel and turned his attention toward the worship leaders. He was grateful for life, family, and new friendships.

Yesterday he was really surprised when his mother revealed her decision to place Pops in a nursing home. When she suggested he invite Angel over for Sunday dinner, Wes almost tumbled out of the chair. Wanda had smiled at him the way a mother did when she knew best.

He had asked her, "Are you serious?"

Wanda responded, "Yes, I've been thinking long and hard. I couldn't stay angry at you. I've been in the same situation with Dad too many times to name. It occurred to me, you are a young man, and the only thing that should be on your mind is your career and, of course, producing some grandbabies for me."

Wes had laughed. "Now I see the reason for you trying to play matchmaker!"

"I'm not doing any such thing. I know what I know. Now, you invite Angel over for dinner tomorrow. The first time she came over, we didn't do a proper sit-down and talk. Now that I know you have been visiting with her family, we might as well include her in our family time too."

With his mother's blessings and nudging, Wes had called Angel and had asked her if she would like to attend the eleven o'clock service at Victory Gospel Church with him.

He had laughed when she asked, "Wes Cade, are you asking me out on a date?"

"Well, it's church. I wouldn't call it a date."

"You are slick. Of course, I'm not going to say no. How about I meet you there?"

"Sounds like a plan."

So here they were, sitting next to each other, listening to Reverend Freeman preach. After the service, they walked out together.

"I hope you have some time to stop by for Sunday dinner," Wes said. "Wanda has expressed to me that I must show up at the house with you."

"Are you sure? I think the last time I interrupted family time, and what about . . ." "It's okay. I think we were caught off guard the last time, but I think it would do Pops some good to have some company, like Nick's granddaughter."

"My uncle is with Grams, so I would love to hang out. I'm not turning down a good meal."

"Well, this is good. I like a woman who knows how to eat. You can follow me over."

It took some maneuvering, but they finally arrived at the Cade home. When Wes opened the front door, he was delighted to be greeted by the aroma of one of his favorite dishes, smothered pork chops.

Wanda came out from the kitchen, an apron over her dress. She hugged Angel. "It's so good to see you, and don't you look good in white today. Let me see if I can find something to cover up your pretty dress."

"Thanks, Wanda. I appreciate you inviting me to your home."

"My pleasure. Wes told me about you singing at Southern Soul Café on Friday night. Maybe I will get to hear your beautiful voice. Girl, your mother used to bring tears to my eyes." Wanda pointed and shook her finger at Angel. "I bet you have not even tapped into what God can do with your voice. Hold tight. I will be right back." Wanda disappeared into the back of the house.

Wes smiled. His mother was right. He knew Angel was hesitant about singing, but there hadn't been anyone in the audience who wasn't mesmerized by Angel's vocals. Wes still could remember the goose bumps he felt from hearing her voice. Her voice was so pure, and he could tell she was singing from a place deep within.

Wanda returned and handed Angel a shirt. Wes noticed it was one of his flannel shirts. Wanda said, "Here you go. I'm sure Wes doesn't mind and wants to keep you clean. That shirt over your dress should help you out at the dinner table."

"You brought a girl home, Wes." Pops had walked in silently behind them.

Wes turned around and said, "Yes, I did."

Pops said, "Well, she looks like an angel."

They laughed. Wanda said, "Dad, her name *is* Angel. This is Nick's granddaughter."

Pops blinked and then said, "Oh. I thought I recognized your face. You look like your mother."

Angel smiled. "Thank you."

Wanda shooed them toward the dining room table. "Okay, let's eat. Now, it's been a long time since I cooked, so I hope everything is good."

Once they sat down, Wanda asked Wes to say grace. His mother really did justice with the smothered pork chops, rice and gravy, and sautéed green beans.

Not bad, Mom," Wes said after everyone had cleaned their plate.

"Thank you, son. Oh, I forgot to bring out one more dish." Wanda went into the kitchen and returned holding a pie pan and a stack of small plates.

Angel said, "Wow, Ms. Cade. You baked too."

"Yes, one of Wes's and Pops's favorites. Peach cobbler."

Wes was delighted to see his mother in her element. She hadn't been this happy and animated in over a year.

Wanda asked, "Dad, you want a piece of this peach cobbler? It's piping hot, just like you like it."

Wes looked over at Pops and noticed he seemed to be focused on Angel. "Pops, you okay?" he said.

Pops asked, "Where's Nick?"

Wes and Angel looked at each other, while Wanda stopped slicing through the cobbler. Her smile faltered as she looked at her dad. "Dad, Nick's not here, but his granddaughter is visiting with us."

Pops leaned over and pointed his finger at Angel. "Elisa, you and Nick need to listen. I've told you to watch out for him. Something's not right about that boy."

Wes asked, "Pops, who are you talking about?"

Pops shook his head. "I told Nick, you are too trusting. Not me. I saw the handwriting on the wall. Decided it was best to leave the group."

Wes looked at his mother. "Mom, what's he talking about? You know, he was focused on the day he left the group when we were at the park. Why?"

Wanda shook her head and placed pieces of cobbler on the small plates. "I don't know. This is new to me, Wes. Let's just enjoy the peach cobbler. I want to catch up with Angel."

Wes took the plate of cobbler his mother handed him. He looked back over at Pops, who was now quiet. It was like he'd just left them in the middle of the conversation. Wes couldn't help but think Pops was trying to tell them about someone, but who was it?

# Chapter Thirty-nine

Angel followed Wanda into the living room, while Wes helped Pops to his room. Wanda settled into her favorite chair. She smiled and asked Angel, "How's the nurse working out for your grandmother?"

"Good," Angel answered as she sat down on the couch. Even though she had talked to Wanda a few times, she felt a bit self-conscious. After all, her feelings for the woman's son had grown in a short time. Angel swallowed and continued. "I like Ella Mae a lot. She helps during the day, and I'm able to help Grams at night. Wes mentioned to me that you decided to put your dad in a nursing home. I'm sure that was a hard decision."

Wanda sighed. "Yes, I prayed and cried over what to do. I would do anything for my dad, but I need to work too. I took time off and tried working part-time with the neighbors' help. It was starting to be too much. I feel so responsible for him because he was a really great dad. He was there for me. We had some great times together."

Angel said, "I can imagine it must be hard to watch his memory slip away."

"It's very difficult. I try to concentrate on the good memories for him."

"Detective Cade is blessed to have a daughter like you. I guess Jacob may feel that way about Grams. I mean, with seeing her go from being so vibrant to being a lot more dependent."

"Jacob loves his mother. He always got along with her better than with Nick. I remember he told me one time that Fredricka just understood him. That's what moms do."

"You said the other day, Jacob used to be fun. I wonder what happened to him."

"Your mother happened. Then there was me," Wanda responded quietly.

Angel didn't say anything at first, surprised by how much she was learning about her uncle from Wanda. Angel had sensed there was a little more to Jacob and Wanda's relationship than just a friendship. "You and Jacob were a couple?" she finally asked.

"No, no." Wanda rubbed her hands together as if they were cold. "We have known each other all of our lives. We were comfortable with each other. I think as we grew older, Jacob had more feelings for me than I did for him. I loved . . . still love him like a brother—"

"But he wanted to be more than that to you," Angel said, interrupting her.

Wanda shook her head. "I fell head over heels for Wes's dad in high school. It hurt my friendship with Jacob. We didn't even talk to each other on graduation day and for a few years afterward. He just became distant. But I heard he moved on. What's his wife's name?"

"Liz."

"Right. They are still married and doing well?"

Angel wasn't sure how to answer the question, knowing Jacob and Aunt Liz's marriage was pretty rocky at the moment. She answered, "They are still together." To avoid any awkwardness, Angel said, "You mentioned my mother. You know, I sensed just recently that Jacob really . . . I don't know. . . . He kind of despised her. Is that true?"

Wanda looked at her thoughtfully, like she was weighing her answer. "Your mother was a ball of energy. She could light up a room, and sometimes she could darken a room."

"You mean she had mood swings?"

"Bad mood swings. I don't know how much your grandparents talked about it, but your mother would dip up and down so much. Jacob told me they took her to see a doctor. They were on eggshells around her. Nick would do whatever he could to make Elisa happy."

"It's funny you mentioning that, but I do remember her being really sad, and then she could be happy like a little kid."

Wanda added, "There were some extremes. Even just the way Jacob and Elisa were treated differently. I know one year Jacob really wanted to learn to play the drums. He was all tuned up to do it. By that time your mother had been singing on a pretty regular basis at church and at local talent shows. Anyway, with entertainers in your family, it seemed appropriate for Jacob to follow suit, but Nick was against him learning to play."

Angel frowned. "Really? Why?" She was becoming more disturbed about her family as Wanda talked.

Wanda shrugged. "I don't know. I do know there was this big blowup. Jacob kind of never felt the same about his dad. He also couldn't stand the drummer in Southern Soul."

"Are you talking about Eddie?" Angel inquired.

"Yes. Eddie joined Southern Soul when he was nineteen. I think Jacob was twelve. Anyway, Eddie brought more spunk to the aging band's sound. I could remember my dad wondering why they brought such a young guy into the group. I thought he was pretty cute. Just a really cool guy. I believe Jacob's desires to play the drums formed because of Eddie. But Nick wanted his son to pursue an education, versus the entertainment business."

"Wow, you really know Jacob. I had no idea." Angel had always wondered about the rivalry between Jacob and Eddie. Both men clearly didn't like each other. Now she understood a little bit. It didn't seem fair that her grandparents had let her mother push forward with pursuing her singing career but held Jacob back. She wondered if that was why he was so intense. Maybe her uncle hadn't pursued his passion in life.

Angel said, "You know, Eddie used to hang out with our family all the time. I affectionately called him uncle. I grew up with his daughter, Denise, and we were close, I guess much the way you were with Jacob."

"Is that so? Southern Soul is just one big family, a bit dysfunctional, like any family, though."

Angel laughed with Wanda. Both women turned around when they heard Wes entering the living room. He was talking to someone on his cell phone. Angel noticed that his brows were furrowed, like he was upset. She heard him say, "Are you sure? Yes, I will be there right away."

After Wes clicked off his phone, Wanda asked, "Son, what's going on? You aren't going to run out on your guest now, are you?"

Angel looked at him. "Yeah, Wes. Is everything okay?"

Wes shook his head. "No. Angel, you might want to come with me. I hate to break this to you, but I just confirmed with Serena that Southern Soul Café is on fire. She's down there now, covering the story."

Angel jumped up from the couch. "What? Oh no!" They had just been at the restaurant on Friday. She'd spent all of Saturday uploading the videos from the talent show to the YouTube page. "This can't be happening! Was anyone there? They would have a huge lunch crowd from church now."

"I don't know. If you are up for it, let's go find out."

Wanda walked behind them as they headed out the door. "You two be careful and keep me updated."

Angel practically sprinted behind Wes, who was moving pretty fast toward his car. All Angel could see in her mind was the photo of her mother on the restaurant wall, with flames licking around the edges.

# Chapter Forty

Wes noted how Angel gripped the seat as he drove. He wasn't sure if she was tense because she couldn't believe Southern Soul Café was on fire or because of his driving. He eased off the accelerator. His mind was racing with questions as to how this could have happened. Sundays were usually the busiest day for the restaurant.

"How could this have happened?" Angel's comment mirrored his thoughts. "Did they say if anyone was inside?"

Wes shook his head. "Serena arrived on the scene. She said the building was engulfed in flames and the firefighters were working hard to contain the blaze. I asked her if there was anyone in the restaurant, but she didn't know yet." Serena had called him, knowing his history with the place.

He knew Angel was probably thinking of all the history the owner had collected over the years. All the photos and souvenirs on the walls documented many of their grandfathers' memories. Then there was the photo of Elisa, which he remembered from the day he'd met Angel for lunch. Knowing how much she cherished memories of her mother, he hoped Angel had a copy.

Wes pulled off the exit nearest to where the restaurant was located. From a distance, they could see smoke billowing. He dreaded what they would find as they approached the café and wondered if they would even be allowed to get close. Sure enough, as he rounded the corner, he came upon a police cruiser with flashing lights. The officer was diverting traffic away from the street where Southern Soul Café was located. Wes parked nearby. He and Angel walked as close to the café as they could. A crowd stood behind the yellow police tape. Wes could see several television vehicles with reporters and camera crews up and down the street.

Angel tapped him on his shoulder and told him, "I see Eddie's daughter. I will go see if she can tell me anything."

"Sure. I will catch up with you in a bit."

Wes headed over to Serena, who was talking live. "We have confirmed from at least four employees that upon arriving to work this morning, they noticed smoke and called nine-one-one. As of now, the fire-fighters have been able to contain most of the fire. From what we have been allowed to see, it looks like most of the well-loved Charlotte-based restaurant has been lost. Stay tuned for more details." Serena spotted him. "Hello, Wes. You burned some rubber getting here. Excuse my pun."

"We were just here on Friday for the talent show. Southern Soul is a special hometown band. A lot of people enjoyed coming here for good Southern food and entertainment."

"It's a shame," Serena said. "Hey, I saw your girl-friend singing. So she did inherit some skills from her mother. I wouldn't normally admit it, but I felt the hair rise up on my skin. She has some powerful chops."

"I didn't know you were there, and I told you, we are just friends. She wasn't a part of the competition, but she did sing with Southern Soul at the end of the show." He looked around for Angel and saw her in the crowd, talking to a young woman.

Serena leaned over. "For someone who is not your girlfriend, you keep tabs on her pretty good. I'm just saying. I am a reporter, and I know what I see."

Wes blushed. Knowing he had spent most of his Sunday with Angel, he wasn't sure why he was denying Serena's observations. Wes saw a familiar face emerge from the crowd and forgot about Serena's meddling. "Hey, what's he doing here?"

Serena replied, "Who?"

"Darnell. I mean, Detective Jackson." Wes had a feeling this fire would unearth something a bit more sinister. "What's homicide doing on the scene?"

Serena narrowed her eyes. "That's my question. This fire has just become more interesting."

Wes looked around. "Where's the owner? Eddie. Have you seen him?"

Serena stared at Wes and opened her eyes wide. "No. I haven't. Maybe he was in there. Makes sense that he would arrive early to open the place."

Wes hoped it wasn't so. Both Serena and he headed over to where Detective Jackson was standing. He had just stepped under the yellow police tape.

Wes called out, "Hey, Detective Jackson, any information about whether anyone was in the place?"

Serena stepped in front of Wes and jabbed him in his chest with her finger. "Mr. Cade, you are supposed to be off work." She turned back to Darnell. "Well, any information, Detective Jackson?"

Darnell looked from Wes to Serena. "Sorry, you two. I can't say anything right now. Once the firefighters clear out the place and say we can go in, you will know what I know."

Wes spun around and searched through the crowd for Angel. He remembered she'd said she was going to talk to Eddie's daughter. He needed to find her. This day could turn out even worse than they imagined.

# Chapter Forty-one

Angel did the only thing she could do. She hugged Denise. Angel looked at the burnt shell of one of her favorite places. The restaurant had been part of their childhood from the time Eddie opened it fifteen years ago.

"I'm so sorry. Are you okay? Where's your dad?"

Denise sniffled. "I don't know, Angel. I've been calling him. I've called him at the house and on his cell. No answer."

"Doesn't he usually open the restaurant?"

Denise nodded, tears streaming down her face. "Yes. Every day he's the first person to arrive and the last person to go home at night." Denise rubbed her shoulders as if she was cold. "What if he was in there?"

Angel stood close to her. "It will be all right." As she tried to comfort Denise, an odd feeling crept up her back. She examined the crowd and found Wes standing next to his coworker Serena. Both reporters were talking to Detective Jackson. Angel frowned and thought, *Why would a homicide detective be here?* Now she was afraid for Denise.

Wes turned around and seemed to be looking for her. She waved. He saw her and approached. Angel stepped away from Denise, who continued to cry quietly and stare at the building. Angel was wondering if her friend was going into some type of shock, because she seemed to have become unresponsive.

"Hey, can we talk?" Wes stared at Denise and then focused on Angel.

Angel eyed Denise as she responded, "Sure. Denise, I will be right over here."

Denise didn't even look at her. Angel followed Wes away from the crowd, keeping her eye on where Denise stood. She told Wes, "I'm worried. Denise hasn't been able to get in touch with her father. Why is Darnell here?"

Wes sighed. "That's why I wanted to talk to you. Nothing is confirmed yet, but we can only assume they found a body in there. The fire marshal will have to investigate if this was arson. If it was and they have found a body, well . . ."

Angel stared at him. "Southern Soul Café is like a home."

"What do you know about Eddie?"

"What do you mean?"

"Is he a likable person?" Wes asked.

Angel couldn't believe Wes would ask that type of question. A man she had known all her life could have died. She sucked in a breath, feeling a sob form in her throat. Angel backed away from him and folded her arms. "Seriously? Don't you think this is a little inappropriate? You don't even know if a body is in there, nor do you know if foul play happened here, but you are ready to jump on a story."

Wes blinked and then reached out to touch her arm. "I'm sorry, Angel. I just wanted to know if anyone would want to hurt Eddie and the restaurant. You never know how the people you meet can turn on you later. Suppose he let go of a disgruntled employee. Wouldn't you want to know that so they could investigate and possibly bring the person to justice?"

She shrank away from Wes's touch. "Of course I would, but you are jumping a little too fast to get a story. My best friend . . ." Angel stopped at those words as she looked at Denise. This was the girl she'd grown up with, the girl she'd spent countless hours with at sleepovers, doing homework, giggling in church. Angel turned to Wes. "Denise is going to fall apart. I don't want you talking to me any more about this. I can't be there for her with these types of questions in my head. I'm going to stay with her. We will work out a way to pick up my car later."

"Angel." Wes looked at her, his eyes pleading with her, but Angel walked away to stand by Denise.

She liked Wes, but she didn't care for his insensitivity right now. Besides, Eddie was like an uncle to her. If something happened to him, it would be one more piece of her world torn away from her. She hoped that nobody was in the restaurant and, above all else, that Eddie was alive.

# Chapter Forty-two

Wes realized he'd reached a dead end. Nothing was making sense to him. The two African American women he'd researched that were in their early twenties when they went missing didn't seem to have as much in common as Elisa Roberts and Melanie Stowe did. He thought if he could tie the missing women to a potential serial killer in the area that might make the similarities between Elisa and Melanie all the more striking. It was probably just a coincidence that the past was tied to the present.

It did cause Wes to pause, though. He found out that about 40 percent of missing persons were people of color. As a journalist, he knew certain missing cases received more attention than others. He decided he would pursue a story about missing people of color later.

Wes noticed the cursor on his computer screen seemed to be frozen. He clicked the mouse several times and then just gave up. He really wanted to call Angel. Wes wasn't trying to be insensitive yesterday, but he had let his enthusiasm for investigative journalism get the best of him.

Wanda had helped him return Angel's car to her yesterday evening. He wouldn't say a word to his mother about why Angel hadn't returned to the house with him, other than he thought Angel wanted to support her friend. His mother had studied his face, but he wasn't going to admit to her that once again he'd let pursuing a story get in the way.

"Hey, kiddo. What are you doing here so early on a Monday?" Serena came over to his desk and studied Wes. She narrowed her eyes and asked, "What's up?"

Wes shook his head and responded, "Just looking into some more leads about the Melanie Stowe case. You know Alan. He wants something to report, like, yesterday."

Serena sat on his desk. She was a bit too close for Wes's comfort, so he rolled his chair back. Serena watched him with an amused look on her face. "Don't worry. I'm not going to bite you. I take it the story isn't going in the direction you'd hoped, due to the expression on your face."

Wes shook his head. "Nope. I was trying to connect some other local missing cases to it. Nothing stands out. I just feel like this twenty-year-old case is somehow connected to this month-old case. Can you believe Melanie's been missing this long?"

Serena sighed. "I know. This is probably not going to turn out good. I just hope that, unlike your nineteen ninety-one missing-person story, they actually can find Melanie." She stared at him. "What else is going on? I saw you leave without your girlfriend yesterday."

Wes cleared his throat. "I don't know how many times I have to tell you, but we are just friends. Angel is friends with the owner's daughter. She felt like she needed to stay. That's all. Has anyone heard from him?"

"No. Which is why I'm waiting on a call from a source at the medical examiner's office."

"Medical examiner?" Wes sat up. "So they found a body?"

Serena nodded. "Yes, they did. From what I've been able to gather, it was a male."

Wes leaned back in his chair and rubbed his head. "So, they weren't able to identify the body? Was it badly burned?"

"Yes, and there wasn't any ID on the victim, so the medical examiner will probably try to get fingerprints. If that isn't possible, then they will compare dental records. We should know soon, I hope. I want to be able to share something for the noon broadcast."

"This is going to be devastating for Angel. Makes me wish I had kept my mouth closed yesterday."

Serena shook her head. "So you did upset her."

"What?"

"Oh, come on. She walked away from you, and it was clear to me she wasn't happy with you."

*Great!* Wes looked at Serena. He really wasn't into confiding in her. "I kind of let my reporter side get the best of me."

"You asked questions that you shouldn't have asked."

"She told me I was being insensitive to the situation. I thought I was just asking questions about the owner. What do you know about Eddie? Is he likable? I just didn't think about the fact that she's known the man all her life."

"Kiddo, it happens. Believe me. I've been through enough relationships to know that the desire to get the story can get in the way. You are ambitious like me. You won't stop until you get at the truth. That can cause trouble."

Wes thought about when he left Pops alone the other night to track down Larry Stowe and how upset his mother was at his reckless decision. He looked at Serena and noticed her face had softened. "Are you okay? "

"Of course." She flipped her hair over her shoulder and looked away from him.

"You are full of advice lately. I know we're both ambitious, and I know what drives me, but what drives you to go after a story with such intensity? Like K-Dawg, for example. To be honest, the twenty-year-old unsolved murder of a rapper doesn't seem to me like the type of story Serena Manchester pursues."

Serena glared at him, but there were clearly tears in her eyes. All these years he had known this woman, he'd never seen her act emotional. Serena was an ice queen.

Serena wiped her eyes. "Sometimes when a story hits close to home, it becomes your obsession."

Wes frowned but didn't say anything as he waited for Serena to continue.

"You know, I came to Charlotte the year K-Dawg was shot. I was eighteen years old and so ready to leave South Carolina. I wanted to get away from the small town and what I considered all the small-minded people. So, my cousin invited me to stay with her for a while, and she introduced me to all the hot places to go. One night, can you believe I actually met a decent guy? We started hanging out with each other, and I just fell for him so hard." Serena sniffed. "I can't believe I'm telling you this."

Wes said, "Sure. I appreciate you sharing with me. So, what happened with your boyfriend at the time?"

"He went out that night. I didn't feel well. I remember I was so upset with him. I wanted him to stay and be with me, but his best friend knew that K-Dawg was going to be at this club. So they went." Tears were visibly streaming down Serena's face. "He didn't come back. You know the focus has always been on K-Dawg, but bullets were sprayed into the crowd too. Three people were injured, and two other people besides K-Dawg lost their lives."

Wes went over to the desk that was behind him and pulled out tissues from a box and handed them to Serena. For the first time, Wes started to see past Serena's flirtatious, but hard-core exterior. This beautiful woman hid behind a world of hurt that started when she was young. She might have lost the one man she loved.

Serena wiped her face. "Wow, kiddo. I can't believe you got me crying in here." Serena composed herself. "Anyway, I've been in touch with contacts on and off, including K-Dawg's mother. She was the only one who recognized that other people lost loved ones that night too. So when she asked about doing a twentieth-anniversary story, of course, I said yes. I want to include the other people."

Wes nodded. "I think it's going to be a wonderful story. Have you been able to reach out to Minister J.D.? I'm sure he would love to be a part of the story."

Serena sighed. "Yeah, I know you gave me his information. I will do that, but in the meantime I need to get something tonight for Southern Soul Café. I'm going to call my contact." Serena pulled her phone out of her bag, which had been sitting on the floor. "Hey, Lou. How are you doing? It's Serena. You got anything for me? We have lots of concerned people." Serena looked over at Wes as she talked.

As he listened to Serena's conversation with the medical examiner, Wes held on to the arms of his chair.

"So, you were able to get a partial fingerprint?" Serena asked.

Wes watched her eyes grow wide. *Please don't tell me it's Eddie.*

"Thanks, Lou." Serena stared off into the distance.

"Serena. Hello? Don't keep me in suspense here. Did they identify the body?"

She turned to him. "Alan is going to flip out. Actually, you might flip out."

Wes leaned forward. "Who was it, Serena?"

"The fingerprints analysis was a match for Larry Stowe."

Wes felt his mouth drop open as he struggled to process what Serena had told him. "Melanie Stowe's dad. Why in the world would he be at Southern Soul Café?" *And where is Eddie Gowins?*

Serena interrupted his thoughts. "Oh, but that isn't all, kiddo. There was a definite gunshot wound to the head, which is probably what killed Larry."

Wes stood and faced Serena. "He was murdered. The fire was about covering up a murder." Wes held his hand to head. Angel might not have been pleased with him yesterday, but he had to talk to her. Their digging had turned into a connect-the-dots game—except none of the dots were connecting.

# Chapter Forty-three

Melanie leaped off the bed to the side. *What is going on?* She could hear items being thrown against the wall and crashing to the floor. Melanie had been stuck in the cabin room so long, she wondered if she would ever see the outside again. Her heart raced as she heard a string of loud expletives. Something or someone had angered Mister. At any moment, Melanie thought, he would burst through the door.

Maybe whatever reason he had kept her here was no longer valid. Maybe he no longer needed to. What was it Mister had told her? *That's up to your father.*

Melanie held her head, which was now throbbing with tension. "Dad, what did you do?"

Something hard and huge bumped against the door. Then she heard the most awful scream. Mister sounded like he was having a nervous breakdown. She covered her ears and looked around her bedroom prison. What could she do that she hadn't already thought of a million times? She thought, *I'm not going down without a fight.* She had watched enough *CSI* episodes to know all she needed to do was to get his DNA under her fingernails.

She closed her eyes and prayed.

As fast as the tornado outside her door had come, it grew quiet.

Melanie opened her eyes. She knew he wasn't gone. What had stopped him?

She didn't have long to ponder. The bedroom door burst open, slamming against the wall. Melanie got up from the floor and stood to face Mister, the bed in between them. She looked at the open door behind the man. If only she could get by him, out that door. It was her chance for freedom. She knew she had to be out somewhere deep in the woods. If she had the chance, she would take her last opportunity to escape among the trees.

Mister stepped into the room. His eyes were crazed, and he didn't smell right today. Melanie subconsciously stepped back, knowing all she had behind her was a wall.

The man shook his head. "What am I going to do with you? Your dad couldn't do it. Couldn't keep his mouth closed." Mister threw up his hands and walked closer to her. "All these years and he suddenly got a conscience."

He paced in front of her. The wide-open door behind him beckoned her to make a run for it. She looked down at the bed and then returned her attention to Mister. He stopped and pointed in her direction. The man was facing her, but his eyes didn't seem to be focused on her. It was like he was having a conversation with himself and she was his audience.

"He took the money. Didn't have a conscience back then. I told him to be careful and that none of this better get back to me. I told him."

Melanie eyed the door, but she wanted to know what Mister was talking about. "Are you talking about something my dad did?"

"Yes."

"I don't understand why you brought me into it. Shouldn't you deal with him?"

Mister smiled. That crazed look in his eyes scared her. What he said next paralyzed her. "I've already dealt with dear ole dad. He's no more trouble."

*He's crazy!* She took one look at him and screamed, "No!" Melanie swerved as if she was going to go around the bed. Mister came around the other side. With all the strength she had in her body, she went back toward the bed and reached for the blanket. She threw the blanket at his head as he leaped toward her. She screamed as she felt his hand touch her leg. With all her strength she kicked hard, feeling her feet making contact with bone.

Melanie stumbled to the other side of the bed, crawled, and then sprinted for the door. She made it through the door, then ran past another bedroom, down a hallway, and into the living area. The front door was ahead of her, but before she reached it, she felt strong hands yank her backward by her shirt.

"No, no!" Melanie screamed and kicked. She swung her hands toward Mister's face and dug into skin. He roared and pushed her hard. She fell against something hard, smacking the back of her head.

Melanie felt her body slide down to the floor as blackness overtook her.

# Chapter Fourty-four

Summer was drawing near, and the daylight was stretching into the early evening. It had been a long day, but Wes had tracked down and interviewed several people who knew Eddie Gowins. He was looking forward to his last stop because he hadn't seen these guys in years. Wes climbed the steps to the porch and approached James "Buddy" Waites and Pete Daniels, two original Southern Soul band members. These guys stopped playing in the band around the same time as Nick Roberts. A new generation of band members came in as replacements, but nobody had the chemistry of the original set.

"Well, I'll be," Buddy shouted from the porch chair, where he held a cold beverage. "It's a treat to have Lenny's grandkid visit us old fogies."

Wes shook Buddy's hand and then Pete's. "I appreciate you guys letting me interrupt your evening."

"No problem," Pete said. "So to what do we owe this pleasure? I saw you in that magazine. Eligible bachelor? Please tell me some lady has snagged you by now."

Wes threw his head back and laughed. He was not going to ever get away from that article. As he laughed, he saw Angel's face in his mind. He took a seat on one of the vacant porch chairs as he answered Pete's question. "Maybe. It would be nice. I think I'm ready to settle down and have a family."

Buddy cackled. His voice was hoarse from years of smoking cigars, and from a short distance away, Wes could tell Buddy still enjoyed having one or two. "Well, that's a good thing. In order for a marriage to work, you have to be willing to try it out."

Pete shook his head. "That's for sure. If you aren't really ready, you might as well stay single. People get together in a hurry and then divorce faster than you can blink your eye."

"I know your granddad will be proud of you. We've known you since you were this high." Buddy held his hand to his waist. "With your granddad only having a girl, he was so proud to have his grandson. How's Lenny doing these days?"

Wes cleared his throat. "He's declining. Mom has decided to place him in the nursing home."

Pete and Buddy nodded. They all remained silent for a moment. Wes knew with the guys being close in age to Pops, that was hard to hear.

"I have some questions about Southern Soul," Wes said, breaking the silence.

Pete clapped his hands. "Sure. Ask away. You know Lenny and Nick Roberts started the band. Now, those two could jam. Nick strummed that guitar, while Lenny beat them piano keys."

"All that was before my time. Pops left the group first."

"Yeah, he got interested in the police academy. Told us he needed a real job to support his family."

Both men laughed and then grew quiet again.

Wes said, "The last few times I talked to Pops, he seemed to be focused on the night he left Southern Soul. Do you remember it?"

Pete and Buddy looked at each other. Pete finally answered, "Lenny actually left because he and Nick couldn't agree over a few changes in the group."

Wes raised an eyebrow. "Oh? What changes?"

"We had lost our drummer. Nick met this young dude. He was really good, but he just didn't fit in with us." Pete rubbed his hand over his bald head. "He was just too young, a little bit reckless."

Buddy grunted. "A whole lot reckless and impulsive. He was a charmer, but something about him always just rubbed most of the guys the wrong way, except Nick. Nick took up for him. Lenny just got tired and decided it was time to move on."

Wes looked at the men. "This guy? He was Eddie Gowins?"

Both men nodded and looked off in another direction, neither focusing on Wes. He asked them, "What happened to the original drummer?"

Buddy sighed. "Levy was killed."

Wes sat up. "Killed? Like murdered?"

Pete nodded. "Somebody stabbed him, left him for dead at his home."

"Did they ever find the killer?"

Buddy shook his head. "Nope."

"So how did Nick find Eddie?"

Pete shrugged. "You know, I don't know. I think we asked him a couple of times. He just showed up, but he could play the drums. I will give him that."

"How did the band feel about him opening Southern Soul Café?"

Buddy narrowed his eyes at Wes and leaned forward. "Is this what this conversation is all about? That restaurant burning over the weekend?"

Wes licked his lips. "Yes. There was a lot of memorabilia from the band. It's all gone."

"He had no right to most of those things," Pete snapped back. "That's what we didn't like about him. We accepted him into a band that had been around over a decade before we let him in. Nick had a lot of that stuff in his home. Somehow, Eddie opened this restaurant and took over all of it like he owned it."

Wes was starting to see another side of the jovial Eddie, whom he'd met just a few weeks ago, when he had lunch with Angel at Southern Soul Café. The older band members resented the man. He didn't want to mention that Eddie was missing, since some of the information, Wes knew, the public didn't know yet.

"You know what was really difficult to see?" Pete added. "Nick allowing Eddie to be such an influence over his little girl."

Wes asked, "Are you talking about Elisa?"

Buddy nodded. "Yep. Elisa was a spoiled child, but she could sure bring tears to your eyes when she opened that mouth. I remember her singing as a small girl. Just took to being in front of an audience like water. Nick really encouraged her."

Wes had really come to talk to the two former band members about Eddie Gowins and was surprised that the conversation had turned to Elisa Roberts. "I heard she had a record deal about the time she went missing. Did you know about that?"

Pete responded, "Nick had told us she was offered a deal. He wasn't happy about it, though. I think by then, Nick was starting to see Eddie wasn't the right person to be managing Elisa's career."

"Huh?" Wes wasn't sure if he'd heard right. "Are you saying Eddie was Elisa's manager?"

"Oh yeah, Eddie called himself managing a couple of young people's careers. He was all about being a star and wanting to be behind the next big star." Pete took out a handkerchief and wiped the sweat from his brow.

Wes rubbed his chin. "I came to ask you some questions about Southern Soul Café, but now you have my mind going in another direction. You mentioned that Nick was against the record deal. Do you think Elisa's pursuit of a singing career had anything to do with her going missing?"

Buddy and Pete looked at each other. Finally, Buddy said, "We are pretty sure that when Nick let Eddie get involved in managing Elisa, he had no idea that the man was going to lead his daughter to her own demise. Eddie was a talker, a charmer, and he always had shady folks around him."

Wes started to think about the body found at Southern Soul Café. Why was Larry Stowe there? "You guys, I have one more question. You said Eddie managed other people. Do you know if he represented any rap artists?"

Pete answered, "Yes, he had a lot of kids under him that rapped."

Buddy leaned forward. "Eddie played with a lot of young entertainers' dreams. But he let them down. Anything that Eddie did was always about Eddie."

Wes took in all that he'd heard. Now he realized that Pops might have been trying to drop hints the past few weeks. He wondered if Pops had suspected Eddie all along but met resistance to the idea from Nick.

He had to get to Angel. They hadn't talked since Sunday, but he needed her to know about the man she referred affectionately to as her uncle. Would Angel believe him, though? Remembering her reaction on Sunday, Wes hoped he wouldn't push her away completely.

# Chapter Forty-five

Angel kissed Grams on the forehead and then smoothed her hair. She wasn't sure if it was her own mood or Grams, but they had had a difficult day. Grams had been extra frustrated by everything today; even Ella Mae couldn't make her smile. Ella Mae had mentioned that her grandmother might experience depression from time to time. She was progressing well, but too slowly for the feisty Fredricka.

Angel said, "If you need me, I will be in my room. I'll come check on you before I go to bed."

She got up from the bed, but Grams grabbed her arm with her left hand, which seemed to be remarkably strong. Angel looked at Grams. "Are you okay?"

"Where's Jacob?" Grams asked slowly.

Angel didn't know what to say. It wasn't the first time Grams had asked about her son, and Angel was not sure what to say about her uncle. It seemed like Jacob had gone off the deep end. Angel was really worried about both Jacob and Eddie. She was hoping Wes would call to update her, but she realized she might have blown it with him on Sunday. He was a reporter, doing what he did best, asking questions. If it wasn't for him, she probably would have never taken the plunge to meet her father.

Angel patted Grams's hands. "I don't know. I'm sure he's fine."

She wished Jacob would come clean about what was going on with him. Maybe he was out looking for a job, although she doubted it. His appearance seemed to grow worse each time she saw him. The clean-cut businessman had disappeared and had been replaced by a man who seemed lost and unsure of himself. Angel reassured Grams again by rubbing her hand. She took one last look at her before she left the room. Despite her condition, Grams seemed more worried about her son than herself.

Angel went to her bedroom and decided to check on the talent show videos. Angel pulled up the VidTube Web site on her laptop. With the fire and everything that was going on, she hadn't been able to check on the talent show results. Did it even matter anymore?

There were well over fifty thousand views to the page. *Wow!* She scrolled through the playlist, and so far it looked like the competition was between the Christian rapper Shadrach and one of the female singers. Angel liked both of them.

She noticed a video had been uploaded this morning, but it had not been included in the contestant playlist. The funny thing was, it had half as many views as the videos that had been uploaded on Saturday, almost twenty-five thousand. Did Daniel upload this other video? She thought they had added all the contestants.

The video was titled simply *Southern Soul*. She opened it. *Oh no!* Angel sat up, feeling panic rise in her chest. This was her singing with the band. Now she wished she'd never let Eddie talk her into singing in public. Her eyes scanned below the video, and she saw that there were comments. Lots of them. She read through the comments. The more she read, the more her nerves calmed down. Many of the comments were from well-wishers who loved both the Southern Soul band and the restaurant.

It brought tears to her eyes when she thought of all the history lost in the fire, but trying to look on the bright side, she remembered all the footage of the café she'd captured on Saturday morning. She'd spent a considerable amount of time there gathering B-roll for the documentary she was putting together as a tribute to her mother. Angel had managed to capture the photo of her mother that hung on wall near her favorite booth in the café and several of the band members on video. She'd derived a bit of comfort from watching the footage today. The phone interrupted her thoughts on what she might do to share these glimpses of the café's interior with the fans.

Angel reached for her phone on her nightstand and looked at the screen. The caller was Wes. She answered the call on the third ring. "Hello."

"Angel. Man, I'm so glad you answered the phone. I'm so sorry about Sunday."

"Don't be. I probably overreacted. I can do that sometimes."

Wes laughed softly on the phone. "Well, I tend to ask too many questions. Look, I called to let you know some news. It's not been released to the public, but since you were there on Sunday, I thought you should know."

Angel held the phone tight. "You're going to tell me they found someone in the fire."

"Yes, but it wasn't Eddie."

She blew out a sigh of relief. "That's great, but who was it? One of the employees?" Angel didn't hear anything on the phone. "Wes, are you still there?"

"The body was identified as Larry Stowe."

"What? Wait, you said Stowe."

"Melanie's dad."

Angel reached up and grabbed the back of her head, which had started throbbing. "What does this mean? Why was he in the restaurant?"

"I'm not sure of the details, but you remember we have been talking about the past and the present, how some dots seem to be connected?"

"Yes."

Wes sighed deeply. "I don't know how well you knew Eddie, but something is not right here. Did you know he was your mother's manager?"

Angel shook her head, forgetting she was talking to Wes on the phone. She responded, "No. I didn't know he was her manager."

"Look, I don't want to upset you again. We will get together and talk later. I'm still trying to put bits and pieces together, and there are some people I plan to talk to tomorrow. Why don't we plan to meet later tomorrow?"

"Okay, fine. We can meet tomorrow." After saying good night, Angel clicked the phone off. *Eddie was my mother's manager,* she thought. She sat back against her pillow. That meant he would have helped her get the record deal. Angel looked at the clock on her phone. She started to call Denise but then thought that wasn't a good idea. What would she ask her? She'd set out to find out more about her mother's life, but now Angel was feeling more confused and no closer to the truth of why Elisa disappeared.

A noise jolted her. *Grams.* Angel got up from the bed and walked down the hallway toward Grams's room. She entered the room and walked over to Grams. Her grandmother was sleeping soundly.

Maybe she was just hearing bumps in the night. Angel left her grams's room and headed down the hallway toward the living room. There weren't any lights on in the front. It was so quiet, though. A lot quieter than usual, at least that was what Angel thought. Her over-active imagination was inching toward paranoia.

She stepped into the living room and stopped. Her entire body tensed. Due to the light coming through the window from the street and the porch lights, Angel could see a figure sitting on the couch. Out of the dark-ness, a voice called out her name. "Angel."

# Chapter Forty-six

Angel took a second to remember to breathe instead of scream. Moving forward into the darkness, she reached out for the lamp that was on a nearby table. The light calmed her, but her uncle did not. He seemed to have aged overnight.

"You scared me, Jacob. When did you get here? Grams has been asking about you."

She walked farther into the living room and sat across from her uncle on the love seat.

"I'm sorry. I was hoping not to wake you."

"What's going on with you? And stop pretending like everything is okay. It's not. Look at you."

Jacob snarled, "Will you lower your voice?"

"Grams has noticed something is wrong with you too. She can't even rest herself because she's worried about you."

Jacob leaned his head against the back of the couch. "This has been the worst time in my life next to your mother disappearing. Losing Dad was one thing, but I didn't see them letting me go at the job. Fifteen years. I gave my best years to that company for fifteen years."

Angel said, "I'm so sorry. Have you been looking for another job?"

"Angel, I'm almost fifty years old. Employers prefer the youngster, who they can pay less. But I have been working, just not doing what I thought I would be doing. More or less just temporary contract work. I still hope to obtain something more permanent with benefits again, but it's been hard. So much has happened at once. I mean, I wasn't expecting Mom to . . ." Jacob sighed and held his head down, but not before Angel took notice of the tears in his eyes.

She remained silent, understanding that her uncle had lost a lot and was probably just as scared.

Jacob interrupted her thoughts. "I ran her off. She's gone because of me. That's what has been haunting me lately." Her uncle stared in her direction, but it was like he was looking through her.

"Liz? Why don't you try talking to her? I'm sure you two can work it out."

"No, no, no." Jacob leaned over and held his head in his hands.

Angel continued, "You've been married so long, there has to be something . . ."

Jacob stared at her. "Angel, I'm talking about your mother."

She sat back on the love seat and eyed her uncle. "My mother? What did you do?"

"Elisa was different when she was younger. She looked up to me as the older brother. I protected her. We grew farther apart the more people encouraged her to sing. It became her obsession. But then she started to change. Elisa's behavior became so manic that she would get angry and lash out at people, and then, all of a sudden, she would just be the happy little sister I knew."

Angel remembered talking to Wanda earlier in the week. She'd mentioned her mother's mood swings. She didn't want to interrupt Jacob, so she remained quiet.

He laughed quietly, his shoulders shaking. "You were the best thing that ever happened to Elisa. She doted on you. Dressed you up. Being your mother gave her a sense of being normal, being a mom. If only she'd stayed on her medicine."

"Medicine?"

Jacob focused on Angel. "Dad didn't want to think anything was wrong with her. If it wasn't for Mom keeping up with her and staying on her, Elisa would have gotten into a lot more trouble."

"What was she taking medicine for?" Angel asked.

"She was bipolar. Elisa would be up one day and then down for days."

"How come no one told me this?"

Jacob shook his head. "I don't know. I do know that she ran away before. She would go off when she was in high school. We would all look for her, and then we would finally find her at some friend's house. Most of us had never met these friends."

"So when she left that night, had she been taking her medicine?"

"I don't know. I suspect not. She was really flying high, just a ton of energy. She was like a kid, going on and on about the record deal and how she was going to be like Mary J. Blige and Mariah Carey."

Angel asked, "Did Eddie know? I mean, about her being bipolar."

Jacob lunged from the couch and paced. "He knew. I tried to tell Dad that Eddie was no good. Yeah, he could play the drums, but he was surrounded by people who were questionable. Even the guys in the band were starting to be weary of him. I still don't know how Eddie talked Dad into letting him be Elisa's manager. He knew she had talent, and he just wanted to make money off her, but Dad was so blind."

Angel stared at her uncle, trying to let his rants sink in. "Well, what did you mean when you said you 'ran her off'?"

Jacob sat back down. "After she argued with your father, I tried to talk to her. I told her Angelino was right. She needed to wait a while longer for a better opportunity. She was so angry at me. I didn't realize she had left, but . . ." Jacob swallowed. "Mom went to check on you, and you asked her where Mommy was going."

"I did?"

"Yes, you were the one who clued us in on the fact that she had left. I knew she was angry with me."

Angel leaned over. "Do you know if she was there the night the rapper K-Dawg was killed?"

Jacob studied her for a second. "What do you know about that night?"

"Wes has been looking into some things for me. There's a theory that she saw who killed K-Dawg, and wherever she went after that, the person responsible did something to her. Do you think that's what happened?"

Her uncle sat quietly for a moment, deep in thought. He looked back at Angel, his eyes glistening. "She was there. Dad sent me to get her. She had been off for a few days. Mom suspected she was not taking her medicine. Someone called Dad and said Elisa was acting a little crazy. I just happened to be home visiting and was sent to fetch my sister."

Angel asked, "Did you arrive when the shooting happened? Do you think she saw something?"

Jacob responded, "I arrived after the shooting. I remember it was just chaos. It took me at least ten or fifteen minutes, but I finally located Elisa. She was standing on the sidewalk, just staring at the car. The police had asked her if she saw something."

"She didn't say?"

"No. Nobody said anything." Jacob sighed. "It's possible she could have seen something, but she never said anything. I just tried to get her back home. She was sitting so still in the passenger seat. I thought maybe she was in shock."

Angel felt close to tears. This was the closest she had ever come to finding out the truth about her mother. She just didn't understand why it had taken so long to pull it out of her own flesh and blood.

Questions still lingered, though. "Jacob?"

"Yeah?"

"Where would my mother have gone the night she left?"

"Angel, cops have been over this time and time again."

"But they missed something, and I need to know." Angel stood. "Did they know she was at the club the night of the shooting? When she was really frustrated, was there someone she turned to? She had to say something to someone."

"Before Elisa disappeared, the only person she would really listen to or confide in was Eddie."

Angel stood still. Wes was right. She was starting to question if she really knew at all the people in her life she thought she knew. When she met with Wes, they would have a lot of pieces to put together.

# Chapter Forty-seven

Wes decided to talk to the last person he knew had talked to Larry Stowe. He walked into the Kingdom Building Church offices. There was a different person, an older woman, sitting at the secretary's desk today. She reminded Wes a little of Minister J.D. in terms of her facial features.

He smiled at her and said, "Hello. I'm Wes Cade, and I'm wondering if I can talk to Minister J.D. I called him earlier this morning."

"Sure." The older woman smiled. "It may be a few moments. He is in with someone now."

"Thanks. I will wait."

Wes walked over to a group of framed pictures on the wall. The first time he came to see Minister J.D., he hadn't noticed the collection. He studied the photos and knew from the clothes people wore that they were taken in the late eighties, early nineties. Wes recognized a younger Minister J.D., along with K-Dawg and Larry Stowe, in one of the photographs. Larry really looked angry in the photo, and it was not just that rap artist swagger, where one was mad at the world for the camera's sake. No, Wes sensed tension in Larry's eyes.

Minister J.D.'s door opened. When Wes turned around, he was surprised to see his friend Detective Darnell Jackson stepping out of the office. Wes walked over.

Both the minister and the detective watched Wes as he approached. Both looked solemn.

Darnell asked, "Now, why did I know you would not be far behind me?"

"A reporter has to get their story," Wes replied.

Darnell turned to shake Minister J.D.'s hand. "It was a pleasure to meet you. Sorry about the loss of your friend." Darnell gave Wes a warning look. "Like I told Serena, be careful with the details on this case."

Wes nodded. "You got it." After Darnell walked away, Wes addressed Minister J.D. "I hope you will still see me."

"Sure. It's good to see you back. Come on in."

Wes followed the minister into his office and sat down across from him. "I won't hold you long, but given the turn of events since I saw you last, I would like to know what relationship Eddie Gowins had with Larry Stowe."

"The last time you were here, we talked about the old Royal Records. It was actually partly owned by Eddie. He brought in demo tapes from all types of artists. He was all about looking for the next star. Well, we were young, and Eddie talked good game. So we decided to let him manage us."

Wes tilted his head. "Big mistake?"

"Big mistake. Don't get me wrong. I liked Eddie. Smooth talker. Loved that restaurant. It's a shame that we lost it. To be honest, I don't know why Larry was there."

"He certainly wasn't trying to resurrect his career," Wes said.

Minister J.D. let out a short laugh. "No. You know, I stayed in touch with Larry while he was in prison. I told him when he got out, I would get him hooked up with a job at the church, but you know, he was more interested in his little girl. He wanted to be able to see her make it in the music industry. When he got out, he talked to me about helping Melanie. It's funny, but that girl wouldn't give him the time of day. You couldn't blame her, but he was trying to make up for his absence. Unfortunately, the bottle took up most of his attention."

"Do you think Larry might have talked to Eddie about managing Melanie's career?"

"I don't know. After K-Dawg died, we all tried to stay in the game for a while, but it all fizzled. Everyone, including Eddie, just gave it up. He went into the restaurant business, and everyone went and did their own thing."

Wes thought about how Larry still dressed like he had when he was in his twenties. "It still seems like Larry hadn't let go. Was there a beef between Eddie and Larry back then?"

"Not that I could tell. But . . ."

Wes encouraged the minister. "Yes. Is there something else?"

"To be honest, Larry was good. He had better skills than K-Dawg on the mic. He could freestyle like nobody else could. I think he always had resentment about not getting his due." Minister J.D. looked down at his desk for a long moment, as if he was in prayer. He finally turned his attention to Wes. "When Larry came to sit in my office, right there in that chair, I almost felt like he was apologizing to me for something. He kept saying, 'I should have stayed loyal to y'all.'"

Wes frowned. "Sounds like he betrayed you in some way."

"I just wasn't sure how or what he was trying to tell me. Now I won't know until we meet on the other side."

Wes's phone buzzed in his pocket. He pulled it out and looked at the caller ID. "Minister J.D., I appreciate your time. I need to get this call." He shook the minister's hand and quickly walked out.

By the time he was outside the office, the voice mail had picked up the call. He listened to Angel's voice. "Wes, I'm not sure what time you wanted to meet today, but there's something I need to do. If you don't hear from me in a few hours, then send the cavalry to come find me." Wes heard a door slam, like Angel was either getting in or out of the car. This reminded him of when she showed up at her father's house a few weeks ago. Wes dialed Angel's number.

She didn't answer.

Wes peered down at his phone. He played the voice mail again. Angel sounded stressed and determined. He felt an urge to find her. *Angel, where are you, and what are you up to?*

# Chapter Forty-eight

After a fitful night of sleeping, Angel sat propped up against her pillow, watching the sun come up. While memories of her mother were usually faded, last night she could picture her mother's face vividly in her dreams and when she awoke. She'd always sensed her mother's moods, especially the extreme ones. Now there was a name for it, and all this time Angel hadn't known. People would tell her Elisa was spoiled and got her way, but her grandparents probably did all they could to keep up with a talented, but troubled woman.

She had read a bit about bipolar disorder before going to bed. If her mother hadn't been taking her medicine, in a manic state could she have confided in the wrong person? Angel had grown weary in her search for answers, but she couldn't rest until she knew the truth. She was the closest she had ever been to learning more about her mother.

A half an hour later, Angel entered the kitchen to grab some coffee, which someone had already started. She peeked into the dining room and found Jacob and Grams talking. Her uncle looked like he hadn't slept much, either, but thankfully, he had shaved his beard. To see her uncle's clean-shaven face gave Angel hope that he was doing better.

"Morning, Angel," Grams said with a familiar smile.

Angel was sure having Jacob around had improved her grandmother's mood. Angel hugged her and then did something she hadn't done since she was a little girl. She hugged Jacob. He accepted her hug, barely touching her as she squeezed him.

He stared at her with questions in his eyes. Maybe he was having second thoughts about being so candid with her last night. "You are up early this morning," he said.

"Yeah, I have some things to do. You two enjoy the day. I will see you later." She exited the house and walked briskly to her car. Today the forecast was for rain all day. It was cool compared to the hot, muggy weather of the past few weeks.

Before Angel started the car, she dialed Wes's number. They had talked last night about meeting but hadn't set a time. He didn't answer, so she left him a message. Angel checked to see if the phone was on vibrate and slipped it into her jacket pocket. As she drove, she felt the phone vibrate in her pocket. Angel concentrated on the road instead of taking the call. She sensed it was Wes, but she didn't want him to try to talk her out of what she was about to do.

Like a few weeks ago, when she went to meet her father, she had felt compelled to let someone know what she was doing. Well, sort of. She was sure her cryptic message would leave Wes scratching his head, but knowing his inquisitive mind, Angel knew she could count on him.

It occurred to her after she started driving that she should think this through. Soon she found herself on the familiar street. Angel hadn't been to the Gowins' home in years. As she drove up to the house, she saw Eddie's Mercedes in the driveway. She did think the man was flashier than the other members of the group, who were more or less good old country boys. Maybe because Eddie was a bit younger.

Angel parked her car behind the Mercedes. She walked to the door, rang the bell, and waited. She stood there for about two minutes before ringing the doorbell again. Angel cupped her hands around her face and leaned against the windowpane. It could have been a reflection, but Angel thought she saw someone moving around inside the house. She had called Denise before coming over to see if she'd heard from her dad, but there had been no response to her calls.

Maybe Eddie was hurt somewhere. He wasn't that old, only in his fifties. With all the health scares and issues she'd seen with her grandparents, Angel would have hated if she walked away and he was hurt. That was the only explanation Angel could think of for him just disappearing. But then that wouldn't explain the dead body found at Southern Soul Café.

She looked back at her car in the driveway and decided to take a look around outside. Angel walked around to the side of the house. When Denise and she were kids, they never went through the front door. Mrs. Gowins was one of those women who did not like children in her living room, so the back door was the main entrance.

While the house looked immaculate from the front, she saw objects leaning against it as she moved closer to the back. There were at least three cars, older cars that Eddie used to drive. They appeared to be in great shape, clean and polished.

Angel thought maybe she ought to have had more than coffee this morning due to the throbbing feeling in her gut. She pulled the latch on the fence to enter the backyard. Angel headed toward the back door. The Gowins used to leave a key under the mat. The black mat was still there. Angel peeled the mat back but didn't see any key. She glanced around the yard. What was she doing here? Certainly the police had been by here, looking for Eddie. She sighed and decided to leave.

As she came around the side of the house, Angel saw that the front door was now open. She walked up fast to the front door. "Eddie? Eddie, are you in here?" Angel placed one foot across the threshold and called out, "I need to talk to you." This was too weird. Angel spun around and yelped.

Eddie was standing behind her. He had a wild-eyed look, which she didn't recall ever seeing before. What happened to his face? she wondered. There were ugly scratches across his cheek, like he'd been in a fight. He smiled. "Angel, what a surprise. Why don't we go inside?"

As she slowly stepped inside the house, Angel looked around. "Denise and a lot of people are looking for you," she told him. She jumped and spun around when the door slammed closed behind her. "Eddie?"

Eddie pointed his finger in her face and walked around her like an animal examining his prey. "You are just like your mother. Showing up at the wrong time. The day you walked into Southern Soul Café with that reporter, I knew you would be trouble."

Angel frowned. "Why would me talking to Wes bother you?"

"Because it meant you were digging and he was helping you," Eddie spat.

"Well, I have learned a lot about my mother, but not enough. You were close to her before she died, so you can tell me the truth."

Eddie glared at her, and then he looked away. "Elisa was my star, the best thing I had going with all those other clowns I had under me."

"You managed K-Dawg, Larry Stowe, and some of the other local rap artists in the area."

"They came to me wanting a demo tape. I said I would help them if I could manage them. It helped me later convince your granddad, although he was real hesitant, to let me manage Elisa's career." Eddie grew quiet as he paced, almost like he'd forgotten Angel was standing in the same room.

Angel nudged him. "Do you know what happened to my mother?"

"It was an accident."

Angel's body tensed, and she crossed her arms. That was not what she'd expected to hear.

Eddie stopped pacing. "She came to my house, here, just like you did today. I knew something had been bothering her. She was all excited and waving her hands. Elisa kept saying, 'I saw him. He had a gun.' That's when I knew she was talking about Larry."

"Wait a minute. Larry? Larry shot K-Dawg? I thought they were friends."

Eddie laughed out loud, his voice harsh and bitter. "K-Dawg was a pretty boy with no talent. The real talent of the group was Larry. I don't know how he had been pushed into being the hype man. K-Dawg was always wisecracking on him. I told Larry over and over again he needed to assert himself more."

"So, if Larry killed him, why would that concern you? Why didn't you and my mother turn him in? Wasn't that what my mother was trying to say?"

"It would have come back to me. I gave him the gun. I also gave him money."

"You hired him to kill K-Dawg? Wasn't he your client too?"

"K-Dawg was smarter than he looked. He'd been digging around my past and was trying to get out of his contract. His ego had gotten inflated once that song blew up on radio stations around the country. To think

I was the one who gave him a chance, when no one would hear him. The real talent was Larry. He wrote the song. Your mother was singing the background hook. It was amazing. Her time was coming. Elisa was a star already."

As Angel listened to Eddie ramble, she couldn't believe this man. What was it about his past that would cause him to be concerned? She stared at the man she'd known all her life. *I don't know him at all.* "You still haven't told me what happened to my mother."

"Larry showed up is what happened. She was babbling about him. I told her to shut up. Larry wanted to shoot her. I told him he was in enough trouble. Your mom took off and ran. I grabbed her, and somehow she fell, hitting her head on the table." Eddie waved his hands around. "It was bad. Blood was coming from her head."

Angel felt like she was going to throw up, she was so nauseated. She cried out, "Why didn't you get her some help?"

"It was too late. She knew too much, and Larry was about to lose it. He wanted to put a bullet in her to make sure she was dead. I told him we had to get her out of there and I knew a place. In fact, we are going there now."

"What?" Angel watched as Eddie leaned over and took something out of a duffel bag on the floor.

Eddie stared at Angel as if he were looking through her. "Angel, why don't we go for a ride?"

Angel noticed Eddie's hand. He was holding a gun. She looked at him, tears flooding her eyes. "Why?"

His eyes didn't move from her face. "You should've left the past alone, girl. It's been so long. You and Larry, I don't know why you both decided you wanted to dig up the past now." Eddie laughed. "Old Larry had the nerve to want to come clean now. He'd served his time and wanted to get right with God." Eddie was yelling and waving the gun.

Angel held her arms tighter around her as it dawned on her what had really happened at Southern Soul Café. Tears fell down her face. Eddie had burned up all those memories to cover up his crime. But it wasn't his only crime. What else had Eddie done?

He turned to look at her. "Stop with the tears. Just move. Go!"

Knowing the gun was at her back, she walked out of the house toward her car. She glanced at the street, hoping cops would show up looking for Eddie. Angel opened the car door and climbed in. She remembered she'd put her phone in her left pocket. As Eddie came around the car, she pulled out the phone and tapped it to see the touch screen. From the corner of her eye, she saw the last phone number she had dialed. She selected the number and slipped the phone into the car-door pocket as Eddie jumped in.

She looked at the barrel of the gun. "What about Denise? She's been worrying about you."

Eddie jabbed the gun into her side, causing Angel to cry out. "Stop asking me questions. Just do what I tell you to do."

She turned the car's engine on and placed her shaking hands on the steering wheel. Her mother was dead, and this man, a trusted family friend, was responsible. What he intended to do with her, she didn't know, but she prayed to God that Eddie would get the punishment he deserved.

# Chapter Forty-nine

Wes had tried several times to get Angel on the phone after hearing her message. He decided to swing by her house to see if her family knew where she had gone. Wes drove into the Robertses' driveway. Though she didn't ask him directly this time, Wes felt led to pray for Angel's safety for some reason. Something in her voice caught his heart. Angel sounded scared to him. In the back of his mind, he knew what she must be trying to do. He just hoped he was wrong.

Wes rang the doorbell. Angel's uncle opened the door. He appeared puzzled and said, "Wes? It's good seeing you again. Are you here to see Angel?"

"Yes, we were supposed to meet up this afternoon. She left me a message about something she had to do. I was hoping she came back home."

Jacob eyed him. "No, she hasn't been back since she left this morning. She did seem a bit preoccupied, though. Do you know what's going on with her?"

Wes was hesitant to say anything. He wasn't sure how much Angel had told her family about her research over the past few weeks. But this was her family, so he decided to take the plunge. "Angel and I have been looking into her mother's disappearance. We came across a few things, and we were going to meet to try and put the pieces together."

"Oh no!" Jacob rubbed his head. "She asked me questions last night about her mother and Eddie. I was wondering why she had so many questions."

Wes frowned. "Well, where do you think she went?"

"Probably to find Eddie. I told her last night that Elisa had gotten really close to Eddie before she went missing. She would confide in him and listen to his advice over our parents' and mine."

Wes's phone buzzed in his pocket. "Hold on a minute. This could be her. I've been calling her for the past hour." He pulled out the phone. "It's her." Wes answered the call and said, "Angel, where are you . . ."

He stopped talking and listened. Angel was talking in the background to someone else. "Angel?"

Jacob stepped forward. "What's going on?"

Wes shook his head and strained to listen. He pulled the phone away. Wes had clearly heard a man's voice say, "Just do what I tell you to do." He swallowed hard, lowered the phone, and said, "We need to call the police and get them to trace Angel's phone. I think Angel found Eddie. He sounds like he's going to hurt her."

# Chapter Fifty

Angel gripped the steering wheel in fear as she calculated every move Eddie would make. What if she jerked the car off the road? *No.* She *wanted* to live. Still, a car accident had to be better than what he would do to her. She had no idea where they were going. Angel could only hope that Wes had picked up the phone and had caught her conversation with Eddie. She knew enough from watching television that it was possible for the police to trace her cell phone.

"Pull over right up here." Eddie turned his hot breath on her. "Do it now."

With as much ease as her trembling body allowed, she slowed the car and pulled to the side of the road. There hadn't been another car for miles on this back road. The sun was hidden behind cloudy dark gray skies.

Eddie cocked the gun toward her chest. "Get out." He swung the passenger door open.

Angel peeked down into the car-door pocket. Her eyes were glued to that phone, and she hoped it wouldn't fail her now. Her hands felt ice cold as she struggled to grasp the door handle.

"Come on!" he growled.

She yanked the door handle and scrambled out of the car to face her abductor.

Eddie waved the gun and yelled, "Start walking."

Sticks and leaves crunched as they walked into the mass of trees. From a distance, she saw lightning streak across the sky. It was the time of year for southern thunderstorms to roll through. A cool breeze whipped through the trees, but it brought Angel no comfort. Her heart raced, as if she had just run a marathon. She choked back a sob. Eddie was going to kill her. She couldn't believe this was happening.

To think how much she had trusted him. It never would have crossed her mind that he would hurt her. More lightning split the sky, and it was followed by an intense rumble of thunder. The trees shook their limbs, as if taunting her for being so naive.

"Stop."

She turned and noticed that Eddie had cocked his head like he had heard something. Was someone else out here?

He swung the gun an inch from her temple. "Get down."

"What?"

"Get on your knees," he snarled.

She fell on her knees, feeling the earth beneath her. Her heart lurched as the thunder roared like an angry lion above their heads. Big drops of rain began to crash down around them. Angel shut her eyes tight, not believing this was her fate. "Please, God, help me," she prayed fervently.

When she opened her eyes, an answer lay near her, barely covered by leaves. She glanced up at him. Eddie's eyes had grown wilder as he paced around her. He seemed to be having a conversation, but she couldn't understand a word he was saying. The rain was falling harder now, soaking her clothes. She peered down at the ground again. Why not? What did she have to lose? She had to do something.

Angel scooped the smooth rock up from the muddy ground. Her dormant softball skills kicked in as she zoomed in on his hand. Not waiting another second, she swung the rock with all her might.

The rock smacked him square on the hand, and he dropped the gun. "No, you . . ."

She leaped forward like a track sprinter and headed into the trees. As Angel ran, the oddest memory of a Sunday school lesson entered her mind. The one about Lot's wife. God told her not to look back, but she did and lost her life.

Eddie's voice bellowed behind her.

"Don't look back," Angel told herself as she ran. "Don't. Look. Back."

# Chapter Fifty-one

Wes and Jacob waited for Detective Jackson to return to his desk from the captain's office. Wes stared at his phone, praying for Angel. He was glad he'd activated the mute button, so he could keep the connection without Eddie being aware of conversations.

Jacob asked, "What's the plan? How are they going to find her?"

"Angel was clever enough to call, so her phone can be used to trace her location. It used to be only the FBI had access to tracking technology, but now quite a number of police departments can also track cell phones in case of emergencies, like a kidnapping. Right now they are working to nail down her location, and I'm pretty sure the SWAT team has been called in."

Jacob frowned. "SWAT? You think he has a weapon on him?"

Wes hesitated because he wasn't sure how much Jacob knew, but Angel was his niece. "Look, you know about the fire at Southern Soul Café."

"Yeah."

"There was a body in there with a gunshot wound to the head."

"Are you serious? Who was it? Are you telling me that Eddie killed someone?" Jacob got up from the chair and paced. "I knew it. I knew it. All this time, I knew that man was no good."

Wes noticed Jacob's tightened fists. "Okay, calm down. If we can't keep it together, they won't let us go with them to find her." Wes wasn't actually sure if they would or would not, but he hoped his buddy Darnell could pull some strings. Wes had to be there to help them find Angel. He said, "You know I talked to some of the members of Southern Soul, Pete and Buddy. They seemed to not care too much for Eddie, either. Neither did my pops. Do you know why Nick was the one that always seemed to be in Eddie's corner?"

Jacob shook his head. "Wes, that's the million-dollar question. I don't know why my dad was such a fan of Eddie's. Don't get me wrong. I remember admiring him when I was a kid. I think I was twelve when he joined the group. He was different, younger, and he could play the drums. I wanted to play the drums just watching him. But I don't know. . . . He had a way of being manipulative when he wanted something. He just turned on the charm, but there was something else about him that just never sat right with me."

Jacob sat down. "My dad had this one-track mind. When he made up his mind about something, it was hard to convince him that he could be wrong. I remember I was accused of being jealous. Nick was my dad. He was on the road a lot, and I wanted his time. Eddie would come by with his problems, and Dad would stop and listen. You know, later I learned he bailed him out of jail."

Jacob threw up his hands. "This dude was arrested and put in jail. If that wasn't the handwriting on the wall, I don't know what it was. None of the guys in Southern Soul were perfect, but they all were God-fearing men who had families."

Wes nodded, agreeing with Jacob's rants. To bring Eddie into a group that had already been in existence for quite some time, and especially with his age difference, did seem a bit odd. He asked Jacob, "What was Eddie arrested for?"

"Assault and battery, I believe," Jacob answered. "Eddie claimed the guy he used to work for had called him a racial slur, so he hit him. The man called the cops, and Eddie was arrested. I believe the guy dropped the charges, because nothing happened, or at least I didn't hear anything more."

Wes looked up and saw Darnell walk out of the captain's office. He was wearing a bulletproof vest. He walked over.

"Okay, SWAT has been called, and the signal from Angel's phone has her up near the Lake Wylie area," he told them. "There are cabins out there. Do you, by any chance, know if Eddie has property up there?"

Jacob stood. "No, he doesn't have property, but before he became the drummer with Southern Soul, he worked at a place with cabins. In fact, he worked there for a while even after he joined Southern Soul."

"You remember the name of the place?" Darnell asked.

Jacob looked at Wes and then focused back on Darnell. "I was just telling Wes about the time my dad bailed Eddie out of jail. He had been arrested for assaulting the owner of a cabin resort. I don't remember what the place was called. Misty Pine, maybe. I remember the name of the place had the word *pine* included."

"Okay, okay. That might help us narrow down the search. Do you remember what year Eddie was arrested?" Darnell asked.

Jacob blew out a breath. "I don't know. This was probably early eighties. It was right before I graduated from UNC Chapel Hill."

Wes asked Darnell, "Eddie's fingerprints should be in the system, right?"

"Yes," Darnell answered. "After hearing Jacob's story here, I'm curious to know a little bit more about Eddie's background. I've been looking into leads on him since the fire on Sunday. Eddie kind of doesn't have anything on him prior to Southern Soul. I think I'm going have his fingerprints run in the AFIS database. I will get someone on it. Right now, Angel's safety is our focus. It appears they stopped at some location and haven't moved, unless her battery died."

Wes followed behind Darnell as he headed toward the door. "You are going to let me go with you, right?"

Darnell turned and looked at Wes, then at Jacob.

Jacob shook his head. "I'm fine. I need to get back to my mother. The nurse was nice enough to come in on her day off. Fredricka doesn't know what's going on, but I have a feeling this will be on the news." Jacob looked at Wes.

Wes nodded. "I know Serena is on this. She's going up in the WYNN helicopter, but I'm not interested in going to get the story. I want to be there for Angel."

Darnell said, "Wes, you can't be trying to play hero. We have trained professionals who will handle Eddie."

"I know that, man. Angel is going to need a friendly face when you find her. She's probably totally freaked out."

Darnell sighed and looked over at the captain's office. "Fine. We'll get you a vest, and you are not to get in anyone's way. Understood?"

"You got it!" Wes said.

A few minutes later, Darnell sped down the highway with Wes in the passenger seat. Wes still held tight to his phone, praying that they would reach Angel in time. After what seemed liked forever, Wes could see flashing lights ahead, along with the SWAT truck. He could see several officers standing in a group, dressed in gear.

Wes sat up and pointed. "Oh, man, there's Angel's car." He reached for the door handle while the car was still moving.

"Okay. Stay cool, man." Darnell pulled the car over, and both of them got out. Wes kept up with Darnell's long strides. From what he could see, no one was in Angel's car. He looked over into the woods. Eddie must have taken Angel into the woods.

Wes watched as the SWAT officers suddenly took off into the woods.

He asked Darnell, "How are they going to find her in there? Does she still have her phone on her?"

Darnell had been talking to a technician who had been examining Angel's car. He shook his head. "No, she left her phone in the car, which was probably a good thing. She wouldn't have wanted Eddie to know she had kept it on. The team has mapped out the place and is spreading out now. It looks like this road leads up to the back of Pine Meadows. Some of these cabins haven't been open to the public in a while. This is probably the place where Eddie worked at earlier in his life, and he probably knows the area well."

Wes felt fear surge through his body as helplessness set in. Angel would need more than just the SWAT team. He prayed, *Lord, please protect Angel. Send your angels to surround her and protect her from evil.*

# Chapter Fifty-two

Angel's chest felt like it would burst as she struggled to breathe and run. Eddie wasn't far behind her. Amazingly enough, as she ran, zigzagging around the trees, her anxiety about being in the woods a few weeks ago was low on her priority list. She stumbled over a rock but jumped back up quickly. The bottoms of her jeans were muddy, as were her hands. She told herself, *Just move*. She'd watched enough horror movies to know to keep running.

She slowed for just a second to decide where to go next. "Angel." She heard her name echoing through the trees. That motivated her to go right. If he hadn't taken her keys, she could have run to the car, except she had no idea how to get to the car or how far she was from the road. She could only hope to find camouflage in the heavily wooded area. At some point she would need to stop and hide.

The sound of her feet pounding the ground was probably drawing attention to her location. She had a feeling Eddie had outdoor skills she didn't possess.

Angel glimpsed a cabin ahead, but as she approached, there weren't any lights visible from the outside. Angel ran up to the door, banged, and then yanked on the door handle. Nothing. She ran around to the side of the cabin, and there appeared to be a shed. Maybe she could at least go in there and catch her breath. She needed to think.

More importantly, she needed a miracle. God had already answered one prayer. *Lord, please help me.* She hoped Wes had been able to hear what was going on through the phone and had sent the cavalry after her. It could be her imagination, but she thought she heard the deep hum of a helicopter hovering above.

Angel pulled on the shed door. She cringed when it creaked open, and entered the darkness. It took her eyes a few minutes to adjust. Angel bumped into a sharp object and sucked in her breath to keep from crying out her pain. In the distance, she heard her name again. Angel gingerly stepped around what felt like a lawn mower or some type of cart. She went to the other side of the shed and squatted down. Her wet clothes clung to her.

She realized if she didn't stop panting like a dog, she was going to give her location away. Angel gulped air and reached up to grab the object in front of her to steady herself. She snatched her hand away as the remnants of a cobweb wrapped around her fingers. Angel wiped her hands on her jeans. No need to get freaked out by the creepy crawlies now. It was either the little creatures or the crazy man outside. Angel looked up at the object that had been covered with cobwebs. It was a shovel. Her mind was moving fast. *It's a weapon.*

No match for the gun, which Eddie had probably recovered from the ground, though. Maybe she should have stayed and gone for the gun. Now all she was doing was second-guessing herself. She'd never shot a gun in her life. All she knew was she could be dead by now.

"Angel." Eddie's voice ricocheted close by.

She reached for the handle of the shovel and inched her way around to behind the shed's door, careful not to step on anything. Maybe he would come through the door; maybe he wouldn't. She was going to be ready for him. Angel spread her legs and held the shovel in her hands.

"Angel, you can't hide from me. Just come out. You wanted to find out about your mother. I told you I would take you to her."

Angel gripped the shovel tighter. As she thought back to what Eddie had revealed earlier, she started to get the picture. Larry and Eddie had got rid of her mother's body. She swallowed hard, but tears flooded her eyes. Her mother had been buried up here in these woods. No wonder no one could find her. She wiped her face with her sleeve, willing Eddie to walk through the door.

She would have her wish. Eddie had to be right outside as he shouted, "Angel, I loved your mother."

Angel listened. What was Eddie talking about?

"It hurt my heart to see Nick in pain about Elisa. But in some ways it made up for my pain. I grew up without him in my life. He'd just left my mother, not that I blamed him. She was crazy."

*What?* Angel almost lost her grip on the shovel. Eddie really was her uncle. Her granddad had never mentioned that Eddie was his son. That was not a secret her granddad would have kept. Her head started spinning. She couldn't believe a word Eddie was saying. Maybe he was just trying to draw her out. She dug her heels in again and watched the door.

"Angel." Eddie dragged out her name.

The door of the shed creaked open. Angel waited, looking for the gun.

Eddie didn't disappoint. The gun came through the door first.

Angel slowly pulled the shovel back and hoped the darkness of the shed would conceal her. Eddie's tall frame appeared fully inside the door, the gun out in front. He turned slightly to the left. Angel took that as her cue to smash the shovel across Eddie's head.

"Ah!" Eddie screamed. The gun went off as he stumbled and fell.

Angel ducked, and then adrenaline surged through her body. She jumped up and slammed the shovel hard across Eddie's back. The gun spun out of his hand and landed somewhere inside the shed. Something primal surged through her body, and she screamed and picked up the shovel again. *This man.* She slammed down the shovel. *Killed my mother.*

"Angel!" She stopped, holding the shovel and breathing hard. Several people behind her were calling her name. She slowly stepped back out of the shed with the shovel. Angel turned to see several men with guns pointed in her direction.

One of the officers stepped out from the group. "Angel. Angel Roberts?"

She nodded.

"It's okay. We're here. Eddie in there?"

She dropped the shovel and nodded again. One of the officers came over and pulled her away as the others swarmed the shed. The officer led her over to the steps of the cabin. After the officer left her side, she sat and cried. Angel shed tears over the loss of her mother and the split second when she wanted to take Eddie's life.

Angel wiped her face, which she was sure was a dirty mess now. She looked at the scene before her, trying to make sense of it all.

"Help."

Angel turned her head. There was so much commotion around the shed and the cabin now that maybe she was just hearing things.

"Please help me."

She sprang up from the steps, her heart still pounding, and pressed her ear against the cabin door. Angel banged on the door. "Is someone in there?"

Angel could hear a female voice. She sounded young and weak. "Yes. Please help."

Angel waved her arms and yelled at the officers around her. "Someone is in here. Please, she needs help."

Angel moved out of the way as members of the SWAT team rammed the door open.

"Angel, are you okay?"

She turned around to see Wes running toward her. Knowing she looked a hot mess, she gladly accepted his arms around her and buried her face into his shoulder. She cried hot tears again, grateful that God had worked out a way for Wes to save her.

"Oh my!" Angel heard Wes say.

"What?" She turned and saw a young woman being carried out on a stretcher. "Who is she, Wes?"

"Angel, I believe you found Melanie Stowe."

Angel tore herself away from Wes's arms to move closer to the woman. It was her. Eddie had kidnapped Melanie. Seeing the caked blood on Melanie's face, Angel guessed that Eddie had left her for dead. That explained where the scratches had come from on Eddie's face.

She looked over at the man as officers escorted him out of the shed. Angel had left her mark on Eddie too. He appeared disoriented. Rage surged through Angel again. She tried to run toward Eddie, but Wes and Darnell snatched her back.

"Whoa, Angel! Let us get Eddie into custody, okay? He has quite a few charges coming his way," Darnell said to calm her. "Don't worry. He will get prison time."

She turned to Darnell. "He buried my mother up here. You make him tell me where she is."

Wes and Darnell both looked stunned.

Darnell nodded. "All right. We'll have to get the medical examiner's office up here to see what they can recover. In the meantime, you need to get back to your family. I know Candace is blowing up my phone, she's so worried about you."

Angel nodded.

After Darnell walked over to the other officers, Wes reached his arms around her. "It's going to be okay."

Angel held her head against Wes's shoulder. She hoped so. It had turned out to be a day she would never forget. In her quest for the truth, she'd unlocked so many secrets, she wasn't sure if she would ever be the same.

# Chapter Fifty-three

*A year later . . .*

Angel wiped the tears from her eyes. She knew someone was going to come looking for her, but she needed just a few moments to herself. She was grateful to Reverend Freeman and Lenora for allowing her to screen *The Elisa Roberts Story* at Victory Gospel Church. She had spent many nights determined to pull the memories of her mother's tragedy together. Some nights she had wept as she edited and spliced together photos and precious footage from family videos.

She was hesitant about including Eddie's footage, but he was a part of the story. Eddie's claims that he was Nick's son still hadn't been proven. From what Wes could dig up, it appeared that her granddad was briefly involved with Eddie's mother. Why Eddie had made it his goal to claim Nick Roberts as his father was unclear. Whether he was really her uncle or not, she didn't care. The trial would start soon, and if all went well, Eddie would spend the rest of his life in prison.

Sadly, any opportunities to rekindle a friendship with Denise had been lost. Denise and Kenneth had called off the wedding and had gone their separate ways. She'd seen Kenneth around, but Denise had taken little Kenny down to Florida.

Someone knocked on the bathroom door. "Angel, are you okay?"

"Yes." Angel went over and opened the door. She laughed and said, "Wow. Grams must have sent the cavalry after me."

Candace eyed her. "Girl, you know no one is about to let you disappear." Both Candace and Lenora walked into the bathroom and stood on either side of her.

Lenora reached for more tissues from the box on the sink. "I understand this was emotional for you. I believe there aren't too many dry eyes in the room. Even Reverend Freeman shed some tears."

Candace added, "Darnell tried to play hard, but I caught him wiping his eyes too."

Angel giggled, and then she caught sight of Candace's hand. "OMG! What is this?" She grabbed Candace's hand. "Is this . . . ?"

"Yes, child, that man proposed." Candace beamed as she showed off the diamond on her hand. "You know I accepted. We grown folks, and it was about that time."

Lenora laughed. "You know you are both going to have to make an appointment with Reverend Freeman right away for marriage counseling."

"I'm going to start following you two around with my video camera so I can get some good footage for that wedding video." Angel reached over and squeezed her friend. "I'm so happy for you two."

"Thank you, honey. Speaking of happy, we need to get you out there before Fredricka gets up with her walker and starts looking for you herself."

The three women walked out of the restroom and into the Victory Gospel Center. Most of the guests were lined up around the tables, adding food to their plates. Angel saw Grams looking around for her. Sitting at the same table were Jacob and Liz, along with Wanda. Angel hadn't realized Liz had made it down for the screening. She thought it looked a bit awkward to have Liz and Wanda at the same table, but Jacob looked good. Her uncle looked happier than he'd ever been. As Angel approached, Grams struggled to stand.

"No, Grams. You can sit," Angel told her.

"No. I don't want to. I'm standing to hug my Angel."

Angel bent down and let her grandmother reach up to hug her. It was a strong, comforting hug. Grams whispered in her ear, "I'm proud of you, and so is your granddad."

Angel thought she would burst out and cry again, but she held it in. She moved around the table, hugging Wanda next. "How's Lenny?"

Wanda said, "He's as good as he can be. He would love to have you visit with Wes again. I heard you sang for him the last time."

"I enjoyed the last time I visited. He really seemed happy when we played some of Southern Soul's CDs."

"Oh, he loves music. Best medicine for him."

Angel walked around and hugged Liz. "It's good to see you. Both of you."

Jacob stood. "She surprised me." Liz and Jacob were still separated, but they were keeping in touch. Her uncle reached down and hugged her. "I'm proud of you, kid."

"Thanks." That meant a lot coming from her uncle Jacob. "How are the business plans coming along? My dad said you were going to take off in no time."

Angelino and his family couldn't make it to the screening, but Angel had been enjoying spending time with her dad and his family. She had quite a bit in common with her younger half sister. Surprisingly, Jacob, who was making his way back from his bout with depression, had struck up a friendship with Angelino.

"Your dad is something else," Jacob commented. "I think there will be another entrepreneur in the family. I owe it to you for being an inspiration."

"Ah, stop. I'm liking this new uncle."

"I'm your only uncle."

"You are right about that." Angel hugged her mother's brother again, her thoughts turning to the other man she had affectionately called uncle most of her life. As she pulled away from Jacob, she tried to hide a shudder that had moved up her body.

"You okay?" Jacob asked.

"Yes." She smiled. Her mouth stretched wider as she saw Wes walk over. His eyes were all for her.

"I have someone who wants to see you," he told her.

Angel looked at him. She had questions, but Wes's eyes were sparkling. "Okay."

She placed her hand in his as he led her down a hallway and into a conference room. Sitting in a chair facing the window was a woman. Angel walked around Wes to see her face more clearly.

"Melanie." Angel ran over to her as she stood. "How are you? You look so good."

"Thank you. Sorry I'm late. I had to come."

"I'm glad you were able to make it to the screening. I know coming back to Charlotte was hard."

"Yeah, well, it was good to be in Oklahoma. Being around my aunt, I felt connected to my mother."

"That's beautiful." Angel looked behind her to where Wes stood at a distance. She lowered her voice. "How are you sleeping now?" Angel looked into Melanie's eyes and squeezed her hand. "I know. We will keep praying for each other. It will get better. I know neither one of us wants to be near the woods anytime soon."

They both giggled at Angel's attempt at a joke. The two young women had shared an experience together that had forever changed them both but had bonded them as friends. Not only had Melanie been saved, but the authorities had recovered Angel's mother's bones. It was a bittersweet thing for Angel.

She asked Melanie, "Are you singing?"

Melanie nodded. "I am. I feel more like myself when I am singing. I saw the video. You need to get out there more."

Angel nodded over her shoulder at Wes. "Believe me, I hear that all the time."

Melanie peeked around at Wes. "You got a good one. Thanks again for everything, my sister." They hugged each other.

Angel watched as Melanie walked out.

Wes came up and placed his arms around her. "Did you see Candace's hand?"

Angel smiled. "I did. Darnell did well with the ring."

"He did all right."

Wes and Angel had been dating—or as Candace liked to say, courting—for a year now. Angel didn't know how she would have made it through the past year without Wes. Some days she had pushed him away as she struggled with her long overdue grief and anger. Wes had stood by her with a listening ear and prayers.

She smiled at Wes. "What? You think you can do better?"

"I don't know. Let's find out."

Angel watched as Wes dropped to one knee in front of her. She gasped as he pulled out a ring box from inside his jacket.

He opened the box. "Angel, I would love for us to make a lifetime of memories together. Would you marry me?"

The joy that flooded her soul sparkled inside more vibrantly than the diamond Wes held out to her. She beamed down at Wes and answered, "Yes."

# Discussion Questions

1) At the beginning of the book, Angel becomes frustrated with her grandmother for bringing up her mother's disappearance on her birthday. A bit later, Fredricka suffers a stroke. Angel already feels horrible about her outburst, and then she experiences guilt about her grandmother's condition. Have you ever had a conflict with a person prior to a medical emergency or a tragedy? How did you deal with the guilt?

2) Despite his celibacy vow, Wes finds himself in a compromising situation with his coworker Serena. If he hadn't been saved by the phone, he could have broken his vow. Has there been a time when you found a temptation so enticing, you almost broke or actually broke a vow/promise?

3) Angel finds herself directly involved in caring for her grandmother, while Wes encourages his mother to seek help caring for his Alzheimer's-stricken grandfather. Have you been involved in the care of an aged or disabled loved one? Have you offered your services to or assisted a caregiver?

4) Readers learn that four years ago, Angel was betrayed by her former best friend and her boyfriend. Consequently, Angel is hesitant to reach out to others, almost isolating herself to focus on her business.

# Discussion Questions

When Angel befriends Candace Johnson, she gains not only a new friend, but also a sister in Christ. The two women bond over their losses. Have you suffered the loss of a friendship? If so, how did you handle the loss? How did God bring new friends into your life?

5) With the absence of her parents, Angel was raised by her grandparents, who encouraged her to be all that she could be. They helped her pursue her passion for videography, which stemmed from Angel's desire to capture memories. At the age of twenty-five, Angel owns her own business and does work she loves to do. Where are you at in your career? Are you passionate about your work? Do you have dreams of owning your own business? If you haven't pursued those dreams, what's stopping you?

6) When the Overcomers Women's Ministry discusses the lesson on forgiveness, Angel voices her concerns about forgiving people who have betrayed her. Candace explains to Angel the true benefits of letting go and forgiving. Have you truly forgiven the person(s) who hurt you or betrayed your trust? Have you denied your true feelings? Or are you hanging on to those feelings, using them as your motivation to remain bitter?

7) As a reporter, Wes is determined to seek the truth, to the point where he takes risks. In fact, Wes's quest for the truth pushes Angel to take a risk that she wouldn't normally consider. Wes learns to pray for Angel, but he also needs to learn to pray for himself. Have you ever been driven by ambition to the point where you made a risky decision? Did you

seek God in prayer prior to making the decision or afterward?

8) Angel has a beautiful voice like her mother. She refuses to sing in public due to childhood fears and misunderstandings about her mother's disappearance. Slowly, God draws Angel out of her shell so she can share her gift and glorify God. What talents and gifts has God given you that you are not using to uplift His Kingdom building plans?

# Resources

### Alzheimer's Disease
The <u>National Institute on Aging (NIA)</u> is dedicated to understanding the nature of aging, supporting the health and well-being of older adults, and extending the healthy, active years of life for more people. http://www.nia.nih.gov/alzheimers

### Heart Disease and Stroke
The <u>National Stroke Association's</u> mission is to reduce the incidence and impact of strokes by providing education and programs focused on stroke prevention and on treatment, rehabilitation, and support for all impacted by stroke. http://www.stroke.org

### Missing Persons
The <u>National Missing and Unidentified Persons System (NamUs)</u> is a national centralized repository and resource center for missing person and unidentified decedent records. This free online system can be searched by medical examiners, coroners, law enforcement officials, and the general public from all over the country. http://www.namus.gov/

<u>The Doe Network</u> is a volunteer organization devoted to assisting law enforcement in solving cold cases involving unexplained disappearances and unidentified victims from North America, Australia, and Europe. http://www.doenetwork.org/

## Resources

<u>Let's Bring Them Home</u> operates a national missing adults program that provides services and coordinates between various government agencies, law enforcement, the media, and the families of endangered missing adults. The organization also offers safety education for all ages. <u>http://www.lbth.org/</u>

# About the Author

Tyora Moody is an author and entrepreneur. Her debut novel, *When Rain Falls,* was released in March 2012. This is the first book in the Victory Gospel Series.

Tyora writes romantic suspense and cozy mysteries. She is a member of Sisters in Crime and American Christian Fiction Writers. She served as a judge for the Christy Awards for three years.

She owns and operates TywebbinCreations.com, a design and marketing company. For over twelve years, she has worked with authors, small business owners, and nonprofit organizations to develop their online presence. For free tips, how-to guides, and eCourses, visit DIYwithTy.com.

When Tyora isn't working for a client or doing something literary, she enjoys spending time with family, catching a movie on the big screen, traveling and, when the mood hits her, baking cookies. You can visit her online at TyoraMoody.com.

## ORDER FORM
## URBAN BOOKS, LLC
### 78 E. Industry Ct
### Deer Park, NY 11729

Name: (please print):_____

Address:    _____

City/State:    _____

Zip:    _____

| QTY | TITLES | PRICE |
|---|---|---|
|  | 3:57 A.M  Timing Is Everything | $14.95 |
|  | A Man's Worth | $14.95 |
|  | A Woman's Worth | $14.95 |
|  | Abundant Rain | $14.95 |
|  | After The Feeling | $14.95 |
|  | Amaryllis | $14.95 |
|  | An Inconvenient Friend | $14.95 |
|  | Battle of Jericho | $14.95 |
|  | Be Careful What You Pray For | $14.95 |
|  | Beautiful Ugly | $14.95 |
|  | Been There Prayed That: | $14.95 |
|  | Before Redemption | $14.95 |

Shipping and handling-add $3.50 for 1st book, then $1.75 for each additional book.
Please send a check payable to:
   **Urban Books, LLC**
Please allow 4-6 weeks for delivery

## ORDER FORM
## URBAN BOOKS, LLC
78 E. Industry Ct
Deer Park, NY 11729

Name: (please print): _____

Address: _____

City/State: _____

Zip: _____

| QTY | TITLES | PRICE |
|---|---|---|
| | By the Grace of God | $14.95 |
| | Confessions Of A Preachers Wife | $14.95 |
| | Dance Into Destiny | $14.95 |
| | Deliver Me From My Enemies | $14.95 |
| | Desperate Decisions | $14.95 |
| | Divorcing the Devil | $14.95 |
| | Faith | $14.95 |
| | First Comes Love | $14.95 |
| | Flaws and All | $14.95 |
| | Forgiven | $14.95 |
| | Former Rain | $14.95 |
| | Forsaken | $14.95 |

Shipping and handling-add $3.50 for 1st book, then $1.75 for each additional book.
Please send a check payable to:
**Urban Books, LLC**
Please allow 4-6 weeks for delivery

ORDER FORM
URBAN BOOKS, LLC
78 E. Industry Ct
Deer Park, NY 11729

Name: (please print):_____

Address:      _____

City/State:   _____

Zip:          _____

| QTY | TITLES | PRICE |
|-----|--------|-------|
| | From Sinner To Saint | $14.95 |
| | From The Extreme | $14.95 |
| | God Is In Love With You | $14.95 |
| | God Speaks To Me | $14.95 |
| | Grace And Mercy | $14.95 |
| | Guilty Of Love | $14.95 |
| | Happily Ever Now | $14.95 |
| | Heaven Bound | $14.95 |
| | His Grace His Mercy | $14.95 |
| | His Woman His Wife His Widow | $14.95 |
| | Illusions | $14.95 |
| | In Green Pastures | $14.95 |

Shipping and handling-add $3.50 for 1st book, then $1.75 for each additional book.

Please send a check payable to:

**Urban Books, LLC**

Please allow 4-6 weeks for delivery

## ORDER FORM
## URBAN BOOKS, LLC
78 E. Industry Ct
Deer Park, NY 11729

Name: (please print):_____

Address:        _____

City/State:     _____

Zip:            _____

| QTY | TITLES | PRICE |
|-----|--------|-------|
| | Into Each Life | $14.95 |
| | Keep Your enemies Closer | $14.95 |
| | Keeping Misery Company | $14.95 |
| | Latter Rain | $14.95 |
| | Living Consequences | $14.95 |
| | Living Right On Wrong Street | $14.95 |
| | Losing It | $14.95 |
| | Love Honor Stray | $14.95 |
| | Marriage Mayhem | $14.95 |
| | Me, Myself and Him | $14.95 |
| | Murder Through The Grapevine | $14.95 |
| | My Father's House | $14.95 |

Shipping and handling-add $3.50 for 1st book, then $1.75 for each additional book.
Please send a check payable to:
**Urban Books, LLC**
Please allow 4-6 weeks for delivery